BEYONDBELIEF

Also by Roy Johansen

The Answer Man

BEYOND BELIEF

ROY JOHANSEN

BANTAM BOOKS

NEW YORK   TORONTO   LONDON   SYDNEY   AUCKLAND

BEYOND BELIEF
A Bantam Book / April 2001
All rights reserved.
Copyright © 2001 by Roy Johansen.

Book design by O'Lanso Gabbidon

Library of Congress Cataloging-in-Publication Data

Johansen, Roy.
Beyond belief / Roy Johansen.
p. cm.
ISBN 0-553-80115-5
I. Title.

PS3560.O2765 B49 2001
813'.54—dc21   00-064245

Published simultaneously in the United States and Canada

Bantam Books are published by Bantam Books,
a division of Random House, Inc.
Its trademark, consisting of the words "Bantam Books" and the portrayal
of a rooster, is Registered in U.S. Patent and Trademark Office and in other
countries. Marca Registrada. Bantam Books,
1540 Broadway, New York, New York 10036.

PRINTED IN THE UNITED STATES OF AMERICA
BVG 10 9 8 7 6 5 4 3 2 1

For Lisa, who is proof enough that there is
magic and wonder in the world.

BEYONDBELIEF

PROLOGUE

They were coming for him.

Shouting men.

Barking dogs.

Flashing lights.

Just like last night. And the night before.

What did they *want*? He was only eight years old; how could he possibly matter to them?

The men were getting closer. Their shouting was getting louder and the lights were getting brighter.

Brighter and brighter until all he could see was white. The light was hot; it burned him. The shouting voices were all around.

The ground shook. He looked down. What was happening?

Two hands burst from the ground and grabbed his ankles.

Before he could scream, the hands pulled him down. He could feel the cold, moist earth around his calves, knees, and thighs.

The voices were icy whispers now, buzzing around his head and ears. He still couldn't understand what they were saying.

1

The ground was now at his waist. He pounded on the earth, trying to keep the hands from pulling him under.

It wasn't working. He went even deeper.

The ground closed around his chest, pressing his lungs.

He couldn't breathe!

God, please help me. . . .

He dug his fingers into the cold ground, scraping dirt with his nails as he went under. The dirt covered his chin, and he angled his head back, staring into the bright light. The earth crawled over his ears, muffling the whispers snaking around him. He struggled to keep his nose and mouth aboveground as he smelled the grassy turf creeping over his cheeks.

No, please God, no . . .

He screamed as his face went below.

Dark.

Cold.

He was pulled deeper and deeper, the rocks and tree roots scraping against his face and arms on the way down.

The whispers were getting louder again: *Jesse . . . Jesse . . . Jesse . . .*

Shadowy figures flying around him.

And those eyes.

Dark eyes. Cold. Menacing.

He knew those eyes.

The shadows called his name.

Jesse . . .

He had to fight. It was his only hope.

Clawing, punching, scratching . . .

He was moving in slow motion, swinging at the figures through the cold earth.

Jesse . . .

One of the figures moved in close, and Jesse struck out with both fists.

Contact.

The figure slumped, oozing blood from its midsection. It was still.

Did he kill it?

The hands around his ankles loosened slightly.

He punched and clawed at the others.

More blood. It oozed through the soil and coated his arms and chest.

The hands around his ankles were loosening with each hit.

He could do this, he thought. He could get free.

He punched and kicked even harder.

Blood everywhere. The whispers were getting fainter.

He kicked free of the hands and clawed upward through the warm, bloody soil. Higher, higher, higher . . .

Jesse . . .

Don't listen to the voices. Just climb.

Jesse . . .

He crawled past the tree roots that had scraped him on the way down. How much farther?

Jesse . . .

He broke through to the surface, clawing and kicking out of the ground. He was covered in dirt and blood.

The ground was shaking.

He jumped out of the way as another pair of hands broke through the ground.

He ran.

Behind him, he could hear the voices. And the dogs. He knew if he turned around, he would see those eyes.

It was starting all over again. Just like the other nights.

He knew it was a dream, but he couldn't wake himself up.

Wake up, he told himself. *Wake up.*

No use. This dream might never end.

Not until it killed him.

1

Maybe tonight was the night he'd learn to believe in magic.

Not damned likely, Joe Bailey thought.

Over the years, he'd received too many calls that promised something extraordinary but never actually delivered. Why would tonight be any different? He unbuttoned his overcoat as he climbed the polished granite front stairs of a mansion on Habersham Drive. He checked his watch: 1:40.

The call had come only fifteen minutes earlier from Lieutenant Vince Powell, who headed the evening watch at the station. There had been a homicide.

"I'm in bunco," Joe told him. "You're sure I'm the guy you want?"

"I know who you are," Powell said. "You bust up all the phony séances, psychics, and witch-doctor scams."

"Among other things, yeah."

"Well, we got something right up your alley. It's scaring the shit out of the officers on the scene. You wanna take a look?"

No, he didn't want to take a look, but he was here anyway. He strode through the open door. It was a cold February night in Atlanta. Mid-thirties, he guessed. He could still see his breath in the air as he walked through the foyer and looked for the uniformed officer who usually secured a crime scene.

Probably upstairs getting the shit scared out of him.

There were voices echoing down the stairway. Not the matter-of-fact grunts he'd heard at the few murder scenes he'd visited; the words were the same but uttered faster and louder. A totally different energy.

But whatever it was waiting for him up there, he was sure it wasn't magic. He always tried to allow for any possibility, but in his six years on the bunco squad, he had yet to see the genuine article. He'd been a professional magician in his twenties and early thirties, so the smoke-and-mirrors stuff had quickly become his specialty. It was still only a small part of his job, but when the squad needed someone to pull apart spirit scams or sleight-of-hand cons, he was the man.

He'd never been asked to investigate a murder.

"Who the hell told you that you could be a *real* cop?" a voice drawled from the top of the stairs.

Joe looked up to see Carla Fisk, a detective he had once worked with on a beauty-juice investigation. The perp had been selling bottles of tonic that supposedly made its female users flower into beautiful specimens of womanhood. Carla, who cheerfully admitted that her face looked like the "before" picture of almost every beauty ad ever printed, had worn a wire and purchased a few of the bottles. She was no glamour girl, but she was one of the most beautiful people Joe had ever known.

He smiled. "It's past your bedtime, Carla. You're not working nights, are you?"

"Nah, I was down the street at Manuel's Tavern. Everyone wanted a look at this one."

"Why?"

"You'll see. How's that little girl of yours?"

"Furious. She wasn't happy about being woken up and shuttled to a neighbor's place so I could go check out a Buckhead murder scene."

"She'll understand."

"Maybe if I come back with Yo-Yo Ma tickets."

"You gotta talk to your kid about the music she listens to. People are gonna think she has a brain." Carla grinned, flashing yellow teeth. Then she cocked her head down the hall. "You'd better get down there. They're waiting for you."

He walked down the long hallway, feeling a sudden chill. Was it getting colder? No, it was probably just his imagination, fed by the nervous voices at the end of the hall.

What was in that room?

He stepped into the doorway and froze. He thought he was prepared for anything, but he was wrong.

Suspended high on the far wall, a man was impaled by a large spiked sculpture.

The sight was so odd, so out of the realm of belief, that Joe looked away, then back, as if another glance would help it make sense.

It didn't.

He was staring into a large room with a tall ceiling, perhaps fifteen feet high. There were grand bookshelves, two towering windows, a seating area, and a grand piano. The corpse was suspended at least eight feet above the floor. The chrome sculpture, a skyline of gleaming spikes, was driven downward into the victim's chest, sticking him to the wall like pushpins into a paper doll. A pool of blood had collected on the floor below, along with one of the man's shoes.

"Unbelievable," Joe murmured.

"Is that your professional opinion?"

He turned to see a tall, tanned, fiftyish detective standing next to him. The man didn't offer to shake hands.

"Are you Bailey?"

"Yeah."

"I'm Mark Howe, Homicide. Have you ever seen anything like this?"

"No."

"How did this happen?"

"I have no earthly idea."

Howe clicked his tongue. "That's not the answer I wanted to hear. You've never investigated a homicide, have you?"

Joe shook his head. "No, I'm in bunco."

"Right. The Spirit Basher."

Joe sighed. "The Spirit Basher" was a nickname he'd picked up after several high-profile busts in which he had debunked phony spiritualists and psychics. The local papers championed the headline-ready nickname whenever he ventured into that territory.

"Yeah," Joe said. "Some people call me that."

Howe made a face as if he had just bitten into a lemon. "For the record, I didn't ask for you. It was my boss's idea to call you in."

"I'm glad we got *that* straight."

"No offense, but you spend most of your days breaking up insurance scams, gas station pump fixes, and auto repair con jobs, am I right?"

"And you spend most of your days investigating drug deals gone bad and domestic disputes settled at the end of a firearm. I'd say we're both in foreign territory here."

That shut him up.

Joe glanced around the room. Two fingerprint specialists were dusting every flat surface, and a medical examiner was walking from side to side, staring up at the corpse. A photographer was snapping pictures of the scene.

Joe studied the corpse's face.

It wasn't possible.

"Christ. I know this man," Joe finally said.

"What?"

As if this weren't bizarre enough. "I know him. This is Dr. Robert Nelson."

"That's right," Howe said, surprised.

"He was a professor at Landwyn University. He cochaired the parapsychology program."

"Friend of yours?"

"He despised me. I do some part-time work for the university. The head of the humanities department doesn't believe in that stuff, and he brings me in to debunk the psychics and spiritualists they study."

Joe couldn't take his gaze from Nelson. The professor had been in his early fifties, and his strong chin and cheekbones were tensed in a horrible grimace. It almost appeared as though Nelson were still feeling the agony of that sculpture rammed through his chest. Blood had run down his blue oxford-cloth shirt to his khaki slacks and dripped from the cuffs. Another bloodstain ran down the wall behind him, obviously from the exit wound.

"Who found him?"

"Girlfriend. Eve Chandler. She's in the next room. She let herself in around eleven and found him. She said there have been some disturbances here the past few nights."

"What do you mean?"

"Objects moving around, furniture shifting, and that piano tipping over. All by themselves."

"Did she see these things happening?"

"That's what she says. She's sure they were caused by the same person who made the statue fly into her boyfriend's chest."

"And who would that be?"

"An eight-year-old boy."

"That little bastard murdered him, I know he did."

Eve Chandler leaned back on Nelson's sofa. She was an attractive woman in her early forties, and she had obviously taken a heavy dose of sedatives. She was slurring her words, and her eyes were thin slits. Tears streamed down her face, and she occasionally wiped them from her neck with the back of her hand.

"Who is this boy?" Joe asked.

"It's a kid Robert was studying. His name is . . . Jesse Randall. He makes objects move with his mind."

"Even five-foot sculptures?" Howe asked skeptically.

"All kinds of things. Robert was very excited about him. He said this boy was like no one he had ever seen."

"Why would the boy want to hurt him?" Joe asked.

She stared at Joe as if he were suddenly speaking a foreign language.

Howe leaned forward. "Ms. Chandler, are you on medication?"

She nodded. "Valium. Lots of it. I have a prescription. Wanna see the bottle?"

"That won't be necessary," Joe said. "I know this is hard for you, but we need you to focus. It's important." Eve nodded, but Joe still wasn't sure she understood. He spoke slowly. "Can you tell us why the boy would want to hurt Dr. Nelson?"

"He and Robert had some kind of disagreement. I'm not sure what happened, but he didn't want to see Robert anymore. That's when the shadow storms began."

"What?" Howe asked.

"Shadow storms," Joe said. "Supposed psychic phenomena caused by angry or emotional dreams. While the telekinetic sleeps, objects will move around, flying off shelves and smashing against walls—that kind of thing."

She nodded. "It always started just after nine o'clock, which Robert said was Jesse Randall's bedtime. All hell broke loose after nine o'clock."

"You saw these objects moving around?" Joe asked.

"Mostly we heard them, but a couple of times we saw things flying through the air."

"Can you show me what you actually saw moving?"

"They were both downstairs."

"We'll go down with you."

Howe shook his head. "We have some other things to sort through first."

"Now," Joe said.

"I have a few other questions first," Howe said.

"They'll keep," Joe said. "This is evidence that could be tampered with, stolen, or otherwise compromised." He stood. "Please, Ms. Chandler, will you show us?"

She led them to a sitting room adjacent to the foyer, where she picked up a small decorative musical instrument made up of five bamboo reeds tied together by red twine. She handed it to Joe. "We heard this playing from the next room. Every time we went in to look, the playing stopped. Once, when Robert went to look, it flew out of the room and almost hit him."

Joe inspected the instrument, but there didn't seem to be anything unusual about it. "Did either of you see it rise from the shelf?"

"Hell, we saw it flying toward his *head*."

"That's not quite the same. Did you see it rise from the shelf?"

She thought for a moment. "No. He may have though." She

wiped more tears from her face and neck. "Jesus, I can't believe this."

Howe offered her a handkerchief, but she waved it away. "Keep it," she said. "I gotta be pretty close to running dry."

Joe sympathetically pressed her arm. "Can you tell me what else you saw?"

She nodded. "It was in the kitchen. I'll show you."

They followed her into the large, magnificently decorated kitchen, which was centered by a ten-foot marble-topped island. A rack hung above it with dozens of pots and pans.

"Sometimes, during the night, these pans would swing by themselves and start banging together." She shuddered. "They'd make a terrible sound."

Joe pushed some of the pans, and the eerie, hollow clanging sounded like dozens of out-of-tune gongs.

"Imagine hearing that in the middle of the night," Eve said. "We came downstairs, and as we got closer to the kitchen, the pots started to bang together harder and harder. By the time we made it in here, a few of them were even flying off the hooks and hitting the island and floor. We watched them swinging and clanging into each other for more than a minute, making that horrible sound. Then they just stopped."

"You have no idea what caused it?"

"Robert had an idea."

"The little boy and his shadow storms," Howe said sarcastically.

"Yes." Eve's expression hardened. "Can you arrest him?"

Howe shook his head. "There's the matter of proof. We don't have any evidence that links the murder with Jesse Randall."

"How else could it have happened?"

Howe turned to Joe. "You wanna take that one?"

Joe faced Eve, but he was speaking to Howe as much as he was to her. "Ms. Chandler, in my experience, telekinesis does not exist. Part of what I do in my job is to expose con artists who try to convince others that they have paranormal abilities. I've never seen a psychic claim that couldn't be explained in another, more plausible way."

Her face flushed. "I know who you are and what your feelings are, Mr. Bailey," she said fiercely. "Robert told me how difficult you made his job. I loved that man, and his life's work was based on the fact that this phenomenon *does* exist. If you refuse to believe that, then maybe they should throw you off this case."

Howe put a comforting hand on her arm. "There's no need to get upset. I'm in charge of this investigation. We've just asked Detective Bailey to come here and see if he can help explain what happened." He turned to Joe. "Do you want to take another look at the scene?"

Joe nodded. Howe would obviously have better luck finishing Eve Chandler's interview alone.

He left the house and walked toward his car. It was colder now, and a harsh, biting wind had kicked up. He opened his trunk and pulled out a large black suitcase. Its leather finish was worn and scuffed, and the brass latches and hinges were tarnished. It was his spirit kit, which he used to inspect the scenes of séances and psychic demonstrations. Made up of an odd assortment of sophisticated test equipment and ordinary household items, he generally kept it in his car trunk, where it would be handy for both his police investigations and his debunking work for the university. The last time he left it at the station, some joker had plastered a *Ghostbusters* "no ghosts" insignia on its side, and the sticker had adorned the case ever since.

He carried it back into the study, where the police videographer was filming every inch of the room with a digital camera. The still photographer was now chatting with a few of the officers who came to gawk at the sight.

The nervousness among the officers had given way to morbid humor. Joe overheard cracks about Nelson's taste in decorating, and how a nice tapestry might have been a better match for the wall.

They were trying to be funny, but he could hear a slight edge in their voices. Lieutenant Powell had probably been right about his men getting the shit scared out of them.

Joe had just popped open the suitcase's lid, when Howe walked into the room. "Where's Eve Chandler?" Joe asked.

"Passed out downstairs. Between the Valium and you running her all over the house, she was wiped out. Thanks for neutralizing my witness, Bailey."

"You'll get more out of her tomorrow anyway." Joe pulled a small black box about the size of a hardcover book from the spirit kit. Its high-impact plastic case surrounded a five-inch view screen.

Howe squinted at the instrument. "That looks like a bomb squad gadget."

"It is. It's a McNaughton handheld sonar pulse reader that I grabbed from the bomb squad's scrap heap. It's a little out of date, but it still does the job."

"*What* job?"

Joe attached a battery pack to the unit's top edge. "It tells me if there's anything on the other side of these walls I should know about. It throws out sonar waves that detect any mass behind scanned surfaces. It was made to find explosives, but it also works to detect flying rigs, projectors, or anything else phony spiritualists use." He screwed a telescoping rod onto a bracket on its base and extended the rod out to its full eight-foot length. He flipped the red power switch, and the unit revved to life with a high-pitched whine.

The other cops in the room stopped talking as he slowly swept the reader across the walls and ceiling.

Ping . . . Ping . . . Ping . . .

Joe took note of a few spots where the sonar reader detected areas of greater mass. He was hoping to find some evidence of a contraption that could have sent the sculpture flying into Nelson, but the readings indicated only support beams.

He glided the reader along the wall where Nelson was impaled. No significant variances.

Damn.

He put down the reader and pulled out a large aerosol can. He turned toward the other cops. "Are you guys finished in here?"

One of them nodded. "Knock yourself out."

Joe sprayed the can high on each wall and over the entire ceiling.

Howe snorted. "If it's the smell you're worried about, that usually isn't a problem until the corpse has been around for a few days."

"It's not room deodorant. It's phosphorous clearcoat."

"What?"

Joe was used to the smart-ass comments and questions. Most cops had only the vaguest notion of what he did, and he always tried to patiently explain the tools of his trade. "It coats everything with phosphorus that will show up under an ultraviolet light. If there are any thin wires or mesh up there, this will light them up."

Joe reached back into his kit and produced a high-wattage battery-operated fingerprint lantern. He switched it on. A faint purple light emanated from its rectangular lens plate, and the phosphorus that had settled on his sport jacket took on an intense white glow. He aimed the lamp toward the ceiling and slowly walked around the room. Except for a few cobwebs in the corner, nothing showed up under the light.

He turned off the lantern.

Howe's lips twisted. "Well, *that* was impressive."

"It wasn't meant to impress you." Joe's patience was almost at an end. "It was only supposed to narrow the field of possibilities, which it did."

"Uh-huh. So what you're telling me is that you're no closer to figuring out how it was done."

"You're always closer if you can eliminate some of the possibilities."

"Now I'm *sure* you don't know what you're doing. You're actually spouting the bullshit that McCarey and Stevens teach at the academy."

"McCarey and Stevens?" Joe smiled faintly. "They must have been before my time."

"Screw you."

"This isn't their bullshit. It's mine, and it's what made your boss call me at one in the morning when you couldn't even begin to figure out what was going on here."

"I can handle this."

"I'm sure you can, and after tonight, I'm sure you will. I'm just here to scope things out and help where I can."

"Which doesn't appear to be much."

"We'll see."

Howe relaxed slightly. "Hmm. Were McCarey and Stevens really before your time?"

"Yep."

"Damn, that's depressing." Howe turned toward the door. "I'm gonna roust Ms. Chandler and see if she needs a lift anyplace. I'll check back with you."

"Fine."

Joe pulled out a tape measure and extended it to the base of the sculpture, which was angled up at a forty-five-degree angle. Eleven feet four inches from the floor.

He measured the entire room, noting the height and width of the one door and two windows. The measurements could come in handy later, when comparing various heavy lifting methods typically employed by magicians and psychic scam artists. He could immediately eliminate the Harrison winch due to the rig's large size and lack of portability, and others, like most pulley systems, would not work due to the high center of gravity necessary to drive the sculpture so forcefully into the wall. And he knew of no rig that could explain Nelson's elevated position.

A sharp crack sounded in the room.

Joe spun around.

It was Nelson's other shoe. It had finally slipped off his foot and fallen on the floor, spattering blood against the wall.

As Joe walked out the door, no one was making cute comments about Nelson or anything else. It was obvious they just wanted to get the hell out of there.

He headed downstairs, trying to make sense of what he had just seen. Even if he could figure out how it happened, who would kill Nelson in such a bizarre manner? And why?

He stood in the foyer, jotting down a few last impressions of the crime scene, when Howe came through a doorway with Eve.

"Any ideas?" Howe asked.

Joe put his notebook away. "Not yet. I need to do some checking around."

Howe nodded. "I'm going to take Ms. Chandler home. We'll touch base tomorrow."

Howe said it more like an order than a simple statement. Joe let it pass.

Eve walked toward him until her face was only inches away.

"Just what *do* you believe in, Mr. Bailey?"

He stared back, unsure how to respond.

. . .

It was almost four by the time Joe arrived at his converted loft apartment in Decatur. The building was a former elementary school that he had, in fact, attended during the fourth and fifth grades. The redbrick three-story building had given him some of his worst childhood memories, but it had offered plenty of space to build and rehearse his elaborate illusions. Its charm kept him there long after he had abandoned his magic career, and it amused him to think that he slept on the same spot where the evil Miss Lydecker had lorded over generations of terrified students.

Joe bypassed the noisy freight elevator out of consideration for his sleeping neighbors. Wanda Patterson, a sculptor who lived down the hall, had taken in Nikki after he was summoned, and his daughter barely stirred as he picked her up and carried her back to their apartment. He tucked her in and glanced around the room. Posters of Yo-Yo Ma and Sarah Chang decorated one wall, and *Teen Beat* pages of Leonardo DiCaprio covered another. So different from other girls her age, yet so much like them.

He stood up and leaned against the doorframe, watching Nikki sleep.

What do you believe in, Mr. Bailey?

Eve Chandler's parting words had been bothering him ever since he left Nelson's house. He wasn't a religious man, and he didn't believe in the afterlife. But he did believe in himself and in the little girl who slept on the other side of the room.

He'd also believed in his wife, Angela.

God, he missed her. Had she really been gone two years? In some ways it seemed like decades, in other ways just a few weeks. Angela's battle with ovarian cancer had taught him more about courage and strength than he ever thought possible, but there had been nothing noble about her final days. They had been cruel and ugly, torturous and sad. She had literally wasted away, her body racked with pain, her mind dulled by medication.

When Angela had finally let out her last long breath, he had wiped the tears from her face and held her close until the sun rose on a world much more wretched and lonely than he had ever known.

His eyes still stung to think about it. He instinctively turned from Nikki even though she wasn't awake to see him crying.

He must be strong for Nikki.

His daughter had given him so much joy. He loved seeing the world through her eyes as she made fantastic discoveries in the mundane, finding beauty where he'd thought none existed.

She hadn't seen her mother during that terrible final week, but Nikki was convinced that her mom was in a better place now and that one day they would all be reunited.

If only he could believe that.

Even now, sleeping, Nikki seemed to be smiling. She had told him that her mother was in her dreams almost every night. Was she dreaming about her? Was Nikki laughing with her mother, eating peanut butter and banana sandwiches and working in the rooftop garden, just like in the old days?

He hoped so. He wished he were there too.

He could never remember his dreams.

Jesus, he was a scary man.

Natalie Simone leaned against her Range Rover 4.6HSE while Garrett Lyles stared disapprovingly at the automatic weapons spread out on the back floorboard. They were standing on a dark side street in Atlanta's south side, chosen by Natalie for its isolation.

She was used to dealing with tough characters, but there was something about Lyles that terrified her. It wasn't his looks; he was a tall, good-looking man in his mid-thirties, and he had broad shoulders and long brown hair. His striking blue eyes softened his chiseled features. Maybe she was reacting to the stories she'd heard.

He glanced up. "Is this all you have?"

Natalie tried to pretend that his sharp tone didn't rattle her. She was thin and twenty-eight, and many of her customers thought they could intimidate her. She lit a cigarette. "It's not like I had a lot of notice. You're lucky I'm even here, soldier boy."

"Did I disturb your beauty sleep?"

"No, but you're making me miss one hell of a rave party."

"I'll make it worth your while."

"Then stop whinin' about the selection."

Lyles picked up the Lanchester. He palmed the grip a few times and softly rubbed the grooved trigger with his index finger.

Natalie smiled, blowing smoke through her pursed lips. "This is where the sickos get a hard-on. Glad to see you're not one of those."

"The night is young."

She thought he was joking, but she wasn't positive. "What brings you to town? *Soldier of Fortune* annual convention?"

"No."

"I heard about that little maneuver you pulled in the Balkans. Your employers were very happy. Pretty smart, soldier boy."

"I don't know what you're talking about."

"Uh-huh."

"How much for the Lanchester?"

"Eleven hundred."

"Too much. You're taking advantage of me."

Natalie took another puff from her cigarette. She'd put on a strong front, but she was afraid he could see her trembling hand. "I don't negotiate."

He looked at her as if he wanted to snap her neck, but he finally nodded. "Fine." He reached into his pocket, pulled out a thick roll of cash, and counted out eleven one-hundred-dollar bills.

Natalie handed him the Lanchester.

"You should wear a thicker jacket," Lyles said. "It's pretty obvious you have cannons up your sleeves. What do you have, a pair of Rugers?"

She dropped the cigarette, flicked her wrists, and two snub-nosed revolvers suddenly appeared in her hands.

Lyles nodded. "Berettas. My mistake."

"You still didn't tell me what brings you to town."

"In your business, you should know better than to ask questions."

She did know better. If he hadn't made her so nervous, she never would have made that mistake. "Sorry."

He smiled and tucked the gun into his jacket. "But I don't mind telling you." He didn't look back as he walked away from her. "Let's just say I'm here to get in touch with my spiritual self."

2

"Is it for real, Dad?"

Joe woke up to find the morning newspaper on his chest. Nikki was standing over him. Joe tilted the paper up to see a large color photograph of Dr. Nelson impaled on the wall of his study.

"Jesus!" He jerked upright in bed.

"Did that really happen?"

Who could have taken that picture? As he studied it, he realized that it had been shot from outside Nelson's house, through the upstairs window. A photographer with a long zoom lens could have taken it from the house across the street. Or a scanner geek might have shot it from a tree outside. "Yes, honey. It's real. I can't believe they printed this."

"I've seen worse."

"That doesn't mean I want you looking at it. I'd expect this from a New York tabloid but not splattered across the front page of *our* paper."

Nikki made a face. "Splattered? That's not even funny."

"It wasn't meant to be. And where have you seen worse?"

"Monica and I watched a video where, like, ten people got slaughtered by a guy in a mask."

"Remind me to talk to her parents about that. Anyway, this is different."

She pulled her strawberry blond hair away from her face. "I know. This is real."

Joe drew her close. She *did* know the difference. Her mother's death had been a crash course. For months afterward she had tried to ignore the pain, but she had gradually opened up about her feelings.

He pushed her back and rolled up the newspaper. "This is why I had to drag you over to Wanda's last night."

Nikki's eyes widened. "No way! You were there?"

He climbed out of bed and headed for the kitchen. "I'm afraid so."

She followed him. "Why didn't you wake me up and tell me about it?"

"Oh, *that* would have been a nice bedtime story."

"It would have been a lot less scary than listening to Wanda scream cuss words on the phone to her ex-boyfriend."

"Remind me to talk to her about that."

"Don't talk to her, just get Vince next time."

Vince was her favorite baby-sitter, an aspiring young magician who often watched her when Joe worked late.

"Vince had a late-night gig, and there's no way I would've given you the gory details that our local paper did."

"Why were you there? You don't do murders."

"I don't *investigate* murders. Until now. They wanted me to come down and see if I had any idea how it happened."

"Do you?"

"Aren't you late for school or something?"

"Nope. Do you know how it happened?"

"No."

"Awww, what good are you?"

"The people I work with are probably asking themselves the same question. But don't worry, I'll figure it out."

"Oh." She fell silent.

"You okay?"

"You're gonna work on a murder case?"

"It looks like it. At least until I can figure out what happened."

"Can't somebody else do it?"

"Why?"

She looked down. "It's a *murder* case. Won't it be dangerous?"

Joe turned toward her, but she wouldn't meet his gaze. She'd grown much more protective of him since losing her mother. "I'll be all right, baby. They only need me to advise them."

"Uh-huh."

He lifted up her chin. "There's nothing to worry about."

She managed a smile. "Okay."

Joe stared into her eyes. It wasn't okay. He hoped like hell they could wrap this up quickly.

"You'll see." He motioned toward the kitchen. "Now, is it my turn to make breakfast, or yours?"

Joe arrived at work at the windowless ten-story police head-quarters building located on the periphery of the Georgia State University campus. "GSU's biggest dorm," the students joked, as the building also housed the Atlanta city jail.

He entered the squad room, where tacky green felt acoustic panels did little to quiet the bustle of activity from fourteen cops at their desks. The receptionist, Karen Nevois, stopped him.

"Joe, you'd better get over to Lieutenant Gerald's office in Homicide."

"Now?"

"Unless you'd like to keep the chief of police waiting."

"You're kidding, right?"

No smile. She wasn't kidding.

He rapped on the door of Gerald's office and stepped inside. Gerald, Howe, and the police chief, Paul Davis, were standing around the desk, looking at the morning newspaper.

Gerald didn't look as if he had slept. "Close the door behind you, Bailey."

Davis stepped forward and extended his hand. "Good morning."

Joe shook hands with him. Davis was a fiftyish man with white hair and horn-rimmed glasses.

"What the hell happened there last night, Joe?"

"I'm sure Howe filled you in. I surveyed the scene. There was no evidence of lifts, pulleys, or any kind of winch. The sculpture that went through the victim normally rested on the other side of the room. It was angled downward, which means force had to have been directed from a height of over eleven feet. Do we know the weight of that sculpture?"

Gerald nodded. "One hundred and sixty-two pounds."

"Heavier than I thought. I'd like copies of the videotapes and photographs that were taken."

"You got it."

"Lieutenant, I have to tell you, I have a pretty heavy load of my own right now."

"Not anymore. I've already spoken with Henderson. You're on this full-time, and you'll be working with Howe."

Joe cast a glance at his new partner. Howe obviously wasn't happy.

Davis held up the paper's front page. "You know, of course, this is only the beginning. Tonight it will be on *Hard Copy, A*

Current Affair, and *American Journal.* By tomorrow, Letterman and Leno will be joking about it. By Monday, it may be in *Time* and *Newsweek.* Psychic murder, the headlines will scream, along with this ghastly picture. Damn."

Gerald nodded. "We need to put this one away quickly."

The chief looked at Joe. "Anything you need, any help you require, just ask. And I don't want any statements to the press unless it has been cleared through my office. Are we all clear on that?"

Joe, Howe, and Gerald nodded.

"Now, what about this ridiculous story about the boy and his powers?"

Howe produced his notebook and deliberately stepped in front of Joe. "His name is Jesse Randall. He's eight years old, African American, and lives on Avenue K in Techwood. Dr. Nelson had been studying what he believed to be the boy's telekinetic abilities, and the two staged a demonstration for several other parapsychologists in Dallas last month. Every scientist there was convinced that Jesse Randall is the genuine article."

Joe shook his head. "It was an easy crowd to convince. He probably wouldn't have lasted ten minutes in front of a group of professional magicians."

"Or you?" the chief asked.

"Or me."

"Good. That's your angle. Find out how Nelson was killed, and figure out how the boy does his stuff. A lot of the heat will dissipate as soon as you do that."

"I thought the goal was to find out who did it."

"That's *my* job," Howe said.

"It's *both* of your jobs," Gerald said. "You'll just be going at it from two different directions. Coordinate with each other, gentlemen. Remember the box in your grade school report card that said 'works and plays well with others'? That was to get you ready for this."

Howe obviously wasn't happy as he and Joe walked downstairs.

"Okay, Howe, what's the problem?"

"The problem is that I'm gonna be busting my hump to break this case, when all you'll be doing is deflecting bad PR."

"I'll be doing a bit more than that."

Howe stopped on the landing and spoke in sharp, icy tones. "Our authority is one of the best weapons we have, Bailey. Last night you undercut mine in front of a witness and potential suspect."

"*That's* what this is all about?"

"That and the fact that I've already been poached way too many times."

Joe nodded. Now it made sense. Just as stealing credit was common in the corporate world, it was part of life on the force. He knew quite a few cops who had ascended through the ranks by poaching cases and one-upping their fellow officers whenever they got the chance.

"So you're afraid the Spirit Basher will grab all the glory?"

"That's where this is headed. The second you walked into that room, I was invisible."

"I'm not looking to take anything away from you."

"Whether you're looking to do it or not, it could still happen. I've been screwed more times than I can count. Just stay out of my way, Bailey. You handle the how, and I'll take care of the who and why. Got it?"

"Now we know how you scored on the 'works and plays well with others' box, huh?"

Howe glared at him and continued down the stairs.

. . .

Jesse Randall sat in the corner of the school playground, pushing his Hot Wheels Grand Prix racing car through the dirt path he had just carved with his middle three fingers. Some of the guys called it a "grand pricks" racer, but he knew they were just jealous.

It was recess time at Lackey Hills Elementary School, and Jesse was once again playing by himself. Even though he never did his tricks for the other kids, they had heard about him from their parents and teachers. The word got out that he was someone to be afraid of, and one by one his friends withdrew, closing him out of their fourth-grade cliques.

Fine. He didn't need 'em. One day soon he'd buy a nice house like he and Mama had always wanted. Then he'd have friends in his new neighborhood, and maybe Daddy would even want to come back to live with them. If his tricks could make that happen, it was worth having to play alone.

Jesse looked up and saw three men and a woman walking toward him. They were on the other side of the playground's chain-link fence, and two of the men had large TV cameras. He'd seen cameras like that in Dallas.

He hated Dallas.

In Dallas there were lots of people asking questions, wiring horrible machines to his head and chest. Dr. Nelson said it was okay, but he wasn't nice the way he had been in Atlanta. He sometimes yelled, especially when the tricks weren't working well.

"Make it happen, boy. . . . You want to make a fool of yourself?" he'd shout.

Dr. Nelson later said he was sorry, calling it another experiment.

Whatever.

It didn't make up for the days of tests, interviews, and experiments that measured everything from his eating habits to his sleep routines.

The people with the cameras were now standing at the fence. He'd seen one of them before; the pretty lady was on the news. She shouted at him: "Are you Jesse Randall?"

He adjusted his wire-rimmed glasses and nodded.

She slid off her shoes and climbed over the fence, looking far less classy than she always did on TV. One of the cameramen handed her his camera and climbed over to join her.

Jesse stood up. He'd climbed that fence many times when a pop fly went over, but he'd never seen grown-ups doing it.

The cameraman pointed his camera at Jesse as the pretty lady shoved a large microphone in his face. "Hi, Jesse. I'm Darlene Farrell from Big Four News. How are you today?"

Jesse shrugged. He wanted to turn and run, but he stood still, staring down at that microphone with the big "4" on it.

She moved in closer. "Tell me, Jesse, did you kill Dr. Robert Nelson?"

Jesse stared at her in bewilderment. What was she talking about?

The other reporter, now awkwardly climbing the fence, chimed in. "Did you use your powers, Jesse? Did you murder Dr. Nelson with your powers?"

"Dr. Nelson?" Jesse said, still not grasping the question.

Other kids in the playground had noticed the cameras, and they were starting to approach to see what the commotion was about.

Darlene Farrell leaned closer. "You know he's dead, don't you, honey?"

"He is not!" Jesse shouted.

She handed him the morning paper, then stepped out of the way to allow the camera to catch his reaction.

Dr. Nelson . . .

Jesse threw down the paper. "This isn't him!"

Darlene stepped closer. "I'm afraid it is him, Jesse, and some people think it's your fault. How does that make you feel?"

Jesse pushed her. "Go away! Just go away!"

How could this happen? Dr. Nelson . . .

"Honey, do you want to talk about it?"

"I want you to go away!" His nose was running, and he could feel the tears starting to well up. He wanted to turn away from her, but he didn't want the other kids to see him crying. He kept his head low and backed away.

"Not yet, honey. I need to talk to you first. Would you show us how your powers work?"

"No. Go away!"

She smiled sweetly. "Please, Jesse. For me?"

"Get the hell away from him!" Jesse's mother appeared from the other side of the swingsets. Latisha Randall hurled herself at the cameraman and knocked him to the ground.

"That's a fourteen-thousand-dollar camera!" Darlene yelled.

"If you don't get out of my face, that's going to be fourteen thousand dollars up your ass!"

Darlene backed off.

Latisha glared at the TV journalists. She was a tall, thin woman with pronounced cheekbones and a no-nonsense attitude that dared anyone to cross her. She held Jesse close. "It's okay, sweetheart."

"Dr. Nelson!" he wailed.

"Shh, I know. I just heard it on the radio, honey. I came right away."

The reporters yelled at Jesse.

"Did you kill him?"

"Do your magic, Jesse!"

"Show us how you did it!"

Latisha picked him up and walked across the playground with him, hurrying to stay ahead of the reporters and cameramen.

"Have you ever hurt anyone else with your powers?"

"Miss Randall, are you afraid that your son may be taken away from you?"

Across the street from the playground, Garrett Lyles sat in the cab of his Ford Explorer pickup truck and gripped the steering wheel hard. How dare those reporters treat Jesse Randall with such disrespect. Wasn't that professor's death enough to show them how powerful he was?

Of course not. They were fools.

Too bad the mother had come; it would've been nice to see Jesse take care of them himself. *That* would have been something to see. He could easily imagine the pretty reporter choking on her microphone, with the cord twisting and turning around her thin neck.

But Jesse wouldn't do that. Only now was he beginning to realize the full extent of his powers, and his most spectacular displays hadn't even been executed by his conscious mind. Jesse was new at this, and he needed guidance. He also needed protection against the scum that would prey upon him now that his abilities were widely known.

That's what *he* was there for. Excitement coursed through him at the thought. It was time to take action.

He started up the truck and put it into gear.

"You've got to be kidding."

Sam Brewster ran his hands through his thick white hair as he studied the crime scene photos of Nelson's murder.

"I wish I *were* kidding," Joe said. "Any ideas?"

Sam put the photo down on the sales counter in front of him. He was the eighty-five-year-old proprietor of Sam's Magic, a hole-in-the-wall shop in the downtown neighborhood of Five Points. Joe had been a regular customer since he was eight years old, and he suspected that Sam had been operating the store at a loss for years. Sam, however, was still quite active designing spectacular stage illusions for world-renowned magicians, and his shop was an indulgence he could well afford. It was located only a few blocks from police headquarters, and Joe still stopped by the store at least twice a week.

"Is there a chandelier or any other kind of lighting fixture I'm not seeing here?"

"Nope."

"This is reaching, but would it have been possible to drive the arm of a crane through an open window?"

"The window is too small. It's framed in oak, and there weren't any marks on it."

Sam shook his head. "If you figure this one out, let me know. I could sell it to Copperfield for a mint."

Sam's assistant, Vince, appeared from the back storeroom. Vince was a nineteen-year-old former street hustler who had once practiced his sleight-of-hand scams on tourists and conventioneers along International Boulevard. After Joe busted Vince almost two years before, Sam put his talents to use as a salesperson in his store. Vince was on his way to becoming a fine illusionist, and Joe was sure that his rugged good looks and charisma would translate across any stage. Vince already had a fan in Nikki, who lobbied for him every time Joe needed a baby-sitter for the evening.

"Hiya, Joe. How's my girl?"

"She's furious with you because you weren't able to watch her last night."

Vince smiled. "It was open-mike night at the Punchline, and I made my comedy magic debut."

"How'd it go?"

"The magic part went great. The comedy part, well, let's just say it was a humbling experience."

"I'm sure it wasn't that bad."

"It's the toughest crowd I've had since a group of Hell's Angels caught me palming an ace in a curbside draw poker scam."

"At least you walked out of the Punchline in one piece."

Vince chuckled as he walked to the front window. "With scars that will never heal."

Sam handed the photos back to Joe. "You got your work cut out for you, kid. I'll ask around and see if the local talent has heard anything."

"I'd appreciate it, Sam. Everyone's watching me on this one."

"If you screw up, you can always go back to your old line of work."

"And spend the rest of my life performing escapes to a disco version of 'My Heart Will Go On'? No thanks."

"And I guess that busting palm readers is more dignified?"

"Well, at least it won't bring abject humiliation to me and my family."

"No, your paycheck takes care of that."

It was an argument he and Sam had been having ever since he quit the magic business. Joe had grown up with a romantic vision of illusionists like Houdini, Thurston, and Kellar, but their dignified brand of showmanship didn't exist anymore. Now it was all about cheesy music, dopey patter, and laser light shows.

He had tried to play that game and had even been fairly successful at it, picking up occasional opening-act gigs in Las Vegas and Atlantic City. But it hadn't taken him long to realize that it wasn't for him, and he resented the long weeks it kept him away from his wife.

"But why a cop?" his friends always asked in disbelief.

He usually responded with a shrug and the simple statement that his father had been on the force.

Like that really meant anything. But it always seemed to satisfy them.

His father *had* been on the force, a desk sergeant in the tiny Vinings station, and hardly a day went by that Dad didn't talk about how miserable the job made him. He now owned a revival movie theater, the Celluloid Palace, in Savannah.

The irony of the situation didn't escape Joe: He was a cop, and Dad was in the entertainment business. But Joe had always liked the camaraderie in the department, and when he began to think about changing careers, it had been a comfortable choice to make. He had known many of his fellow second- and third-generation officers since childhood, and he felt at home wearing Dad's worn Brigade holster.

Sam lifted his spectacles and took another long look at the photo. "I sure hope you nail the bastard who did this. It takes some kind of sicko to rig this kind of murder."

"I can't argue with that."

"But when you *do* figure it out, I hope you give me an exclusive on how he did it."

Lyles smiled at the pretty television news reporter as she climbed into her Jaguar in the Kroger supermarket parking lot. "Darlene Farrell?" he asked.

She immediately assumed a defensive posture, obviously conditioned from years of dealing with scary fans and hormone-charged stalkers. "Yes?"

"You don't remember me, do you? I'm Harry Martin. I used to date Elizabeth MacKenzie."

She instantly relaxed. Perfect, he thought. Although there was still no way she could recognize him, the mention of a familiar name was enough to put her at ease. If only she knew that he had just come from the Emory University library, where he had spent forty-five minutes poring through her college yearbook. Elizabeth MacKenzie had been a fellow anchor of Darlene's on the campus closed-circuit television broadcasts.

She smiled. "Harry! Of course I remember. How are you?"

Lyles was impressed; the phony bitch was giving a terrific performance. Almost as good as his.

"Great. I own my own software company up in Marietta."

Her eyes widened. "Really?"

They chatted for a few minutes, and Lyles tossed out just enough names from the yearbook to completely convince her that he was a long-lost college friend. He even admitted that he'd always thought she was a *much* better broadcaster than his old girl-friend.

The stuck-up bitch was eating it up.

"So," Darlene finally said, "did you ever get married?"

Bingo.

She was interested. He had no doubt that his looks and charm had swayed her, but he suspected that the competition with her old college coanchor had also played a part.

"Nah," he replied. "I've just been too busy. I guess you know how that is, huh? I see your reports on the news almost every night."

She nodded. "No rest for the weary."

"Hey, would you like to go grab a cup of coffee? There's a Starbucks around the corner."

Darlene appeared to think about it, but she finally shook her head. "I'm sorry, Harry. I have things at home to take care of. Maybe some other time?"

"No problem. Hey, it was nice talking to you."

Lyles climbed into his pickup truck and waved to her as he

started it. She waved back, and he could see that she wanted to give him her number, her card, or anything else that might ensure another pleasant encounter with this forgotten man from her past.

He backed out of the parking space and drove away.

Before he reached the exit, he saw her struggling to start her car. The starter whined, but the engine refused to roar to life. He turned his truck around and pulled alongside her.

"Engine trouble?"

"Yes. I don't understand it. It was working fine."

She reached for her cellular phone, pushed the power button, and stared at the display. "Damn. It's not working. I was using it just before I went into the store."

He flashed her his biggest smile. "Get in. There's a pay phone down the street."

Joe pushed past the reporters camped in front of Jesse Randall's one-story project home in Techwood. Located near both the Georgia Tech campus and Coca-Cola's worldwide headquarters, Techwood was known for its low-income housing and vicious gang activity. Despite the bad rap given to it on the evening news almost every night, Joe knew that most of Techwood's residents were honest, hardworking people who took pride in their modest homes.

As he walked to the front door, he noticed that one of the news cameramen was getting a shot of a rusted car on blocks across the street.

Sure, Joe thought. Never mind the beautiful flower garden only twenty feet away.

He held up his badge and knocked on the door. There were footsteps and a rustling sound that told him he was being examined through the peephole. Finally the door opened and a slender woman stared at him.

"Ms. Randall?"

"Yes?"

"I'm Detective Bailey, Atlanta P.D. I'd like to talk to you and your son."

"Why?" she asked sharply.

"May I come in?"

Her eyes narrowed. "Those people on the sidewalk want to come in here too. Why should I treat you any differently?"

"Because I'm a police officer," he said gently. "And because you want all those people to go away. The sooner I figure out what really happened to Dr. Nelson, the sooner they'll be out of here. But I can't do my job unless you help me."

She stared at him for a moment, then swung the door open for him to enter.

It was a pleasant, cheery home filled with knickknacks and an exotic collection of salt and pepper shakers. Cushions were strategically placed over the parts of the furniture that were obviously worn or split, and Joe assumed that the awkwardly positioned area rug covered a stain or hole in the carpet.

He looked at Latisha Randall. She was an attractive woman in her mid-twenties, but it was obvious that the day's events had taken their toll on her. What in her life could have prepared her to be thrust into a situation like this?

"How are you holding up?" he asked.

"Stupid question. Reporters are camped outside, the phone's been ringing off the hook, and my little boy thinks maybe he killed a man."

Joe nodded. "Do *you* think your boy killed Dr. Nelson?"

She paused. "How will answering your questions get those people away from us?"

"If I do my job right, they're going to know that your boy isn't responsible. Do you really believe in the shadow storms?"

"I don't know what I think. Jesse has a gift, but how do I know what happens when he's asleep? If his subconscious does take over, that's not his fault, is it?"

"Have you ever seen any of his . . . phenomena here while he was sleeping?"

"Never. Dr. Nelson started noticing it in his house earlier this week."

"His girlfriend said that all hell would break loose after nine o'clock. Dr. Nelson felt that Jesse's disturbing dreams may have been causing it?"

"That's what he said. Jesse *has* been having bad dreams. Since he discovered his gift, he's been afraid people would take him away from me. But it got much worse after Dallas. Dr. Nelson wanted to take him to a psychic research institute in Switzerland. Jesse didn't want to go, and I didn't want him to go either. Jesse was upset with Dr. Nelson. That's a lot of pressure for a little boy to take, you know? He started having terrible nightmares."

"He's not the first child to have bad dreams."

Latisha nervously wiped her sweaty hands on her jeans. "Jesse isn't going to be in any trouble, is he?"

Joe shook his head. "I can't imagine how he could be. I'd like to talk to him though. Is he here?"

"He's in his room." She jabbed a finger into his chest. "But if you say one thing to upset him, I'm throwing your ass right out of here."

She turned and led Joe down a narrow peach-wallpapered hallway. She opened a door and spoke softly. "Jesse, honey, there's someone here to see you."

Joe couldn't hear a response, but Latisha walked into the room and motioned for him to follow. It was a small bedroom, perhaps eight by ten feet, decorated with rap group posters and an assortment of *Star Wars* models dangling from the ceiling on fishing lines.

Jesse was lying on the twin bed, and Joe was surprised at how small and fragile he seemed. Jesse was probably average height for an eight-year-old boy, but Joe realized that he had expected someone more theatrical, like so many of the fake psychics he had made it his business to expose. He'd never studied a kid before.

"Hi, Jesse. How are you doing?" He never talked down to children, remembering how much he'd hated adults talking to him as if he were a moron.

Jesse's head didn't rise from the pillow. He adjusted his wire-rimmed glasses. "Hi."

"You don't have anything to be afraid of, Jesse. I'm just trying to figure out what happened to Dr. Nelson."

Jesse turned away. "I don't know what happened."

"Did you dream about him last night?"

Jesse didn't answer.

Latisha softly rubbed her son's arm. "Honey, it's okay. You can tell him."

Jesse looked at his mother, then back at Joe. He nodded.

"Were you hurting him in your dream?"

Jesse sat up. "*He* was hurting *me* in my dreams! I was trying to run away, and he kept coming after me. He wasn't just one person. . . . He was a lot of people. They all had his eyes. He even came up from the ground and tried to pull me under. I kicked him and hit him so he'd let me go."

"Well, that's what *I* would do to someone who was chasing me. Did you like Dr. Nelson?"

"I used to like him a lot."

"What happened?"

"He got mad at me."

"Why?"

Jesse shrugged. "He wanted me to go away to Switzerland so they could study me. I didn't want to go, and he said I was letting my mama down."

Latisha sat on the bed next to him. "Honey, you never told me that."

"Jesse, how long had you known Dr. Nelson?"

He wrinkled his brow and looked at his mother.

"About four months," Latisha said. "When we discovered the things he could do, I called the university. I talked to Dr. Nelson, and I started taking Jesse there for tests a couple of times a week. Jesse and Dr. Nelson spent a lot of time together."

"Jesse, how did you discover you could do these things?"

The boy looked at his mother again. She nodded her encouragement.

Jesse swung his legs over the side of the bed and leaned closer to Joe. "I was visiting my uncle in Macon, and my cousin always cheated at checkers. He moved the pieces when I wasn't looking. If I tried to move 'em back, he'd pound me. I just wanted to move 'em to where they belonged, and I found out that if I thought about it hard enough, the pieces would move by themselves. Pretty soon, I could make almost anything move by itself."

"My brother called me from Macon," Latisha said. "He was so excited that he was almost out of his mind."

Joe nodded. "I can understand why he would be." He reached down to the floor, picked up a pair of *Star Wars* action figures, and put them on the night table. "Do you think you can make Darth Maul and Yoda move for me, Jesse?"

Latisha stiffened. "He doesn't have to do that."

"Of course he doesn't," Joe said. "But it would help me understand. You want to give it a try, Jesse?"

Jesse was clearly uncomfortable, but he nodded. He took off his glasses and stared at the figures, taking deep, slow breaths.

The change in Jesse's demeanor was startling. He was suddenly still.

Focused.

Determined.

Where was the eight-year-old boy who was just here?

Joe's glance shifted back and forth between Jesse and the figures.

The boy's eyes opened wide, and then . . .

Nothing.

No movement.

Maul and Yoda didn't budge.

Jesse slumped. "I'm sorry."

"Come on, try it again," Joe said. "I have time."

Something snapped within Jesse. His expression twisted with anger. *"Don't you do this to me,"* he said, emphasizing each word.

Joe involuntarily stepped back before he could catch himself. Jesus, this was only a kid. Yet Jesse's manner was not that of a child. It was positively chilling.

"Sometimes it just doesn't work," Latisha said. "Can't you see he's been through enough already today? This is the last thing he needs."

Joe hadn't taken his eyes off Jesse. The boy was still glaring at him.

"Fine," Joe said. "I'll come back."

How could a woman who had appeared so strong, so confident, leave this world in such a pitiful manner?

Lyles watched Darlene Farrell burn in the hastily gathered pile of leaves and branches. He'd made Darlene gather her own funeral pyre, and the woman had cried the entire time, offering him money, influence, and even sex to spare her miserable life.

She should have known better than to hurt Jesse Randall.

Lyles knew that Jesse could have taken care of her himself, just as easily as he had dispatched the professor. But it was his honor to serve the Child of Light.

Are you happy with me, Jesse? Did I serve you well?

Lyles breathed in the tart smell of the roaring, crackling fire.

Burning flesh.

He knew that odor well. He wished he didn't, but there was no erasing the past. He could, however, *atone* for his past, and if he could direct his talents and abilities toward a higher purpose, salvation might be at hand.

He climbed into his truck and drove back to Highway 23, which would take him to I-85 and Atlanta.

He couldn't escape that tart, tangy smell.

Was it on his clothes? It couldn't be; he hadn't been *that* close to the fire. It was always the same: Long after the sights and sounds of his kills had faded, the smells remained. Whenever he smelled freshly cut grass, he thought of the nine dead soldiers in Ireland. Gasoline? The vanload of journalists in Colombia.

Now Darlene Farrell had her own scent.

This time, at least, it was for a good cause.

It had been almost two years since his new life began, when he met Bertram and Irene Setzer of Birmingham, England. They were a well-heeled couple who had hired him to escort their corporate officers out of Sarajevo during a particularly violent period of civil unrest. He had accomplished the mission with his usual efficiency, and as a special reward for his efforts, Bertram and Irene invited him to spend his summer at a villa on their eleven-hundred-acre estate. He knew that they probably just wanted to keep him handy for other jobs that might come up, but he welcomed the opportunity to spend time in the beautiful English countryside. He frequently dined with the Setzers, and it was during those long evenings that he became acquainted with their unusual beliefs. At first, he found their ideas odd and confusing, but as the weeks wore on, he discovered a strange comfort in their philosophy.

No regrets. No guilt. No remorse.

There was more to it than that, of course, but he realized that it was exactly what he needed in his life. The years had taken their toll on his psyche, but this new way of life stripped away much of the pain and anguish that had been consuming him.

Now he couldn't imagine life without the Millennial Prophets. He wasn't worthy yet, but he soon would be.

If only he could get away from that horrible smell.

It was a few minutes past nine by the time Joe came back to his apartment building. As he stepped into the cargo elevator and pulled the accordion-style metal doors closed, he performed his nightly ritual of trying to shake off the job. He rolled his shoulders and breathed deeply. Let it go.

He pressed the button for the third floor. He couldn't help but think back to his meeting with Jesse Randall and how quickly the boy's demeanor had changed. He'd pushed Jesse to perform, which had probably triggered unpleasant memories of Nelson and the other testers.

From one moment to the next, Jesse had transformed from a meek little boy to an angry, venomous child. Nelson had sure done a number on him.

Joe rolled his shoulders again. Not now. Leave it behind. Keep it from interfering with—

He went still. There was something different about the elevator tonight.

The floor was shaking, rattling.

A low metallic groan echoed in the shaft below.

He punched the button again.

The vibration intensified, jarring him backward. The elevator car trembled and creaked, and the hanging light fixture bounced crazily overhead.

Before he could regain his balance, the bottom dropped out of the elevator.

He clawed at the air, finally catching the accordion-style door in front of him. His fingers curled around the sharp diagonal bars as his body slammed against the oily shaft. The floor plate clanged downward, echoing in the void below.

The elevator car abruptly stopped. Still dangling from the door, he tried to get his bearings. What the hell had just happened?

He looked down. Darkness. Shadows.

Death.

He swung his legs back and forth, trying to get a toehold somewhere in the shaft. Not a chance.

Shit.

The door bars, pulled by the tension of his weight, pinched like nutcrackers around each finger. Blood oozed over his hands. He couldn't hold on much longer.

Nikki. He'd never see her again.

Sounds from above. Clanging. Whirring. Gears shifting?

The elevator car lurched downward.

His hands were numb, and he knew that he could lose his grip at any second. He kicked outward, trying to keep his body from brushing against the side of the shaft.

The car moved faster. And faster.

Was it falling? Not quite, he realized, but almost.

The second floor flew by. He was headed for the basement. Though he couldn't see it, he knew that the cement floor of the shaft was rushing toward his outstretched legs.

Climb, he told himself. Now.

He gripped the next row of diagonal metal strips and pulled himself up. It hurt like hell. He grabbed the next row with his throbbing left hand. The elevator was picking up speed. He could hear sounds echoing off the bottom of the shaft.

Climb.

He swung his legs up.

Bam!

Contact.

The force of the impact threw him backward onto the floor of the shaft. He was caked in oily sludge.

He stood up and realized the shaft had been cut about three feet deep into the basement. He forced open the doors and hoisted himself up to the floor. He crossed his arms in front of him, tucking his bleeding hands under his armpits.

The crippled elevator hummed, taunting him as he staggered away. Thank God Nikki hadn't been with him.

He leaned against the dark basement's concrete wall, shaking.

All hell broke loose after nine o'clock.

For some crazy reason, Eve Chandler's voice was ringing in his ears.

Joe angled his watch into a shaft of light cutting through the basement's glass brick window.

Nine-fifteen P.M.

Twenty-four hours after Nelson's murder.

Fifteen minutes after Jesse Randall's bedtime.

If his hands weren't still hurting so badly, Joe might have chuckled. He knew what the Landwyn University parapsychology team would say if they heard about this: another shadow storm. He had upset Jesse, and the boy's subconscious was striking back.

Joe looked back at the humming elevator and the overhead light that was still swinging back and forth.

The spook squad would have a field day with this one.

3

Joe walked into the Landwyn University Humanities Building. He'd hoped to get there earlier, but he had spent much of the morning with the elevator service technician, who couldn't offer any explanation for the previous evening's malfunction. He had shown Joe how the floor panel fit snugly in the base of the car; no reasonable amount of force could pry it loose, and even if it had somehow happened, the elevator's base panels would show the stress. The panels were rigid and straight.

Forget it, Joe decided. It had been an accident, like the dozens of other elevator accidents that occur every day. Nothing spooky about it.

A female grad student was standing guard outside the parapsychology testing room. "Wait here, please. Séance in progress."

Joe looked up at the video monitor over the door. The picture was dark, but there were the requisite spooky sounds, bumping furniture and amazed exclamations from the supposedly objective research team.

The grad student looked Joe up and down. "Dr. Kellner will be out in a couple of minutes. Are you a seer?"

"No."

"Spiritualist?"

"No."

"Telepath?"

"No."

"Healer?"

"Afraid not."

"Then what are you?"

"Police detective. My name's Joe Bailey."

"Ah. Skeptic."

"My reputation precedes me."

"You could say that."

Joe knew that he was probably the single most despised person by the parapsychology program's faculty and students. The head of the humanities department, Daryl Reisman, was a fellow skeptic, and he often hired Joe to debunk the group's findings. Reisman felt that the parapsychology program was an embarrassment to the university, but the group was protected by a wealthy benefactor, Roland Ness, who provided not only most of the program's funding but also many of the university's other endowments. Any movement to abolish the program would certainly be quashed by a board of regents eager to keep Ness's cash rolling in.

Nothing like a little reality to piss everybody off.

The testing room door opened, and the program members filed out smiling, chattering, and gesticulating wildly, as if they had just ridden the Space Mountain ride at Disneyland. The only one who wasn't positively glowing was the medium herself, Suzanne Morrison. She was a strikingly beautiful woman, and it was Joe's experience that attractive people made the best mediums for the same reason they made the best con artists: Dupes *trusted* attractive people. Joe had witnessed one of Suzanne's séances the week before, and although it had been the most impressive display he'd ever seen, he had no doubt that he would expose her trickery after another session or two.

"Congratulations," Joe said. "It looks like you just gave them an E-ticket ride."

"What?" She stared blankly at him.

Joe suddenly felt old. Suzanne was in her late twenties, too young to have ever fussed with the old Disneyland ride tickets.

"Arcane reference. Consider it officially dropped from my vocabulary. It looks like you really wowed them. Of course, you're preaching to the choir."

"Aren't there bad guys out there who need to be caught, Detective?"

"How do you know the bad guys aren't here? How do you know I'm not talking to one of them right now?"

She flashed him a radiant smile. "Are you here to arrest me, Mr. Bailey?"

"Messengers to the hereafter can call me Joe."

"Does that mean I've made a believer of you?"

"It means that you can call me Joe. And that I'm scheduled to attend another séance of yours next week and I fully intend to expose you."

"Promises, promises."

"You don't think I can do it?"

"I think you can *try*."

"I've never failed yet."

She shrugged. "There's a first time for everything."

She walked down the hall.

Joe smiled. He admired her nerve and sense of humor. Suzanne Morrison didn't take herself as seriously as most others in her profession.

"I'm telling you, Bailey, she's the real thing," Dr. Gregory Kellner said as he walked toward him. Kellner was a small, balding man whose face was always flushed red, as if he had just been trying to blow up a balloon that wouldn't inflate.

"We'll see about that. I'm here on official business today, Kellner."

Kellner nodded. "Is this about Nelson?"

"Yes."

"Since when are you a homicide cop?"

"Since a murder was made to look as if it had been caused by telekinetic means."

"Do you have proof it wasn't?"

"It doesn't work that way. Extraordinary claims require extraordinary proof."

"I take it you've discovered a more likely method."

"Not yet, but I will."

Kellner smirked, as he always did when Joe appeared to be stumped by some reputed psychic phenomenon. "I already spoke to Detective Howe about Nelson."

"I'm more interested in the boy. You were studying Jesse Randall, weren't you?"

"He was primarily Nelson's case, but yes, we ran some tests here."

"Why wasn't I called in?"

"Our testing hadn't progressed that far yet. We didn't want to inhibit Jesse by introducing a foreign element."

"A 'foreign element'? I've never been called *that* before."

"A nonbeliever's presence can severely inhibit psychic activity. It's been well documented."

"Uh-huh."

Kellner sighed. "What would you like to know?"

"In your opinion, is Jesse Randall a true telekinetic?"

"Not that my opinion has ever mattered to you, but yes, I believe he is. And I'm not the only one who thinks so. He was subjected to rigorous testing at a paranormal studies conference in Dallas, and he made a believer out of everyone there."

"I understand that Jesse and Nelson had a falling-out. Was Jesse's experience in Dallas part of the reason for that?"

Kellner considered the question. "Jesse wasn't happy. He wasn't used to that kind of scientific testing, and, I admit, it was quite invasive. But when you find someone with a gift as astonishing as Jesse's, you have a responsibility to study every variable you can, while you can. Children often outgrow psychic powers, and we needed to quickly glean whatever information we could."

"Is that why Nelson wanted him to go to Switzerland?"

"Yes. I know Jesse didn't want to go, but for him to spend six months at the Lindstrom Institute for Paranormal Studies would have been a tremendous opportunity."

"Opportunity for whom?"

Kellner didn't answer.

Joe nodded. Just what he thought. "Do you really think, even if Jesse had been psychically capable of it, he would have murdered Nelson?"

Kellner vigorously shook his head. "Not consciously. I think Jesse was fond of Nelson, but he was upset with him, and that anger and resentment manifested itself in a series of disturbing dreams."

"And you believe that those dreams caused these so-called shadow storms, including the one that killed Nelson?"

"I do."

Joe nodded. "All right. I need to take all of the Jesse Randall session videotapes shot here, in Dallas, and anywhere else you may have tested him."

"I'm sorry. I'd need a court order for that."

Joe reached into his jacket pocket and pulled out a sheaf of tan papers. "One court order. How did I know I'd need this?"

"How does he do it?"

Nikki was on the floor in front of the television, mesmerized by Jesse's demonstrations. She and Joe had been watching session tapes for the better part of the evening, captivated as small objects shook and rolled across tabletops, papers sailed across testing rooms, and pieces of metal bent and broke in Jesse's hands. Almost every test was accompanied by pulsating rap music, which Jesse claimed he needed to concentrate.

Joe shook his head. "I can't say for sure how he does it until I see him do these things in the flesh."

"Maybe he *does* have special powers," Nikki said. Her eyes twinkled the way they did whenever she teased her father.

"Maybe *you* have special powers," Joe said.

"If I did, my math teacher's hair would have caught on fire ten times already."

"Hmm. Is that your way of warning me about your next report card?"

She grinned. "You'll just have to wait and see."

"I can't wait. Let's do a little experiment here. Do you still have your fork?"

Nikki picked up her fork, which was still sticky from the bread pudding she had eaten in front of the television.

Joe held her wrist and looked at the utensil. "Okay, honey. I want you to hold that handle and concentrate. I want you to imagine the molecules in the center of this fork dissolving away, turning to mush. Can you picture that?"

Nikki gave him a doubtful look. "Yeah. . . ."

"Do it. Look at this fork and imagine those molecules breaking to pieces, making this metal weaker, weaker, weaker. . . ."

Joe lightly rubbed the lower handle between his thumb and

forefinger, just as Jesse had rubbed silverware and other metal strips on the videos. "The metal is breaking down. I can feel it. Whatever you're doing, it's working. Look!"

The fork suddenly bent.

Nikki's eyes widened.

"Keep it up," Joe said. "Let's see how far you can take this."

As he lightly rubbed it, the fork bent even farther, until the end was at a ninety-degree angle. The end wobbled, then completely broke off.

Joe sat back. "Wow. I guess your math teacher had better watch out."

Nikki made a face and tossed the fork handle at him. "Okay, how did you do it?"

"Probably the same way Jesse did. I'll show you." Joe picked up his own fork. "I really shouldn't be destroying more of our flatware, but we'll chalk this up as a valuable learning experience for you."

"Yeah, whatever."

Joe held the fork in both hands and bent the handle. "See how easy that was?"

Nikki crossed her arms in front of her. "That's *not* the way you did it before."

"Didn't I? If the subject can get to the objects before the tests, there are all kinds of things he can do to them." Joe bent the fork back and forth. "Every time I do this, the bend gets a little weaker. Of course, you don't want it to be *too* weak, so you have to find just the right touch." Joe slowed down and showed Nikki the handle's back side. "Look here. See the bend? Let me know when it becomes a thin crack, okay?"

Nikki nodded.

"This takes some practice, because if you let the crack appear on the top side, the jig is up."

"There! I see a crack!" Nikki shouted.

Joe stopped bending. "Okay, here's where it gets *verrrry* delicate. We bend just two or three more times to deepen the crack, and *voilà*! It's a psychic miracle waiting to happen."

He showed her the fork, and from the top it looked perfectly normal. Even from the bottom the hairline crack was barely visible.

"Go ahead and rub it between your thumb and finger. See if you can make it bend."

Nikki rubbed the handle until it bent and fell apart. She smiled. "Cool!"

"You were getting a little too impressed with Jesse, so I took the fork off your plate while we were watching the last tape. I worked it over and put it back."

She put the fork's remains on the coffee table. "But what about the other things he can do?"

"I can't say. Metalworks demonstrations are one thing, but those moving objects put him in a class by himself. However he does it, he's incredible. I need to see him do this stuff in front of me."

"Do you think Vince can do those tricks?"

Joe smiled. As usual, the conversation had come around to Vince. She had a monster crush on him, even if she refused to admit it.

"There aren't many people in the world who can do those tricks, honey."

Nikki turned back to the screen, where Jesse was waiting for another test to be set up.

"You know, I think I'd like him," Nikki said, still staring at the screen. "But he looks sad."

Joe studied Jesse's face. When he was performing his bits of wizardry, he wore the same intense expression he'd had in his bedroom. But in between setups, his eyes drooped and his mouth fell into a frown.

"See what I mean?" Nikki said.

"He may have been uncomfortable with all those people look-ing at him. He's only eight."

"He probably wishes they would all leave him alone. I bet he wishes his life would get back to normal."

Joe put his arm around Nikki. After Angela's death, his daugh-ter had endured a parade of well-meaning friends and relatives, each trying to fill the hole in her life by taking her on roller-skating outings, movie parties, and an endless succession of pic-nics. The teachers at school had briefed Nikki's classmates on how to behave with her, even offering them a laughable illustrated booklet titled "Barbara's Mommy Went Away."

"Does Jesse have any friends?" she asked.

"I'm sure he does."

"I don't know. He looks really sad."

He motioned toward the screen. "Would you like to meet him sometime?"

"Sure."

Jesse slowly opened the creaky screen door, careful to avoid waking his mother. The door seemed to make so much more noise at a quarter after six in the morning. He'd decided to go to school early, using his own special shortcuts, so the reporters wouldn't bother him again. Mama didn't want him leaving the house without her, but he knew he'd have a better chance of sneaking out on his own.

He crawled toward his skateboard, which was parked at the edge of the porch. Lying flat on his belly on the skateboard's rough surface, he pushed away and slowly rolled down the con-crete walkway to the back gate. He grabbed the gate's thin metal frame, pushed it open, and rolled into the redbrick alley. He looked around.

So far, so good.

He reached for brick after brick, pulling himself down the alley as the news crews waited on the other side of the houses. He'd never noticed how loud his wheels were on the bricks.

Clatter-clatter-clatter-clatter-clatter . . .

He finally reached the end of the block. No reporters in sight. He picked up the skateboard, slung his knapsack over his shoulder, and walked down Edgewood Avenue toward the school.

He was halfway there, when he felt a sharp jab on his left shoulder.

"Are you gonna kill me, dickweed?"

Jesse didn't have to turn to know that it was Al Whatley, a kid who was twice as big as any other kid in the neighborhood and twice as stupid. Whatley went to Willingham, a school for students with disciplinary problems, which meant that he had to get up early to catch his crosstown bus.

Jesse kept walking, but he felt another jab. And another. And another.

Two strong hands gripped his shoulders and spun him around. It was Whatley all right, and he had two buddies, Matthew and Josh, with him.

"Look at me when I'm talking to you!" Whatley's face was marred by a myriad of cuts and bruises.

Jesse backed away. "I gotta get to school."

"Everybody says you're a killer," Whatley said. "But I think you're just a little wuss. You think you can hurt me? Let's see you try!"

He pushed hard against Jesse's chest. Jesse turned to run, but Whatley's buddies grabbed him.

"I knew it," Whatley said. "You're just a scared little wussy boy!" He smiled through his chapped lips and punched Jesse in the stomach.

Matthew and Josh twisted his arms behind him until he was sure his limbs would break. He could feel his eyes stinging.

Please, please don't let me cry, Jesse thought. If that happens, they'll *really* cut loose.

A tear ran down his cheek.

"Aw, look at baby Jesse!" Matthew said.

"Whatsamatter, baby?" Whatley taunted.

Jesse raised his head and glared at Whatley. He could feel his heart beating faster and the rage coursing through his entire body.

Whatley stopped laughing.

The next moment Jesse's glasses flew off his face and struck Whatley's chest. The glasses clattered to the ground.

Matthew and Josh released Jesse and stepped away.

Whatley appeared to be shaken up, but he tried to shrug it off. "It's just a trick," he said.

Jesse was still glaring at him.

The cigarette tucked behind Whatley's ear suddenly flew away. "It—it was the wind," he said, as if trying to convince himself.

Jesse turned and stepped toward Josh.

Josh backed away. "We were just kidding, Jesse. We were just having some fun."

Jesse continued toward Josh, staring straight at him.

"We didn't mean nothing by it."

Josh was clutching his notebook against his chest. Suddenly the papers began to flap and wave under his chin. Josh screamed, dropped the notebook, and ran. Matthew was right behind him.

Jesse turned back toward Whatley, who nervously licked his lips. "My dad says it's all bullshit. You can't hurt me."

Jesse said nothing.

"I'm not afraid of you," Whatley said.

Jesse nodded.

Whatley stepped over to where Jesse's glasses lay on the sidewalk. He cast a glance back at Jesse and placed his foot over the wire-rimmed spectacles.

Still Jesse did not move.

Whatley took a deep breath and slowly lowered his foot. Then, seemingly out of nowhere, a large hand gripped him by the neck and lifted him into the air.

Jesse gasped. He'd never seen such a strong, powerful man. He looked like a character in a video game.

"What do you think you're doing?" the man said with soft menace.

Whatley made a gurgling noise from the back of his throat.

The man cocked his head toward Jesse. "Stupid, don't you know that little kid could splatter you against that garage door? Just like I'm going to do."

The boy started crying.

Jesse backed away. He wanted to run, but he couldn't take his eyes off the giant.

Still holding Whatley up by the neck, the man slammed his head against the garage door.

"A little piece of rat shit like you isn't fit to walk the same planet as this boy."

Whatley's head was bleeding. He began to sob.

The man looked like he was about to slam Whatley's head again, but the voices of a group of joggers coming around the corner stopped him. He gave a low curse and dropped Whatley in a heap to the ground. He turned toward Jesse. "Come with me."

Before Jesse could respond, the man scooped him up and carried him around the corner to a pickup truck. He threw Jesse into the passenger seat, then climbed behind the steering wheel and started the engine.

"Everything's going to be okay."

Jesse frantically reached for the door handle, but it wouldn't work. The childproof locks had been activated.

"Let me out!"

"Don't worry. You're safe now, Jesse."

"How do you know my name?" Jesse said.

The man stared at him in disappointment. "You don't know who I am?"

"How could I? I've never seen you before."

"But I thought sure you'd be able to—that's all right. You can call me Lyles. We'll have plenty of time to get to know each other."

Lyles gave him a brilliant smile as he put the truck into gear and stepped on the gas.

4

Joe ran up the front steps of Lackey Hills Elementary School and yanked open the door. Before his eyes could adjust to the dim atrium, a forceful, overweight African American woman was in his face.

"Police?" she asked.

"It shows?"

"It *always* shows. I'm Laurel Adams, the principal."

"Detective Joe Bailey."

"This way."

The principal led him down the corridor, past several colorful construction-paper collages that offered the inner-city kids hope of a life beyond their depressed community. Anti-gang messages were everywhere.

Laurel opened her office door and ushered Joe inside. Jesse Randall stood near the window.

"What happened, Jesse?"

The boy turned toward him. "I already told Ms. Adams."

"Tell *me*."

Jesse related the morning's events to him, pausing to describe the giant in as much detail as he could. Joe jotted down the description.

"So this person just dropped you off in front of the school and left? Did he say anything about getting in touch with you again?"

"No, but he said his name was Lyle or Lars. He said we'd have a lot of time to get to know each other."

"What did he mean by that?"

Jesse shrugged. "Can I go now?"

"You're absolutely sure you've never seen this man before?"

Jesse shook his head. "Never."

Joe turned to the principal. "How's the other boy?"

"I called the principal at his school a few minutes ago. Eleven stitches in his forehead, but he'll be all right. I think he's home now."

"And he doesn't know this man either?"

"No."

Joe turned back to Jesse. "If you ever see this guy again, I want you to stay away from him and tell your mother, okay?"

"Why?"

"Do it," Joe said. "We don't know anything about him."

"He *helped* me," Jesse said.

"*This time.* But there are a lot of crazies in this world, and we don't know what this man is capable of."

The principal nodded. "I called Jesse's mother. She's the one who suggested contacting you. She's coming to take him home for the rest of the day."

"Good."

There was a soft clattering sound in the room. On a low shelf next to Jesse stood a series of wooden figurines representing the children of the world.

One by one, the figures were falling.

The principal gasped and stepped back.

Joe glanced at Jesse. The boy's glasses were off, and his eyes were open wide as he stared at the dropping figurines.

Jesse looked away.

The figures were still.

No one spoke for a moment.

Joe motioned back toward the shelf. "Can you make the rest fall, Jesse?"

Jesse shot a quick glance at the shelf.

Another figure dropped.

"Like that?"

The principal was hyperventilating in a corner of the room.

Joe kneeled next to the shelf, his eyes only inches from the remaining figurines. "Do it again. Please."

Jesse stared at them. And stared.

"Sorry," he finally said. "No more today."

Joe wanted to push for more, but he stopped himself. He'd already seen Jesse's reaction when he felt he was being pushed. "Okay, fine. Show me your hands, Jesse, and slowly back away from the shelf."

Jesse tensed. "Why?"

Joe didn't take his eyes off the shelf. "I'm just securing the location. I don't want anything disturbed."

Jesse raised his hands and backed away. Joe's eyes flicked between the boy and the shelf.

Joe spoke over his left shoulder and motioned toward the figures. "Ma'am, is it okay if I borrow these?"

The principal nodded and made a squeaking sound from the back of her throat.

Idiot, Lyles thought.

He parked his pickup truck on the street in Cabbagetown, a

lower-class neighborhood built around a long-defunct cotton mill. He gathered his Lanchester and maps and climbed out of the truck. If he were lucky, a thief would pick it up and it would be in a chop shop by midnight.

He'd made a mistake by letting Jesse see him. Now everything had to change. Not only did he have to get rid of the truck, he'd have to change his appearance and adopt new surveillance strategies.

Shit.

What an amateurish thing to do. But he was no amateur. He'd just gotten impatient, starved for contact with the One who had been the center of his world for months now. It had seemed like the perfect opportunity; what better way to make a good first impression than to save him from that punk?

But he was wrong. It was a stupid, stupid thing to do.

He walked to the King Memorial MARTA mass transit station and jumped on a train that would take him to Midtown. He sat in the rear of the car and pulled a manila envelope from the gym bag.

"K.Y.O.," he muttered under his breath.

K.Y.O.—know your opponent—was a rule he swore by; he'd watched too many men die because they didn't know what they were up against. Fierce bravado and an arsenal of weapons were no match for a warrior who could anticipate his opponent's every move. Lyles pulled a photocopied personnel file from the envelope.

The cover page read: BAILEY, JOSEPH.

K.Y.O.

"The kid creeps me out, Bailey." Howe shuddered. "I watched one of his test videos this morning, and it chilled my shit."

Joe sat at his desk in the squad room, squinting at one of the principal's figurines through a large illuminated magnifying glass. "Really? My little girl thought it was cool."

"Cool? Then she'd probably creep me out too."

"I'm sure the feeling would be mutual."

"How are you so sure he's not the real deal? Between what I saw on that tape and what you're telling me about those little dolls this morning . . ."

Joe snorted. "Don't get wiggy on me, Howe."

"Then explain it. Do you see anything under that glass that tells you how he made those doodads fall?"

"Hmm."

"Stumped?"

"No, I'm just trying to figure out how long it's been since I've heard the word 'doodad.'"

"You're a riot, Bailey."

Joe put down the figure and magnifying glass. "There are other possible explanations."

"Like what?"

"Jesse was alone in the principal's office when I got there. He could have anchored a thin length of thread to the back of the shelf with a tiny piece of chewing gum. Then maybe he wrapped the other end around a button on his sleeve. A slight pull of his wrist, and the thread starts knocking down the figures."

"Did you see any thread?"

"No, but by the time I got closer, he could have yanked it free. I looked around, but I didn't see any sign of it on the floor. Short of frisking him, there was nothing I could do."

Howe picked up the little wooden figure. "He's just a kid. How could he be good enough at this to put one over on you?"

"That's one of the common characteristics of a paranormal fraud: apparent inability to manifest any complex form of trickery. People said the same thing about two English girls when they produced pictures of themselves with what appeared to be fairies. People said there was no way they had the technical knowledge they'd need to doctor the photos."

"So how'd they do it? Double exposures?"

"No. They cut little figures out of a children's book and posed with them. Sometimes people make things out to be more complicated than they really are."

Joe punched the door buzzer and waited for a reply from the tiny speaker next to it. It was 11:45 A.M., and he was at the warehouse digs of Cy Gavin, a part-time magician and levitation specialist. He had known Cy for over twenty years, ever since they were teenagers vying for a piece of the local birthday party magic show biz.

"Yeah?" Cy's raspy voice was barely audible through the speaker.

"Cy, it's Joe Bailey. Can we talk?"

Silence.

"Cy?"

"Yeah. Sure. Come on up."

The door buzzed open and Joe climbed the stairs to the fourth floor. The building had been a glass factory, but it now appeared to be home to mostly artists and weekend craftsmen. The hardwood floors squeaked as he stepped through the open doorway to Cy's studio.

"Is this a bust?"

Joe turned to see Cy on the other side of a large table saw. He wore faded jeans and a tattered flannel shirt and was thinner than Joe remembered.

"It's not a bust as long as you don't light up any more of that pot I smell."

"You got it. Hey, I know it's been a while, but I was sorry to hear about your wife, Joe."

"Thanks, Cy. How are you doing?"

"Could be better. I guess you got out of the biz at the right time."

"And you've managed to hang in there?"

"Only because I know how to use these tools. These aren't new illusions I'm working on here. It's a bedroom set for the couple that lives next door to me."

"Nothing wrong with that."

"If you say so. What brings you here?"

"Did anyone come to you in the last few weeks for help with some levitation gags?"

"How do you mean?"

"Pots clanging together, a reed instrument playing and flying around . . ."

"I like to think that my illusions are a little more compelling than that."

"They're plenty compelling in a dark house in the middle of the night."

"Spirit gags? I may have fallen pretty far, but I wouldn't whore myself out to a phony spiritualist. Jesus, I hate those people as much as you do."

"I know you do. But you're probably the best levitation guy in the city, and I thought someone may have asked you—"

"No. No one asked me anything."

"Then let *me* ask you. I'm looking into the Robert Nelson homicide. I know heavy lifting isn't your specialty, but there were some smaller occurrences in his house earlier in the week." Joe held up a sheaf of papers. "I sketched everything out and jotted down a brief description. Maybe you can look at them and give me your thoughts."

"Put them on the table. I'll try to get to them later." He

gestured toward a board clamped to the workbench. "If you don't mind, I have a headboard to finish now."

"Devil child, burn in hell!"

Jesse cranked up the LL Cool J tape, trying to drown out the chanting crowd outside his house. The fundamentalist wackos had been clustered on the sidewalk when his mother brought him home from school. They had screamed, yelled, and spat at him.

"Devil child, burn in hell!"

People had never looked at him that way before. He'd seen shock, amazement, and even envy, but never anything like this.

Hate. Pure hate.

They'd kill him if they had the chance.

"Devil child, burn in hell!"

It was worse than any nightmare.

His mother had turned on the television in the living room. She was trying to drown out the chants too. She had shielded him as they ran past the crowd to the front door, and she'd sent him back to his room in case any gunshots were fired through the front windows.

Would he have to sleep in the bathtub, as he had the time a neighborhood gang war had flared up? There'd been so many drive-by shootings, everyone on the block had been afraid to sleep near their windows.

"Devil child, burn in hell!"

As he changed tapes, he heard his mother gasp.

He ran into the living room. She was only watching TV, he realized with relief. Then he saw himself on the playground with that lady reporter who had shown him that awful picture of Dr. Nelson.

The anchorman grimly read the story: "Big Four News reporter Darlene Farrell's disappearance was first noted when she failed to arrive here for last evening's eleven o'clock newscast. Her car was found earlier today in this shopping center parking lot, but there has been no sign of her in almost twenty-four hours. Her most recent story was an exclusive interview with Jesse Randall, a central figure in the bizarre murder of Landwyn University professor Robert Nelson."

For the first time, his mother realized he was in the room. "Go back to your bedroom, Jesse."

"What happened to her?" he said.

"Now."

"What happened?"

"You don't need to see this, honey."

He screamed through clenched teeth: "Tell me now! *I want to know!*"

She gasped and stepped back.

He hadn't meant to scream at her.

His mom suddenly looked . . . *different.* He'd never seen that expression before, at least not when she looked at him.

She was afraid.

Afraid of *him.*

No. Not her too.

He turned and ran into his room.

"Devil child, burn in hell!"

Joe had heard about Darlene Farrell's disappearance by the time he arrived at the Landwyn campus, thanks to *Steve and Foz,* an afternoon talk radio show. Listeners were split as to whether Jesse Randall should be burned at the stake or pressed into service to help the Falcons football team climb out of last place.

He'd seen Darlene Farrell's report on the previous evening's news. What a self-serving bitch. She'd probably hoped that her story would land a nice juicy spot on the national telecasts. Which was, of course, precisely what had happened. Her reward for bullying a scared little boy.

Strange that Farrell disappeared only hours after ambushing Jesse . . . Still, there was no evidence of foul play, and it was Joe's job to maintain focus on Jesse and Nelson.

He walked to the office of Daryl Reisman, head of the humanities department. The secretary waved him in.

"Good to see you, Joe," Reisman said from behind the beautiful mahogany desk that was slightly too large for the room. "Any report on that spiritualist woman yet?"

Joe sat down. "Not yet. Actually, I'm here on police business today."

"I heard you were investigating Nelson's case. Dr. Kellner informs me that the investigative expertise of the parapsychology team is at your department's disposal." Reisman winked. "I believe he's drafting a press release to that effect."

Joe smiled. "We respectfully decline their offer."

"Good boy."

"I want to talk to you about Nelson. I realize that you and he weren't close."

Reisman snorted. "Understatement of the year."

"Did he have any reason to fear for his life?"

"From me?"

"From anyone."

"You know as well as I do that there are many people here who consider that program an embarrassment. In the academic world, our worth, our currency, is based on our reputation and the reputation of the school where we teach. Dr. Nelson was bringing down the value of the neighborhood."

"But do you kill a neighbor if he doesn't cut his lawn and leaves a car up on blocks in his driveway?"

"Of course not. I don't know anyone who would have reason to kill him. We had our differences, but he disliked me more than I did him."

"He didn't particularly care for me either."

Reisman smiled cheerfully. "Oh, he *hated* you."

"I pretty much figured."

Reisman's smile faded. "Joe, how close are you to breaking this case?"

"That's impossible to say. What's the matter?"

Reisman sighed. "There's a magazine article coming out this week insinuating *I'm* to blame for what happened to Nelson."

"What?"

"It's been suggested that I placed too much emphasis on results, and that's why Nelson was so hard on the boy."

"That's ridiculous."

"Maybe, but that's the angle. You'll be interested to know that you'll be featured in the article too, Bailey."

"Why?"

"Your discrediting Nelson's other discoveries is seen as another contributing factor. He was desperate, and it drove him to push Jesse Randall until the boy just snapped."

Joe shook his head. "If a scientist claimed to discover a new method of cold fusion, fifty review boards would be scrutinizing every single stage of his research. But because you wanted one man to check Nelson's results, you're a monster?"

"You and I both know that these people aren't held to the same standard as other scientists. *Real* scientists."

Joe sighed. "Who does this reporter write for?"

"A magazine called *Nature Extreme.* Are you familiar with it?"

"Sure. I read it whenever I need to catch up on the latest alien abductions, ghost stories, and Bigfoot sightings."

"Well, the fellow's name is Gary Danton. Be careful what you say to him."

"I won't say anything to him."

"How many frauds have you exposed for us, Bailey? Ninety, a hundred?"

"Something like that."

"I didn't think it would take half that many to convince the board of regents to be done with those idiots."

"I guess some people will believe only what they want to believe, Reisman."

Joe had three messages waiting for him at his desk, one from the *Nature Extreme* reporter and two from Cy. Joe called Cy back. Answering machine. He left his pager number.

As he hung up the phone, a clear plastic freezer bag loaded with cash landed on his desk. Howe was standing in front of him, grinning like an idiot.

Joe picked up the bag. "If you're trying to bribe me to walk off the case, it'll take more than this."

Howe folded his arms in front of him. "Twenty-five thousand dollars. I found it in Nelson's night table."

"Are you serious?"

"Yup."

Joe examined the neat, paper-banded stacks of fifty-dollar bills. "Have you checked it against the financials?"

"It doesn't appear on any bank or investment statement *I* can find. You knew him. Any idea why Nelson would have twenty-five grand sitting in a night table?"

"We weren't exactly buddies. Maybe he just liked keeping cash on hand."

"He hasn't had it for long. Most of these bills were minted in Denver less than ten weeks ago."

"And it didn't show up on his financials? With that kind of undocumented cash lying around, I'd usually look to drugs, but that really wasn't Nelson."

Howe picked up the plastic bag of cash. "How are you coming on your end?"

Joe was still surprised by Howe's news. "I'm still checking with experts about the levitations. I saw a guy today who may have something for me."

"Good. Pretty strange about that reporter disappearing, huh?"

"Very."

Howe smiled. "Be careful how you interview that kid, Bailey. Make him mad, and we may be peeling *you* off the wall."

Joe hadn't heard back from Cy by the time he left work, but the warehouse was only a little out of the way home. What the hell.

It was dark by the time he rolled to a stop in front of the building. There was a light in Cy's window.

Joe climbed the stairs, cringing at the battle of the bands that had erupted between the alternate-rock-white-boy rap groups rehearsing on the second and third floors. The low bass throbbed through the walls, shaking the floorboards with each pretentious riff. Thank God Nikki wasn't into this crap. Yet.

Cy's large sliding metal door was closed but not padlocked.

Joe rapped on it. "Cy, it's Joe again. I got your message."

Silence.

"Cy?"

Footsteps. The floorboards buckled and whined.

Thud.

Something hit the floor hard. Joe yanked the door open.

Cy was lying near a futon in the corner of his dimly lit studio. His eyes were open, and he was softly mumbling.

"Cy?"

Cy looked at him pleadingly, then rolled his eyes and vomited.

Joe rushed over and turned him on his side. "Take it easy. Just relax."

He vomited again. Foamy and white. Christ.

"Hang in there, Cy. Where's the phone?"

Footsteps. Behind him. Joe spun around and saw a figure in a denim overcoat sprinting out through the open doorway.

"Stop! Police!" Joe yelled. He jumped to his feet, but Cy began choking and gagging. Shit.

Joe turned him over and slapped his back. He tried to clear his mouth, but Cy continued to sputter.

"Hang on. You'll be okay."

Joe had had a feeling that Cy wasn't going to be okay, but he had never imagined that less than an hour later he'd find himself staring at the levitationist's corpse in the Grady Memorial Hospital emergency room.

Cy had been beyond help even before the paramedics arrived at his loft, but they still struggled to rekindle some spark of life. You can always get lucky, an emergency medical technician once told Joe.

Cy had never been lucky.

The emergency room doctor, a tall Latino man, tossed his rubber gloves onto the instrument table. "You knew him?"

"Yeah," Joe said, still not able to take his eyes off Cy's face. "For a long time. Since we were kids."

"Did you know he was a drug addict?" the doctor asked.

"No, I didn't."

The doctor motioned toward Cy's needle-scarred arms and torso. "He was a pincushion. It was bound to catch up with him."

"Are you sure that's what killed him?"

"We'll have to wait for the test results to be sure, but his symptoms were consistent with a heroin-cocaine mix. Unfortunately, we've gotten pretty good at knowing what those symptoms look like."

Joe nodded. Poor Cy. It was easy to look at his face and see the gawky teenager he used to compete with for those pathetic birthday party gigs and Rotary meeting shows. They had lost touch over the years, but he'd always admired the guy for sticking by his dream. Only now, judging by those ugly needle marks, was it apparent how much it had cost him.

The guy in Cy's apartment was probably his supplier, Joe realized. A cop was the last person a dealer would want to talk to, especially if he had just accidentally administered a lethal speedball. Still, the timing was suspicious. Cy had been trying to call him for some reason.

"Can you help us contact his family?"

"He didn't have any. He's been alone for almost as long as I've known him."

Joe gently pulled the sheet over Cy's scarred arms.

Lyles spread out the flat ivory squares on the passenger seat of his new Jeep Cherokee, positioning them to form a large circle. He'd purchased the vehicle that afternoon and had the windows down to dissipate the putrid new-car smell everyone else seemed to love.

His hands worked quickly over the squares. Bertram and Irene had given them to him shortly before he left England. He had carved Latin words on each square, even though most Millennial Prophets chose to write them with indelible ink. This was more *real*, he thought. More permanent.

Like the scalp tattoo now buried beneath his thick brown hair.

He didn't let the squares rule his life as he knew some of the other believers did. He thought the squares offered alternatives, another way of looking at life, but nothing more.

He completed the circle and placed his small sport compass in the center. He picked up the squares at due north, south, east, and west, then placed them in a row.

Modo. Mortis. Creo. Vita.

Modo. Only.

Mortis. Death.

Creo. Create, or make possible.

Vita. Life.

He chuckled. *Only death makes life possible.*

In his present circumstances it could have been interpreted a few different ways. But here, parked on this stretch of Corsair Street, the meaning was clear.

Lyles looked up at the large third-floor window of the building in front of him, where he could see little Nikki Bailey talking on the phone.

"I'm fine, Dad, except that Vince is ignoring me." Nikki spoke into her pink cordless phone, pacing back and forth in front of the living room windows. She shouted across the room. "Aren't you, Vince?"

"Yeah, yeah, yeah . . ." Vince was hunched in front of the television, watching Jesse Randall's Dallas test sessions.

"He's beating his head against the wall because he can't figure out the miracle boy's tricks," Nikki said.

"He can join the club." Joe's voice broke up as it always did when his portable phone passed between the tall downtown buildings. "I'll be home in a few minutes, okay?"

"Okay, bye."

Nikki pressed the talk button to cut the connection. She stared at the street below and wrinkled her brow. A man was sitting alone in a Jeep.

He had been there the entire time she'd been talking to her father. She might not have noticed, but Wanda, her next-door neighbor, had recently filed a restraining order against her ex-boyfriend. It was too dark to tell if this was the guy, but he was definitely facing their building.

"Vince, can you come look at something?"

Vince's eyes didn't leave the television screen. "I'm *already* looking at something."

She turned from the window. "Please . . ."

He sighed. "That's not fair. You know I'm powerless when you ask like that. You girls learn it in the cradle, don't you?" He stood and shuffled toward the window. "What is it?"

"See that man in the Jeep down there?"

Vince squinted. "No."

Nikki turned back sharply. The Jeep was gone. "It was just there!"

"Sure it was."

"I promise!"

Vince laughed and went back to the couch. "Maybe Jesse Randall made it disappear."

She glanced up and down the street. No sign of the Jeep or the driver.

Obviously, the man had driven away, but it made her uneasy that he had left in those few seconds when she'd turned from the window. It was sort of . . . spooky.

She closed the blinds.

Sharp kid, Lyles thought. Like her father. She'd spotted him.

That was okay. He wasn't close enough for her to get a description, and he'd gotten what he needed. He was just doing some preliminary legwork, establishing patterns of behavior, and gathering information.

He wasn't sure he would need the knowledge he'd gathered on

Joe and Nikki Bailey, but it was always wise to arm oneself with as much information as possible.

But was someone else doing the same thing? For a moment, he thought he'd seen a man lurking in the shadows across the street, also looking up at the Baileys' window.

Who the hell was that?

Good morning, Ms. Randall. Is Jesse here?"

Joe and Nikki stood on the front porch of the Randall home early the next morning, trying to ignore the television cameras pointed in their direction.

"He's here," Latisha said coolly.

"This is my daughter, Nikki. Would you mind if we came in?"

"Depends."

"On what?"

"Is Jesse a suspect?"

"Not as far as I'm concerned."

"Then why are you here?"

Joe glanced at the cameras on the sidewalk. "Ms. Randall, at least two of those cameras are connected to high-sensitivity parabolic microphones. They can probably hear everything we're saying. May we come in?"

Latisha looked at the news crews, then opened the door wide for Joe and Nikki. They walked into the small living room, where

Nikki immediately gravitated toward the collection of ceramic salt-and-pepper shakers on the mantel.

"Wow," she said. "Did you make these?"

Latisha's suspicious attitude toward Joe did not transfer to his daughter. "I made some of them, honey, but most of them I bought."

Nikki nodded. "Very cool."

"Thank you. I'm proud of them."

"Ms. Randall, it's important that I be able to talk to Jesse," Joe said gently. "Jesse spent more time with Dr. Nelson than anyone else did in those last few weeks."

Latisha pursed her lips. "But your being here makes it even—"

"He may be able to help me end all of this. That's what we all want, isn't it?"

"Yes." A small voice came from the hallway.

Joe, Nikki, and Latisha turned to see Jesse standing in the doorframe. "That's what *I* want," Jesse said.

"I told you to stay in your room." Latisha turned back to Joe. "He's a prisoner here. He can't leave the house without people bothering him, and they've asked him not to come back to school for a while."

"Why?" Joe asked.

"They say he attracts too much attention." She made a face. "They brought his books and lessons, and they're supposed to send a teacher a couple of times a week. Personally, I think the principal is afraid of him."

"You're probably right about that. I can talk to her if you'd like."

"No, I think he's safer here."

Nikki stepped toward Jesse. "You like *Star Wars,* don't you?"

"Who doesn't?"

"Dad says you have lots of *Star Wars* toys. I have Queen Amidala's spaceship."

"Chrome?"

Nikki nodded.

"I have a Naboo fighter and a bongo."

Joe leaned over. "Maybe he'll show you his collection, Nikki." He looked at Latisha. "If it's all right with you."

Latisha finally nodded. "It's okay, Jesse."

Jesse walked toward his room, and Nikki followed him. When they were out of earshot, Latisha turned back to Joe. "Do you always bring your little girl along on police investigations?"

Joe shrugged. "I thought Jesse would like to be around some-one his own age who isn't afraid of him. It's only natural— Did I say something wrong?"

"No. A little too right, I'm afraid."

"You want to talk about it?"

"No."

"Okay. But can I ask you a hypothetical question, Ms. Randall?"

"You can ask."

"Please don't take this the wrong way, but I'd like you to think about something for me. If, hypothetically, Jesse had a way to fake his special abilities, what would you guess would be his motive?"

She stiffened. "You're calling my son a liar?"

"No. Just hypothetically."

"Don't give me that hypothetical crap. You're asking me to think of him as a liar."

"Okay. Whether or not he was faking his abilities, he obviously hated Dr. Nelson's tests. Why did he go through with them?"

Latisha hesitated. "He didn't always hate them. He really liked Dr. Nelson. I liked him too. In the beginning, he treated Jesse very well. Jesse's father left when he was three, and I think he liked having a decent man around who would take him places and give him some attention, you know?"

Joe nodded.

"Jesse liked going on TV with him, appearing at the lectures and doing the tests. It was fun for him."

"Until Dallas."

"Yes. Dr. Nelson changed. It got to be less about Jesse and more about his own career, I think. Maybe that's the way it was all along, but he just stopped hiding it."

"It's been an upsetting week for Jesse. Has he been having nightmares?"

"More than ever."

"Have there been any more . . . disturbances while he sleeps?"

"None that I know of. But, like I told you, there have never been any shadow storms around here. They were always someplace else."

Nikki sat cross-legged on the floor, lifting the yellow Naboo fighter toy over her head. "I saw your videos."

Jesse put down the Darth Sidious action figure. "What videos?"

"I saw you moving things around a table and bending pieces of metal. It was cool."

"Oh. Yeah."

"You sound real thrilled."

"People are always asking me to do stuff for 'em. I'm surprised *you* haven't asked."

"My dad told me not to."

Jesse leaned against the bed. "Some people were yelling at me from the sidewalk yesterday. An old man who had cancer, and a lady who couldn't hear. They wanted me to help them, but I couldn't. The man started crying."

"Wow," Nikki whispered.

"Yeah." He crossed his arms. "Your dad doesn't believe in my stuff, does he?"

She paused. Her dad had told her not to discuss Jesse's abilities with him, but how could she not? Especially when Jesse didn't seem to mind. "My dad doesn't believe in a lot of things," she said. "He doesn't believe in heaven."

"Really?"

"I know my mom is there, but he doesn't think so."

"Where does he think she is?"

"Nowhere, I guess. Except in our memories."

Jesse looked down. "*I* think your mama's in heaven."

She smiled. "Thanks."

Latisha wrung her hands and spoke softly to Joe. "What I hate most about this is how it's changed my boy."

"What do you mean?"

"He's gotten tense. Irritable. Dr. Nelson and the others put too much pressure on him, and with everything that has happened in the past few days, it's just gotten to be too much."

"Has it occurred to you that maybe he feels guilty?"

"For what happened to Dr. Nelson?"

"No. For fooling Nelson, you, and everybody else." She started to object, but Joe raised his hand. "*Assuming* I'm correct when I say that Jesse is using some kind of trickery, how do you think he would feel right now? This has gone from a few tricks for his family in Macon, Georgia, to a national news event. Maybe the bigger this got, the harder it was for him to see a way out without embarrassing himself, you, Nelson, and all the others. Have you thought of it that way?"

"I've thought of it *every* way."

"Have you ever asked him if his powers are genuine?"

"How else could that boy do the things he does?"

Joe leaned closer. "Have you ever asked him?"

"What is there to ask? He told me that he thinks about things, and they happen. And then he showed me."

Joe nodded. "Maybe you can tell him that it's okay if he doesn't really have these powers. He may need to hear that from you."

"He'll think I don't believe in him."

"Probably. But that might be exactly what he needs. Right now he may be afraid of disappointing you."

She rubbed her temples. "I just don't know what's the right thing to do."

"I know this has been hard on you."

"You have no idea. It's tearing me apart." She bit her lip. "Yesterday, after that TV reporter went missing, Jesse was . . . upset. He looked at me and—I'm not used to seeing him that way, and coming right after hearing about that woman . . ."

"You were frightened of him?"

"Of course not. I could never be—" Tears welled in her eyes and spilled down her cheeks.

"I'm sorry."

"I love him so much, but it's been *so hard*. I never imagined . . ."

"Mama, what's wrong?"

They turned to see Jesse and Nikki in the doorway.

Latisha quickly wiped her eyes. "Nothing, honey."

"What's wrong?"

"It's okay, honey."

Jesse whirled on Joe. "*You* made her cry."

Latisha shook her head. "No, honey."

Jesse glared at him and stepped closer. "It's *your* fault! You made her cry!"

"We were just talking," Joe said gently.

"*Get out!*" Jesse's nostrils flared and his eyes bulged. "*Get out of here now!*"

Latisha grabbed him by the wrists. "Don't you talk to him or anyone else that way, you hear me?"

"Get out! Now!" Jesse screamed. "Leave us alone!"

Joe nodded to Latisha. "I'll be in touch."

"I'm sorry."

"Don't be. Thank you for talking to me."

Jesse was still glaring at him as Joe whisked Nikki out the door.

Garrett Lyles watched as Joe Bailey and his daughter hurriedly left Jesse Randall's house. The little girl was clearly nervous and upset. What had happened?

Perhaps the Child of Light had demonstrated his powers for them. As powerful as the boy was, he did not yet have the patience and wisdom to control his abilities. It was a wonder that more people had not been hurt.

He smiled as Joe and Nikki passed only a few feet from where he stood. He adjusted his video camera and scratched his upper lip. The phony mustache itched almost as much as the long-haired wig. The disguise was entirely in keeping with his cover as a freelancer from Pittsburgh, here to capture footage to sell to independent television stations. The ruse allowed him to keep a close eye on Jesse without arousing suspicion.

The morning's talk on the press line had centered on Darlene Farrell's disappearance. It hadn't occurred to him that Jesse might be blamed for harming her, but it made sense. Nelson had crossed the boy and gotten himself impaled. The reporter had harassed him and been punished.

Good. Let 'em think that Jesse had offed the reporter. Maybe it would make these other creeps think twice before they bothered him.

Even if it didn't, that was okay. Jesse had a protector.

Do you know I'm out here, Jesse? Can you think what I'm thinking? Of course you can.

The time of Alessandro is almost upon us.

Your time.
Our time.

It was after ten that night when Joe took the elevator to the sixth floor of the Landwyn University library. The place was practically deserted. No big surprise. The college library wasn't exactly a Saturday night hotspot.

Although Landwyn had become infamous for its parapsychology studies program, Professor Reisman made sure the library was fortified with a large collection of skeptical literature. Joe was ahead of the curve on psychic fraud techniques, but he still spent most Saturday evenings on the sixth floor, perusing the latest additions. That night he planned to check into any new levitation rigs that might be out there.

Nikki and her friends had a weekly slumber party club in which they rotated from one home to another. It was his turn to host only once every eight weeks, so he was left with many Saturday nights alone. He was surprised how big and lonely the apartment was without her.

Get used to it, he told himself. It wouldn't be long before Nikki would be gone almost *every* night. Surely he wasn't the first parent who wished he could freeze time and hold on to the child who made life so special.

Nikki had been upset by Jesse's outburst that morning, but she didn't hold it against him. "Be for real. If someone made *you* cry, *I'd* be pretty mad," she had said on the way home.

He couldn't argue with that.

He went to the sixth floor and walked to the occult and paranormal studies section. Each row of tall wooden bookcases ran almost the entire length of the room, ninety feet long, with no breaks along the way. Air from the heating vents whistled down the long rows.

He glanced through a few of the newer books, looking for paranormal studies focusing on children. Many of the tests were worthless, since they were so loosely supervised that it would have been extremely simple for the young subjects to cheat. Jesse was clearly out of these kids' league.

Joe thumbed through a few books and put them back on the shelf. Nothing here would be of much—

Crash.

He jumped. It sounded like an explosion.

Crash. Another one. On the other side of the room.

Joe peered over a row of books. The bookcases were falling toward him one by one, like giant dominoes. He was in the middle of the row, far from either side. He turned left and ran.

Crash.

If he didn't make it, a tall oak bookcase would smash him flat.

Faster, he told himself. Run faster.

He wasn't going to make it.

Crash.

He dropped to his knees, curled into a ball, and threw himself into the bottom shelf of the bookcase next in line to tumble.

He kicked and elbowed the books through to the other side, knowing that the heavy volumes would soon be falling on top of him if he didn't get them out. Only one more to go . . .

He gripped the inside of the shelf and pressed his hands and knees against the sides.

Crash.

The shelves in the next row rammed against his. He braced himself as the heavy framework growled and wood splintered above him.

He was going over. The bookcase he was in struck the next one with an ear-splitting crack.

He fell to the floor, and the shelf neatly framed him as it

slammed down a moment later. Hardbound back issues of *National Geographic* magazine from the shelf above pummeled him in the chest and head.

He lay on the floor, recovering from the blows as the rest of the cases fell.

Then silence. It was over.

He clawed through the books and shelving on top of him, rolling bound volumes off his bruised back and shoulders. He pushed his way through one shelf, then another, finally hoisting himself on top. He glanced around at the large room, where there wasn't one bookcase left standing. It looked as if a bomb had gone off.

"Is anyone else in here?" he shouted.

No answer.

He thought he'd been alone in the room, but it was possible someone was pinned beneath the piles of books and shelving.

"Hello?"

Still nothing.

His forehead was cold. He touched it and looked at his fingers. Blood.

Thirty minutes later, a library assistant finished bandaging Joe's head. Campus security had confirmed that no one else had been injured. But no one could tell him how it had happened.

Drew Potter, an older campus cop with a ruddy complexion, shook his head. "Never heard of such a thing, and I've been here for a long time."

"The first case could have been pushed," Joe said.

"By who? The entire weight-lifting squad?" Potter was right. It would have taken tons of force to unbalance it. "Besides," the guard said, "no one down here saw anyone coming or going. Did you?"

Joe shook his head. What a week. Between the elevator and now the bookshelves—

Wait a minute.

Joe checked his watch: 10:38.

Well past Jesse Randall's bedtime.

No way in hell.

He stood up and flashed his badge at the security officer. "Lock the sixth floor. Secure it, stand guard, and don't let anyone inside until I get back." Joe rushed toward the library exit.

"Why?" the guard asked.

"I'm going to get my spirit kit."

"One . . . two . . . three!"

Joe, four campus security cops, and two library assistants lifted one of the massive bookcases onto four McMillan digital scales. It had taken almost half an hour to loosen the bolts securing it to the other cases. The bolts had probably been tightened more than eighty years before.

The scales' digital readouts flashed, and Joe added up the numbers. Four hundred and twenty pounds.

Add another five hundred for the books, multiply that by twenty cases, and it totaled about nine tons for each row. It wasn't likely that a kid had accidentally knocked one over reaching for a copy of *Catcher in the Rye*.

"Okay, guys," Joe said. "Let's clear all books off the first bookcase. However it happened, it all started here."

They cleared away the books. Joe knew they probably thought he was nuts. He could read the faces of the younger library assistants: *It was an accident, man. Get over it.*

But he couldn't get over it. Not after what had happened to him in the elevator. Not after what had happened to Nelson.

This time he couldn't escape the eeriness of the situation.

Again he had angered Jesse, and again he had been almost killed by the force of an inanimate object. It could have been a coincidence, but that possibility was shrinking with each unexplained occurrence. And if it wasn't a coincidence, who was behind it?

He surveyed the scene and asked himself the first question he asked at almost every reputed psychic phenomenon site: How would *he* pull off a stunt like this? In this case he would probably try a pair of power poles.

About the size of a baseball bat, a handheld hydraulic power pole operated on the same principle as a powered automobile jack. Commonly used in factories and construction sites, it exerted a force of hundreds of pounds per square inch. Two or even three poles could have been brought into the library under a large overcoat and braced between the back wall and the first row of shelves.

Joe walked along the toppled shelves, looking for the distinctive pitchfork-shaped marks that a power pole's pronged tip would leave.

No prong marks.

He reached into the spirit kit, pulled out a spray bottle, and coated the shelves with a fine mist.

"What's that?" Potter asked.

Here come the questions, Joe thought. They had been too quiet. He went into autopilot as he slipped on a pair of illuminated goggles. "It's furniture oil mixed with a phosphorous compound. This wood is so old, it shouldn't absorb much of it. But if there are any places that have been pinched or clamped by a vise, the wood there might be softer and more absorbent." He wiped the shelves with a rag. "It should soak in a bit in those places."

Joe put on the goggles and flipped the ultraviolet switch. Although he usually preferred the fingerprint lantern, the goggles were better for close-up work. Again he walked down the row, studying the shelves.

"See anything?" Potter asked.

"Afraid not. Other than a few scratches, there's nothing here."

"Back to the weight-lifting squad theory, huh?"

"Not yet." Joe sprayed the phosphorous oil on the top shelves. It was possible, however unlikely, that ropes might have been used in some kind of pulley arrangement. Here, too, there should have been some softening of the wood.

There was none.

Damn.

He examined the floor where the shelf had rested. The floor-boards had cracked and splintered under the immense weight of the pivoting edge. He picked up a few pieces of the broken floor and placed them into a plastic sample tray.

"Well?" Potter said.

"I'll let you know."

It was after two A.M. by the time Joe got home and went to bed, but he was too wired to sleep.

What the hell was happening?

There was no chance Jesse was responsible. But it was sure being made to look that way.

Why? However he figured it, it didn't make sense. Why would anyone go through all this trouble to kill him, when a simple bullet would do the trick?

Someone obviously wanted the world to believe that Jesse was killing people with his mind. But who? The one person who had the most to gain from such a deception, Dr. Robert Nelson, was dead.

Nothing seemed to fit.

Joe considered the elevator. Had it been rigged somehow? He'd thought it was an accident, but now he wasn't so sure. He tried to put himself back in the moment, imagining all the sights and sounds in the malfunctioning elevator car.

He had some ideas how it could have been pulled off, but he wasn't sure. If he hadn't thought it was an accident, he would have checked it out immediately.

Finally, at a few minutes to four, Joe climbed out of bed and sat in front of the television. He glanced through the tapes of Jesse Randall's test sessions to find the one he was looking for.

Jesse's final session with Nelson.

Joe popped in the tape and pushed play. Jesse was agitated from the start, glaring at Dr. Nelson and scowling at his every request.

In the test, a group of six recruited volunteers were shown a simple drawing and asked to reproduce it on a piece of paper. After that the original drawing and volunteers' reproductions were removed from the room.

Jesse was brought in. "Okay, are you thinking about the drawing?" he asked.

A few of the volunteers nodded.

"Come on, are you thinking about it?" he snapped.

They all nodded and mumbled, "Yes."

"When I count to three, I want you to imagine actually drawing it, one line at a time, okay? Imagine it!"

Again they nodded.

"Okay. One, two, three!"

He stared intently at the volunteers, his eyes flicking between them. Finally, he picked up a marker and moved to a large pad at the front of the room. He drew a circle with a triangle on top of it.

There were gasps from the volunteers, and the original drawing was brought back into the room.

A triangle with a circle on top of it.

Not exactly the same thing, but close enough, Joe thought. Very impressive.

But apparently not impressive enough for Nelson. He spoke sharply: "You can do better than this, Jesse. Do you like wasting everyone's time?"

Joe had never seen Nelson speak that way to any of his supposed psychics. If anything, he usually erred in the other direction, pandering to the subjects and allowing them to run roughshod over the agreed-upon test protocols.

Nelson leaned into Jesse's face. "We're going to stay here until you get it correct five times out of five, do you understand?"

Joe sat forward as he saw Jesse's face change, the expression becoming almost demonic. He knew that expression. He'd seen it before. He also knew the words that Jesse spit out at Nelson a moment later. He'd heard the exact same words from Jesse only hours before almost dying in the elevator shaft:

"Don't you do this to me!"

6

Nate Dillard looked the same as he always had, Joe thought. Even though the guy was pushing seventy, he still had the same rosy cheeks and elastic eyebrows that danced with each spoken syllable. Nate stood on a small stage at the end of the Peachtree Corners High School gymnasium, demonstrating rudimentary magic techniques to a Learning Annex class.

He was a heavy-lifting specialist, and Joe's earliest memories of him were of a flaming trunk rising high over the stage at the Fox Theater. He'd thought of him almost immediately after examining Nelson's murder scene. Although it was unlikely Nate could tell him anything he didn't already know, it was worth a shot to see if there were any rigs out there he hadn't considered.

Joe glanced around the gym, where the class sat on metal folding chairs. About forty people were there, and as usual at these things, men outnumbered women four to one. There were people from all walks of life, Joe guessed, including doctors, laborers, lawyers—

And a spiritualist.

Suzanne Morrison, the attractive medium he'd been studying at the Landwyn parapsychology program, was sitting in the third row. He was scheduled to observe one of her séances the following morning.

Joe smiled. A spiritualist in a magic class?

She was obviously bored. Small wonder, he thought. With the impressive performances she put on at her séances, this had to seem like small potatoes. She yawned and glanced around the room.

He caught her eye. Still smiling, he gave her a quick salute.

A deer caught in the headlights. She turned back to the instructor.

After Nate dismissed the class, Joe ran the particulars of Nelson's murder scene by him. Nate was just as confused as he was.

"Jeez, Joey. I don't know." Nate, like many of the old-time magicians who knew him from his childhood days of hanging out in Sam's shop, still called him Joey. "I'm stumped. Have you stopped to consider that maybe it's *not* a trick?"

"Aw, come on, Nate. Not you too?"

Nate's large belly shook as he laughed. "Who knows? The world's a strange place."

"Uh-huh. Speaking of which, what can you tell me about Suzanne Morrison?"

"Who?"

"She's one of your students. Very pretty—green eyes and long brown hair."

Nate grinned. "Looking for a date, Joey?"

"Hardly. She's been passing herself off as a spiritualist. How long has she been in your class?"

"This is the fourth week of a six-week course. She's been here every time. I don't know anything about her being a medium, but she's smart and catches on quick."

"I don't doubt it."

Joe left Nate with a breakdown of the physical characteristics of Nelson's murder scene, but he could tell the guy wasn't going to be much help.

Joe left the building and wasn't surprised to see Suzanne Morrison waiting for him outside. He smiled. "Well, well, well."

"This isn't what it looks like."

"Really? Well, it *looks* like you were here doing a little occupational research. Did Nate teach you how to rig those séances?"

"No. And they weren't rigged."

"Then tell me this: Why would a spiritualist need to take magic classes? Did Houdini tell you to sign up so you could pass along the latest techniques to him?"

"Are you through?"

"Oh, I'm just getting started."

"I have a good reason for being here."

"This I gotta hear."

"You will, as soon as you lose that smirk."

"It'll take a while to wipe this one off."

Suzanne glared at him.

Joe shrugged and dropped the smile. "As you wish." He looked at her with mock earnestness.

"You bastard. I should just walk away, but I don't want to give you the satisfaction of thinking you've caught me at something."

"Too late. Please tell me."

She glanced away. "I wasn't born with this ability."

"The ability to take magic classes?"

"Do you want to hear this, or not?"

"I'm sorry. Go ahead."

Suzanne took a deep breath. "It started when I was eleven. I had a friend, Daphne, who was killed in a car accident. She was my age. My parents wouldn't let me go to her funeral, but that very day Daphne came to me. She spoke to me. I realized that through her I could speak to other people who had died."

Joe nodded. "I read all this in your case file at Landwyn."

"Then you also read that everyone thought I was crazy. They put me in an institution. I spent my fourteenth birthday in there, and the only reason I got out is that I pretended I couldn't hear Daphne's voice in my head anymore. Later it became more than just the voice. It was moving objects. But ever since I was a teenager, I've been looking for someone who can do the things I do, who's been feeling the things I've been feeling. I go to two or three spiritualists a week, hoping to find someone like me, but they've all been frauds."

"That still doesn't explain why you're taking a magic class."

"I study books and take classes so that I can spot the phonies. I *have* to be an expert. How else will I know if they're putting one over on me?"

Joe stared at her. "That's *good*. Very good. Did you come up with that just now, or had you thought it all out before, in case someone ever saw you here?"

"It's the truth."

"Uh-huh."

"I probably know as much about phony spirit rigs as you do."

"I don't doubt it."

She rolled her eyes. "Fine. Believe what you want. I understand you'll be sitting in on another session of mine tomorrow. Maybe *that* will convince you."

Joe shrugged.

"Am I the reason you came here tonight? Did someone tell you I was in the class?"

"No, I needed to talk to your teacher about something."

"About Dr. Nelson's murder?"

He hesitated before answering. "Yes."

"It's no big secret that you're investigating it. Nate Dillard is a good heavy-lifting guy. Was he any help?"

"Not really."

"Did you consider a Harrison winch?"

"Almost immediately. It wouldn't have worked."

"Center-of-gravity problem?"

"You got it."

A broad smile lit her face. "I guess you haven't considered the possibility that the boy *did* cause it to happen?"

"No. Is that what you think?"

"Not likely. In my experience, pretty much all mediums and psychics are fakes." She smiled again. "Except me, of course."

"Of course."

She gestured down the street. "I'm going for coffee. Would it compromise your objectivity to join me?"

He thought for a moment. "It would have to be *very* good coffee for that to happen."

Joe hadn't planned to make an evening of it, but he found himself enjoying Suzanne's company. If this was part of her con, at least it was an interesting variation.

They bought their coffee and sat at an outdoor table beneath a historical-landmark sign reminding them that hundreds of Confederate soldiers had died horrible deaths on the same spot where affluent young adults now enjoyed cappuccinos and iced mochas.

"You know, we're really on the same side," Suzanne said. "We both hate frauds who pretend to have paranormal abilities, and we both have our reasons to expose them."

"Who, exactly, have you exposed?"

"I don't mean 'expose' in the sense that I arrest them or put them out of business. I just find out what they do and how they do it, and I move on."

"That could fall under the category of occupational research."

"It could if I were a fake. But I'm not. I knew about Merrill Hawkins and the broomstick kids long before you did."

Joe laughed. Hawkins was an elderly woman in Acworth who had convinced Nelson, Kellner, and the rest of the parapsychology program that she was summoning rambunctious spirits to her farmhouse. In reality, the disturbances were caused by the woman's teenage grandchildren, who shimmied in the crawlspace beneath the house and poked broomsticks through removable wood plugs in the floor. They raised tables, knocked over chairs, and caused a general ruckus in the darkened house while their grandmother was in her "trance."

"It took me two visits to figure out that one," Joe said.

"It took me *three* sessions. And my fees weren't being reimbursed by the university or the police department."

"I'm sure you made up for it with your own sessions. You *do* charge, don't you?"

"You know I do. It's how I support myself. I'm a composer, and that doesn't always pay well."

"A composer? Have you written anything I might have heard?"

"I doubt it, unless you've been to chamber music concerts in Dayton or Monterey."

"Damn. I knew I shouldn't have let those concert subscriptions lapse."

"Yeah, right. Symphony orchestras aren't exactly beating down my door with commissions, so I have to get by on what I make as a spiritualist."

"Which, with the reputation you've built for yourself, must be pretty good."

"It isn't bad."

"So, what exactly do you write on your income tax form? 'Musician-slash-Conduit to the Afterlife'?"

"Close. Musician-slash-Spiritual Adviser."

"I'm surprised that you'd let me and the parapsychology team observe you. If you're found out, it could ruin a good gig for you."

"There's nothing to find out. And even if there were, you and I both know the people who usually believe in this stuff aren't about to listen to a police detective and a bunch of academics. I'll bet over half the mediums you've busted are still working right here in Atlanta, and they're probably making more money than ever."

He couldn't argue with that. He'd seen people go *back* to their favorite spiritualists even after they watched him expose them. Their desire to believe was that strong.

"You lost your wife a couple of years ago, is that right?"

"Yes."

"Do you ever ask spiritualists to contact her?"

"No. I won't degrade her memory that way."

Suzanne nodded.

How did she know about Angela? Joe wondered. Had she researched him just as she researched all of her marks? "A lot of people think I should throw down the Angela card every time I go into a session. What better way to know if a medium is blowing hot air? There are a million little things only she and I would know, but I just can't do it. Her memory is worth more to me than that."

"Good. It *should* be," Suzanne said gently.

Joe downed the rest of his coffee. "I have to go."

"I'm sorry. We can talk about something else."

"It's okay. I have to get home to my little girl." Joe stood and tossed a few dollars onto the table. "I enjoyed this. It's too bad I'll have to bust you tomorrow morning."

Suzanne laughed. "I enjoyed this, too, Joe. And it's too bad you're about to lose your perfect record."

. . .

By the time Joe arrived home and released Vince from baby-sitting duty, it was time to put Nikki to bed.

As he drew the covers up to her chin, she smiled. "You look happy tonight."

"Don't I always look happy?"

"Not when you come home from work. What happened?"

Suzanne Morrison happened, he thought. Did it show? Okay, so she was a fraud. And maybe she was playing him the way she played the chumps who paid her to speak with their dearly departed. Still, there was something else there. She actually seemed to welcome the challenge he posed. And it wasn't every day that he talked to a spiritualist who debunked other spiritualists. That was a new one.

"I'd be happier if I didn't have to work so late," he said. "What did you and Vince do tonight?"

"We watched more videos of Jesse. Vince wants to figure out his tricks before you do."

"I hope he does. It would save me a lot of work."

"I told him there was *no way* he would figure it out before you did."

"I guess I'd better get on the stick, huh?"

She giggled. "Yes. Go do it. Now."

He kissed her, walked to the doorway, and looked back at her.

He missed Angela in a thousand different ways, but never more than when he wanted to show her what a great kid they'd made together. She would have been so happy.

He sat cross-legged on the floor in front of the television and popped in another one of Jesse's session tapes. There were still hundreds of hours to look through, and he felt as if he'd only scratched the surface. In this session, Jesse was amazing the members of the parapsychology team with his metal bending. Nothing new here. He'd scan forward and then—what the hell?

He bent forward.

A thin, red-haired man whispered in Nelson's ear between each demonstration. Nelson, in turn, slightly altered the test conditions after each consultation. Was he taking direction from this man?

The pattern continued throughout the rest of the session. Joe had met most of the parapsychology program members, but he'd never seen this guy before.

He popped in a few more tapes, and the red-haired man appeared in roughly a third of them. He generally stood in the back of the testing room, where he didn't speak to Nelson or anyone else. Joe had been watching Jesse so closely that he hadn't noticed him before.

Joe put in a Dallas session tape. The tests were conducted in a surgical auditorium, where the researchers watched through a large observation window.

After one particularly impressive demonstration, Nelson glanced up at the window.

Sitting in the observation room's front row, the red-haired man slowly nodded.

Who was that guy?

At seven the next morning, Joe met Kellner and his team of parapsychology graduate students in a McDonald's restaurant a few blocks from Suzanne Morrison's house. Only three of the spook squad's nine grad students were accompanying Kellner for that morning's séance, and Joe could almost feel their excitement. Theresa Banks, Barry Lawrence, and Earl Pogue were nice kids, he thought. Smart kids. Too bad their academic careers had taken such a ludicrous turn.

After Joe briefed them on his ground rules for the session—no volunteering information, no allowing Suzanne to switch seating positions, no last-minute changes to the test conditions—he asked Kellner about the red-haired man in Jesse Randall's session tapes.

"Sorry. Can't help you."

"Can't help me or won't help me?"

"Can't help you. I know the man you're talking about, but I have no idea who he is."

"You expect me to believe that? You were in the same room with him for weeks."

"Nelson brought him in. He never introduced him to us, and when I asked who he was, Nelson told me to call him Martin."

"First name or last name?"

"Neither, if you ask me. I called him Martin a couple of times, and he had a kind of delayed reaction. It wasn't reflexive. I'm pretty sure it wasn't his real name."

Joe turned to the other team members. "Do you know the man I'm talking about?"

Theresa nodded. "Seen him. Never talked to him. I never saw him say two words to anybody but Nelson."

"And Jesse," Earl chimed in.

"You saw him talk to Jesse?" Joe said.

"A couple of times. Not in front of us, but in hallways and places like that."

"Jesse was alone when he talked to him?"

"Dr. Nelson was there too."

"None of you ever found out who he was or why he was there?"

Kellner shrugged. "We learned not to ask too many questions. Nelson was always trying to drum up financial support for the program. We figured it was some rich bastard he was sucking up to. Maybe someone whose company's stock would take a beating if it came out that he was associating with a bunch of lunatics like us."

"It never hurt Roland Ness."

"He's got billions. When you've got that much money, people expect you to have some quirks. They're disappointed if you don't." Kellner checked his watch. "Ms. Morrison is waiting. Shall we see what she has in store for us today?"

Suzanne Morrison lived in a pleasant two-story home in the Morningside area, only a few blocks from the Woodruff Arts Center. She greeted the team and led them to a small, quaint den upstairs, furnished with a rectangular dining room table, a small sofa, and several bookcases.

Joe and the team sat down while Suzanne drew the curtains and took her place at the head of the table. "Is everyone comfortable?"

"Are you?" Joe said.

"Why wouldn't I be?"

"We're constantly being told that my skeptical thoughts and feelings interfere with the paranormal forces at work."

She smiled. "I'm quite sure the people who say that are frauds. They're afraid of being exposed by you, Mr. Bailey. Your feelings will make no difference to me or our visitors from the other side. That's a lame excuse I will never use."

Kellner, who had accepted that excuse on countless occasions, cleared his throat.

"Why is it necessary to have the blinds drawn?" Joe asked. "Do the spirits have some kind of aversion to light?"

"I'll be able to establish contact under almost any circumstances. But for some reason they're less likely to cause objects to move in bright light."

"You have no idea why?"

"I'm afraid I don't."

"Have you asked your deceased friend?"

"Yes, but she doesn't know. She's not even aware that objects are moving unless I tell her. She's not causing it."

Kellner cut in. "If you have any more questions, they can wait until after the session."

Joe shrugged. "Any time you're ready."

She faced Earl. "I understand we're going to contact someone close to you."

"My brother."

"Good. I want you to think about your brother and just *feel*. Your emotions will draw him here. What was his name?"

"Freddy."

"We'll try to contact him through my friend." Suzanne closed her eyes. "Are you there, Daphne?"

Silence.

"Daphne?" Silence. "I'm having trouble—" Suzanne shook her head. "I'm not hearing her."

"How often does this happen?" Kellner asked.

Her eyes were still closed. "Not often. Give me a little time." She called out: "Daphne?"

Joe glanced around the room, knowing that spiritualists often put tricks into motion while they distracted their marks with preliminary theatrics. No sign of any funny business. Yet.

"I need you, Daphne. There's a man here who needs you too." She stiffened. "I hear you."

Earl leaned forward hopefully.

Suzanne smiled. "Thank you, Daphne. Earl wants very badly to speak to his brother. Can you help him?"

Her right hand went to a small remote control, which she used to turn off the lights. The room was dim, although some sunlight still seeped in around the drawn curtains.

Joe watched Suzanne closely. She was relaxed and casual, as if she were speaking to an old friend on the telephone.

Her eyes still closed, Suzanne turned toward Earl. "You must think about your brother now. Remember the times you had with him, feel how you felt when you were with him. It's the only way to bring him here."

Earl nodded.

"It's not working," Suzanne said after a long pause. "Too many other things are probably clouding your thoughts. Don't try to study me. That's what your colleagues are here for. Put yourself in the moment with Freddy."

Earl closed his eyes and concentrated.

Suzanne gasped. "Your brother is with us now. But you never called him Freddy, did you?"

Earl shook his head. "I called him—"

"Shark," she finished for him.

"Yes."

"When did he pass on? He has no concept of time, at least in our terms. He has no idea how long it's been."

"Four and a half years."

Suzanne paused. "He feels your love, Earl."

"And my mother's?"

Suzanne smiled. "Daphne says he's laughing. Your mother made him leave the house when she found out he had AIDS. He doesn't want to feel anything from your mother."

"Jesus, she's right," Earl murmured.

Of course she's right, Joe thought. She'd probably compiled a dossier on every single member of the team.

"Stay with me," Suzanne said. "There is still anger and resentment in your brother. He took it with him."

The bookshelves shook. Showtime. Joe kept his eyes on Suzanne while everyone else turned toward the shelves.

"But he misses you and your sister," she said.

The sofa's legs pounded on the floor.

Joe leaned forward. Although the sofa was several feet behind Suzanne, it was possible that by applying pressure to a few loosened slats of the hardwood floor she could actually be levering the underside of the couch. He squinted at the floor, but it was too dark to see anything.

The team backed away from the table, staring at the moving couch. It was now rocking violently.

"He still feels the pain. He wonders if it will ever go away."

The pounding stopped. Not because the couch had stopped moving, Joe realized, but because it had levitated off the floor. So much for the floorboard theory.

The couch lifted higher, higher, higher . . .

Now.

Joe leapt from his chair and extended a collapsible magician's cane he'd been nestling in his palm. He switched on a high-powered flashlight and quickly swept it under the couch.

Nothing.

Over the couch.

Nothing.

The sofa levitated even higher, approximately four feet in the air, then plummeted back to the floor. Joe jumped back just in time to avoid being hit.

The couch was still.

"That's all," Suzanne said. "Your brother has no more to say right now."

Theresa switched on the room lights.

Joe stood over the couch, sweeping the cane over the sides. He pulled it from the wall and passed the cane over the sofa's back side. Still nothing.

"Please, everyone leave the room." Joe picked up his spirit kit and placed it on the table.

"It's *my* research project," Kellner said.

"Not this part. Everybody leave, and don't touch anything on the way out."

Suzanne slid back her chair and stood up. "You won't find anything."

"We'll see."

"Suit yourself." She walked toward the doorway. "While Mr. Bailey does his job, I'll make coffee downstairs. Anyone care to join me?"

Forty-five minutes later, Joe strode into Suzanne's living room, carrying his spirit kit under his left arm. Kellner and the team gave him anxious stares.

"Well?" Kellner said.

"Nothing yet," Joe said.

Barry grinned. "Yet? So when, exactly, do you expect to find something?"

Joe sighed. They were eating this up. "I'll need another session."

"That's what you said last time." Kellner chuckled. He stood, and the rest of the team followed his lead. "Thank you for your hospitality, Ms. Morrison. You've been blessed with a wonderful gift."

Suzanne ruefully shook his hand. "It doesn't always feel like a gift."

"It *is* a gift. Never forget that. We'll be in touch."

Kellner, Earl, Barry, and Theresa filed out of the house, leaving Joe alone with Suzanne.

"That *was* amazing," he said. "And I don't impress easily."

"Can I wash my hand now?"

"What do you mean?"

"When you came in the door, your hands were covered in phosphorous powder. You shook my hand so that a good amount of it was transferred to my palm and fingertips. I assume your ultraviolet lantern showed that I didn't leave paw prints anywhere I shouldn't have."

"Very observant."

"Not necessarily. I just use the same techniques that you do."

"Of course. In your never-ending quest to find someone else with your abilities."

"And I assume your sonar unit didn't find any suspicious mass behind the floor or walls."

"No."

"You may have noticed that the floorboards creak in this house, upstairs and downstairs. It would be very difficult for anyone else to be in this house without you knowing about it."

She was right. He'd already considered that. He thought he'd considered *all* the possibilities. No, not all of them. Otherwise, he'd know how she had levitated the couch. "I'd like to see you in the university testing lab," he said. "I know that you've done a session for the spook squad there, but I'd like you to do one for me."

"Anytime." She stared at him. "You won't even admit the possibility that you've witnessed a paranormal experience?"

"No."

"I think that's sad."

"Sad?"

"Yes. Where's the magic and wonder?"

"There's plenty of magic and wonder in the world."

"Where?"

"Everywhere. It's there every time you look at a Monet painting, listen to the Beatles' White Album, or watch Michelle Kwan skate to 'Lyra Angelica.' "

"But is that enough?"

"It has to be."

"No, it doesn't, Joe."

His hand tightened on the handle of his spirit kit as he turned toward the door. "For me it does."

It was just past sunset when Lyles heard the van arrive. He was at the deserted Chattahoochee River Nature Park in north Atlanta, sitting on a large rust-colored rock at the river's edge. It was a peaceful spot, thickly populated by pine trees, small hills, and hiking trails. There was no place else like it in Atlanta, he thought.

He heard the sound of the van doors opening and closing, then the crunching of large, clumsy footsteps on brittle pine straw. Two men stood on the embankment above him, their faces hidden in the shadows.

"Hello, Lyles. You *are* still calling yourself Lyles, aren't you?"

"Yes. And are you still calling yourselves Laurel and Hardy?"

They gave him a puzzled look.

"Oh, sorry. That's what *I* used to call you. Hello, Manning. Hello, Teague."

Manning stepped lower on the embankment. The last tinges of sunlight bathed his plump face in a soft orange glow. "We need to talk."

Lyles smiled. Manning and Teague were always so serious, so intense. So weak. "I think *you* need to talk," he said. "All you want me to do is listen. But first, tell me how you found me here."

Teague worked his way down the bank, struggling to keep his balance in his smooth-soled cowboy boots. He quoted softly, " 'There's nothing like the big rusty rock at the Chattahoochee Nature Park at sunset. The air gets colder, but heat still rises from the stone and massages the soul.' Sound familiar?"

"You know I said that. Who told you?"

Neither man replied.

Lyles cursed under his breath. "The Vicar. What the hell happened to his vow of confidence?"

"It no longer applies once you've broken the seal. We've been out here every night this week. We heard you were back in town, and then, after we heard that you made contact with Jesse Randall, we had no choice but to find you. The Vicar is very displeased."

Lyles stood up. "That's not my concern anymore."

"It should be," Teague said. "Come back to us."

"Is this the Vicar talking, or you?"

"It's all of us."

"That's pretty funny, considering that I was asked to leave the sect only a few months ago."

Manning shrugged. "The Millennial Prophets recognize you as a leader among men. Come with us. We're here to take you for an audience with the Vicar."

"I decline."

"What?"

"I decline your invitation. Tell the Vicar I appreciate his interest."

"You don't understand, Lyles." Teague pulled aside his long jacket to reveal an electric riot-control baton.

Lyles laughed. "What I understand is that the two of you are creeping up on me in one of my favorite places on earth. You gentlemen are probably just confused. The Vicar asked you to bring me in, but I'm quite sure he didn't want you to try to do it by force."

"You underestimate him," Teague said.

"He knows that there is no way the two of you can bring me in against my will. Unless you guys have also fallen out of favor, and this is his way of having you fitted for body bags. . . ."

In an instant, Manning grabbed the baton and leapt toward Lyles. Blue sparks arced from its tip as it whistled through the air.

Lyles jumped to his feet and spun around, flinging the contents of his water bottle at Manning. Water drenched Manning's forearm, hand, and sparking shaft of the baton. He screamed as the electrical current, conducted by the water, surged through him. Before he could recover, Lyles spun and rocket-kicked his lower back. Manning went down, unconscious.

Sparks flew from the baton and ignited the dry pine straw. Lyles turned toward Teague as the fire spread.

"This really isn't your specialty, Teague."

Teague picked up the baton and held it like a batter at the plate. He nervously licked his lips. "Don't come near me."

Lyles shrugged. "Here are the options. Scenario one: You help me put this fire out, you pick up what's left of your buddy, and you live to tell the Vicar not to bother me anymore. Scenario two . . . well, do I really have to go into that?"

The fire was burning blue, fueled by long-dormant underground gases. The blaze crackled and popped.

Teague gripped the baton harder. "You're one sick son of a bitch, you know that?"

"So I've been told." Lyles motioned toward the burning pine straw. "This fire's not getting any smaller."

Teague slowly lowered the baton.

In the next instant, Lyles bloodied Teague's face with an elbow to the nose, crippled him with a sweep across the knees, and suffocated him with a blow to the windpipe.

As Teague lay twitching on the embankment, Lyles picked up the baton and pushed the pronged tip deep into his mouth.

"Good-bye, Teague."

Lyles squeezed the baton's power trigger.

7

ou have visitors," the squad room receptionist, Karen,
whispered to Joe. She leaned over his desk, an excited expression on her face.

He lifted his brows. "What's the matter?"

"It's *him*."

"Who him?"

"Him."

Joe peered over the green and black partition. Jesse and Latisha
were standing near the reception desk.

Joe smiled. "He's not going to hurt you, Karen."

"Maybe not while he's awake."

"Not while he's asleep either. The only one around here who'll
be dreaming about you is Sergeant Ratczek."

She grimaced. "I think I'd rather take my chances with the kid."

Joe stood and walked over to Jesse and Latisha. "Good morning. This is a surprise. Is everything all right?"

Latisha pushed her son closer to Joe. "Jesse has something to
say to you, Detective."

"Yes?"

Jesse looked at the floor. "I'm sorry for how I talked to you the other day."

"In my job, I hear a lot worse."

"It was still wrong," Latisha said.

Joe smiled. "Thank you, Jesse. I know it took a lot for you to come here today, even if your mom did make you do it."

Still staring at the floor, Jesse nodded.

Joe glanced around the squad room and noticed that much of the activity had stopped. Almost everyone's eyes were on Jesse. Joe nodded toward the door. "Come on. Let's go for a walk."

They took the elevator downstairs and started down Decatur Street. "I'm glad you came to see me," Joe said. "I know you had to brave the gauntlet of reporters outside your house."

"It's gotten worse," Latisha said. "Ever since that reporter lady went missing, everyone's convinced it's Jesse's fault."

"*I'm* not convinced."

"You're alone, then."

"Are you still having nightmares, Jesse?"

He gave him a wary glance. "Yeah."

"Was Darlene Farrell in any of your nightmares?"

"No."

"What about me? Was I in any of them?"

Jesse didn't answer.

Latisha spoke quickly. "Lots of people he meets are in his dreams. It doesn't mean anything."

Joe nodded. "Jesse, do you want to talk to me about your nightmares?"

"There's nothing to talk about," Latisha said.

"Ms. Randall, I'm on his side. I don't think he hurt anybody. But, like I told you, I can't help him if he doesn't help me."

"It may be time for a lawyer. I think—"

"You were one of the shadows," Jesse said.

"I was?" Joe asked.

Jesse nodded. "You were one of the shadows in the ground. I could see your eyes and hear your voice. I kicked you until you left me alone."

"When did you have this dream?"

"I had it a few times."

"When did you have it last?"

"Saturday or Sunday."

"He'd just seen you," Latisha said. "He was upset. That's not unusual, is it?"

"When did you go to sleep Saturday night?"

"I get to stay up until ten on weekends."

Joe nodded. The library bookshelf incident had occurred at about 10:30.

"Have you told anyone about the dreams you've been having?"

"I told Mama."

Joe looked at Latisha. "Have *you* told anyone?"

"No."

"Ms. Randall, I wonder if you'd let me and Jesse talk on our own for a few minutes."

"I don't know," she said doubtfully.

"I'm not going to try to trap him. You have my word on that. I don't believe your son has hurt anybody, consciously or unconsciously."

She looked at her son. "Jesse?"

He stared at Joe and then slowly nodded.

"Okay," she said. "I have some business to tend to at the bank. When I come out, I'll be sitting on the bench in front." She reminded Joe, "I have your word."

"Yes. Thank you."

She gave Jesse one more glance before disappearing into the Bank of America building a few yards away.

"Does your mother let you eat churros?" Joe asked.

"Cheerios?"

"No, churros. It's kind of a thin, ridged Mexican pastry." He led him to a snack vendor parked on the edge of the street. "This guy sells the best ones in the city. I'll split one with you." Joe bought a churro, pulled it apart, and gave half to Jesse. He watched Jesse take his first bite.

"Well?"

"It's good. Kind of like a sugar doughnut."

Joe smiled. "Yeah, I guess it is. And just as bad for the waist-line." Joe took a bite. "Jesse, do you remember a red-haired man at your sessions?"

"Yeah, he was there a lot."

"Who was he?"

"I don't know. I thought he was another scientist or a friend of Dr. Nelson's."

"Did you ever talk to him?"

"A couple of times. He never said much. Once he asked me how I liked the tests. Is this why you wanted to talk to me away from Mama?"

"Not really. I want to talk to you about the things you do. Your tricks."

"What about 'em?"

"What do you think people would do if they found out your powers weren't real?"

"But they *are* real."

"Okay, let's just pretend. Everyone suddenly believes that you were fooling them, that you don't have these powers. What would happen?"

Jesse shrugged. "People would be mad at me."

"Who?"

"My mama, all the people at the college . . . everybody."

"It really wouldn't matter to the people who care about you, Jesse. They just want what's best for you."

The boy shrugged.

"What else do you think would happen?"

"The kids at school would make fun of me."

"Why?"

"They'd call me a faker."

"I don't know about that. If I was your age, and I was able to fool all those scientists, reporters, and teachers, the other kids would probably think I was a hero. Especially if I showed 'em how I made monkeys out of all those people."

Jesse took another bite of the churro.

"What I'm trying to say is, it wouldn't be the worst thing in the world to happen," he said gently.

Jesse took off his glasses and wiped them with his shirt. He stopped in front of a No Littering sign, where someone had taped a bright green flyer advertising a local rock band. Jesse lowered his head and stared at it.

It was *the* stare.

The paper started flapping.

Slowly at first, then faster. And faster.

Joe squinted at the flyer. How in the hell was this happening?

Jesse's head tilted to the left. His stare grew more intense. The flyer flapped even harder. It was as if a heavy gust of wind were blowing against it, but the air around them was still.

Was Jesse blowing on it? Joe studied his face. The boy's mouth was closed and his nostrils were pointing down to his chest. Joe slowly raised the back of his hand so that it was only inches from Jesse's nose and mouth. No air.

Holy shit.

The flyer strained against the tiny sliver of tape holding it to the sign pole. Jesse's head tilted to the other side. The sign finally jerked free of the tape. It floated to the ground.

Joe snatched it up and looked at both sides. Clean. He ran his hands over the signpost. Nothing.

Jesse backed away. "I don't want to talk anymore."

"How?" Joe whispered.

"Mama's waiting for me." Jesse turned and waved to his mother, who had just come out of the bank. "I have to go home now."

"How?" Joe whispered again.

Jesse was already walking toward his mother.

All the way back to his office, Joe tried to comprehend what he'd seen. Advance preparation wasn't a possibility. He, not Jesse, had chosen to walk outside, and the boy had had no idea they'd be walking past that sign together.

Between this and Suzanne Morrison's séance, it had been a thoroughly mind-blowing couple of days. Two amazing demonstrations in a little more than twenty-four hours of each other.

He still hadn't recovered from the experience, when he stepped off the elevator to find a billionaire waiting for him.

"Detective Bailey, I'm Roland Ness."

Sure you are, Joe almost said. He was glad he didn't. He'd never met Ness in the years he spent debunking the parapsychology team's findings, but he was sure that the state's second-wealthiest citizen was aware of his work.

Joe smiled ruefully. What next? First an eight-year-old boy stumped him, now Roland Ness was hanging around in the squad room, waiting for him.

Ness extended his hand. He was a tall, robust man in his late sixties, with strong features, gray hair and beard, and bushy white eyebrows. His eyes glistened with what most people might call a childlike twinkle, but they reminded Joe of someone who had just been peeling onions.

"Hello, Mr. Ness. What brings you here?"

"Can we talk?"

"Sure. If you'll walk this way—"

"If you don't mind, I have someplace that may be more private."

"What do you mean?"

"My truck is outside."

"Excuse me?"

"Detective, for a man in my position, privacy is a precious, even vital, commodity. Will you indulge me?"

Ness was obviously used to getting his way, but there was nothing arrogant or insistent about his manner.

Joe turned around, and for the second time in the space of an hour, all eyes in the squad room were on him. He motioned toward the door. "Lead the way."

The "truck" was a thirty-foot RV that could have been driven by his aunt Susie and uncle Thomas on their frequent trips to Branson. The interior, however, reflected a sleek European sensibility, accented by low-key lighting and dark, plush furniture. As soon as Ness closed the door behind them, the vehicle pulled away from the curb. Joe glanced at the spike-haired woman behind the wheel.

"She's my driver," Ness said. "Call me sexist, but I think women make much better drivers than men. By and large, they're calmer, and the highway isn't a video game to them. They're more concerned about getting me where I'm going and less concerned about getting back at the bastard who cut us off five miles back."

Joe sat across from Ness. "What can I do for you?"

Ness smiled. "As I'm sure you know, I have an interest in the supernatural."

"I hear it's more of an obsession."

"Obsession . . . that's a strong word. I prefer 'fascination.'"

"Whatever you call it, I know the Landwyn University parapsychology program appreciates your interest."

"You're talking about the money."

"You're keeping that program afloat."

"I make several endowments to the university. The parapsychology program just happens to be one."

"You're aware of the fact that a lot of the people at the university just wish the program would go away."

"Of course." Ness chuckled. "Many people in my own companies wish it would go away too. But I think it's important to study the paranormal in a scientific manner. *You* should appreciate that, Mr. Bailey. So much of the evidence is purely anecdotal. If my endowment can help advance our knowledge in the field, then it's worth it."

"Does it frustrate you that the program has yet to find one verifiable occurrence of paranormal activity?"

"What about Jesse Randall?"

Could Ness see the tension in his face? How? "I'm still working on that," Joe said.

"And they have a medium who shows promise, don't they?"

"Suzanne Morrison. I'm seeing her again soon, so I wouldn't get your hopes up."

"I see." He paused. "I really wanted to speak to you about Robert Nelson. It's tragic what happened to him, but there's an irregularity that I felt you should be made aware of."

"What is it?"

"I have an auditor who looks after my endowments and sees that the money isn't being spent frivolously. A few months ago we discovered that a substantial amount of the program's funds was being granted to a family in Cartersville."

"Why?"

"I asked Nelson that very question, and after a few weak lies he finally admitted it had all been a mistake. I threatened to pull his funding and have him brought up on charges, but he personally paid back the money into the program's budget."

"Did he ever explain how it had happened?"

"No. My investigator did some preliminary investigation into the family. There's nothing remarkable about them, and they've had no apparent experience with the paranormal."

Joe remembered the $25,000 that Howe had found in Nelson's house. "You think maybe it was a scam? Maybe he was using them to funnel money back to himself?"

"It certainly appeared that way. Especially since he had no trouble coming up with the money to put back into the coffers."

"How much are we talking about?"

"One hundred and sixty thousand dollars."

Joe wrinkled his brow. "Not exactly the kind of money a college professor would have handy. Although he did have a nice house."

"Inherited from his parents," Ness said. "It was all he could do to keep up with the property taxes."

"He told you this?"

"You think I didn't have him thoroughly checked out?"

"How silly of me."

"We carefully scrutinized all of the program's other financial dealings, and this was the only irregularity."

"Tell me something. How much control did you have over the test sessions?"

"None, really. I'm always interested in their progress, but I have other things to keep me busy."

Joe pulled out a small photo of the red-haired man, printed from one of the Jesse Randall session tapes. "Does this man work for you, Mr. Ness?"

Ness glanced at the photo. "No."

"Have you seen him before?"

"No. Who is he?"

"I'm trying to find out. He had input on some of the Jesse Randall tests, but no one seems to know who he is. He and Nelson were pretty secretive about his identity."

"Hmm. Interesting. I wonder, Detective, if you wouldn't mind giving me that photograph. I assume you have another."

Joe put the photo back into his pocket. "I *would* mind. Why do you want it?"

Ness scratched his beard. "I thought I could help. I do have a fair amount of resources at my disposal, and it would be an honor to assist you."

"No, thanks."

"Suit yourself."

Ness looked through the tinted side windows. "Ah, here we are. Back at your headquarters." He handed Joe a typed index card. "This is the address of the family in Cartersville. It may turn out to be nothing, but you never know."

"You never know."

Ness opened the door for him. "It was wonderful to finally meet you, Mr. Bailey. It's not every day that one gets to meet a real-life Spirit Basher."

"Or a real-life billionaire."

Joe stepped onto the sidewalk, and he could still hear Ness chuckling as the door swung shut and the RV pulled away.

"I'm already on it, Bailey. And I didn't need a visit from Roland Ness to tip me off." Howe leaned back in his desk chair.

Arrogant prick.

"And what do you have?" Joe asked.

Howe spoke just loud enough for the detectives at the neighboring desks to hear the seasoned homicide cop enlightening the greenhorn. "I talked to the university finance office, and they confirmed there had apparently been an error, and that Nelson had paid them back in cash. But there was no record of the money ever entering any bank account of his."

"You think this family may have slipped it back to him under the table?"

"Possible."

"Have you checked the family out?"

Howe picked up a yellow Post-it note and squinted at his scribbling. "Ted and Crystal Rawlings. He steam-cleans carpets for a living, she's currently unemployed. They had a teenage daughter who died of appendicitis last year. Their house is a rental, and they have about twenty months left to pay on their Ford Explorer."

"Have you spoken to them?"

"Not yet."

"Let's go."

"Whoa there. I said I'm on it."

"*We're* on it. Cartersville is only an hour's drive. In about fifteen seconds I'll be on my way there. Are you with me or not?"

Howe glanced at the detectives at the nearby desks, giving them a can-you-believe-this-guy? look. He grabbed his badge and keys from the candy wrapper–cluttered desktop. "Sure. Carl Crimestopper's got himself a lead. I don't want to miss this."

Joe had been to Cartersville only once in his life, when his high school basketball team had advanced to the state playoffs. They had lost the game, and for years the mere thought of Cartersville conjured up images of the torrent of paper cups and empty Skoal containers that had been hurled at him and his teammates as they made the sad trek back to the bus. Joe looked at the Budweiser plant as he and Howe drove past, thinking that a lot of those rotten kids were now probably working inside, stirring yeast and cleaning ten-thousand-gallon beer vats.

They found the Rawlings house, a modest ranch-style home in a small subdivision called Bayonet Arms. The name was a nod to the area's Civil War history, but to Joe it still seemed as odd as a neighborhood called Machine-Gun Estates or Grenade-Launcher Villas.

He rapped on the front door, and the sound of barking dogs echoed through the house. After a moment, a frail woman in her late thirties answered the door. "Yes?"

Joe smiled. "Crystal Rawlings?"

"Yes?"

He flashed his badge. "I'm Detective Joe Bailey. This is Detective Mark Howe. We're with the Atlanta Police Department, and we'd like to ask you a few questions. May we come in?"

Her face flushed. "The house is a mess. I wish you'd called first."

Howe stepped forward. "Ms. Rawlings, you don't have to worry about that. I can see already that you have a very nice home, and we just want to ask you a few questions. Okay?"

Joe was impressed. Howe actually knew how to hide his prick-like tendencies.

She managed a weak smile and opened the door. "Okay, but don't say I didn't warn you."

The house smelled of dog, and the couch and carpeting were covered with at least three different colors of canine hair.

She gestured to the couch. "Please sit down."

"No, thank you," Howe said. He fired off the first question: "How did you know Dr. Robert Nelson?"

Her eyes widened. She couldn't have looked guiltier. "Who?" she asked.

Howe smiled. "Let's skip this part, where you pretend you didn't know him and I insist you did, okay? If your memory needs refreshing, he's the guy who gave you a hundred and sixty thousand dollars and then ended up impaled up near the ceiling of his study. *That* Robert Nelson."

Her eyes darted around the room as if searching for a convenient escape hatch. "Maybe you should talk to my husband. He'll be home any minute."

"We'll be happy to talk to him, but we'd like to talk to you first."

Joe leaned forward. "What was the money for, Ms. Rawlings? Why did Dr. Nelson give it to you?"

She bit her lip and looked at the floor. "It came from the school, not from him."

"But he authorized it," Joe said.

"Yes." She took several deep breaths. "It was for a project."

"What project?"

"I can't talk about that."

"*Can't* or *won't*?"

"It was a condition of our agreement."

"An agreement between you and Robert Nelson?"

She nodded.

Howe was getting more annoyed by the minute. "Then why doesn't anyone else in his department know anything about it? This is not the way his program was run. Would you like to continue this conversation at the station? Because I think—"

Joe cut him off. "We're investigating a murder, Ms. Rawlings. I think that pretty much supersedes any agreement you may have had with the late Dr. Nelson."

She crossed her arms in front of her. "I—I gave my word. I can't go against that."

"This is important," Joe said. "I guarantee you it's more

important than anything that happened between him and your family."

She shot a glance at the end table, where there were two framed photographs. A slightly plump teenage girl was in both shots.

"Is that your daughter?" Joe softly asked.

Crystal didn't reply.

"I know you lost her last year. I'm sorry."

She began to tremble. "Oh, sweet Jesus."

"Ms. Rawlings . . . are you okay?"

She nodded, but her trembling continued.

"Is there anything you would like to tell us?"

She looked up. "I didn't do anything wrong, I promise."

"Then talk to us," Joe said.

The front door swung open, and a lanky middle-aged man walked into the house. He stared at Joe and Howe. "What's goin' on here?"

Joe and Howe turned to face him. "We're with the Atlanta Police Department," Joe said. "Are you Ted Rawlings?"

Crystal didn't look at her husband. "They want to know about Dr. Nelson," she half whispered. "They know about the money."

Ted glared at them. "So what?"

"So maybe you should be a little more cooperative," Howe said. "I'm sure the IRS would be interested in all that money. Even if you gave it back to Nelson, you could still be on the hook to the government for tens of thousands of dollars."

"What are you talkin' about?" Rawlings said. "We didn't give it back. We're declarin' every cent and payin' whatever we owe."

Joe frowned. "You didn't give the money back to Dr. Nelson?"

"Hell, no. Why would we do that?"

Joe exchanged a startled glance with Howe.

"I'm not sayin' another word to you fellas," Ted said, moving closer to his wife. "We did nothin' wrong."

"Then what could possibly be the harm in telling us about your relationship with Dr. Nelson?"

Ted gestured toward the open door. "This conversation is over. If you want to arrest us, go ahead. Otherwise, get out."

Joe nodded and gave Crystal his card. "We don't need to go that far today. Talk about it and give us a call. If we don't hear from you soon, we'll be back." He turned to Ted. "We might even have to visit you at your workplace."

"Don't threaten me," Ted said. "It doesn't matter where you turn up. My answer is gonna be the same."

"Have a good evening," Joe said.

Howe strode ahead of him out of the house. Joe paused when he reached the door. Ted Rawlings was still staring at him, but Crystal didn't seem to be aware of any of them.

She was still staring at the pictures of her daughter.

"Where in the hell did Robert Nelson get a hundred and sixty thousand dollars?"

It was Joe and Howe's main topic of conversation all the way back from Cartersville. They compared notes on what they had each uncovered so far, and Joe was impressed with Howe's attention to detail. Howe had an answer for almost every question, and he rattled off the pertinent facts, figures, and dates as if they were his own vital statistics. But when Joe showed him the photo of the red-haired man, Howe was stumped. Nobody seemed to know who the guy was.

They drove to Blues Junction, a dark, smoky club near the Underground Atlanta shopping and entertainment center. Howe had discovered it was one of Nelson's favorite hangouts. They flashed a photo around to the staff, and although a few did recognize Nelson, they couldn't recall anything notable about him.

Joe and Howe sat at a booth, almost shouting over the R&B group wailing on the stage.

"The money still bugs me," Howe said. "I tell you, we did a full financial rundown on him. He didn't have that kind of money."

"He got it from somewhere," Joe said.

"In cash. He must have found it under a rock someplace, because it didn't move through any account he had."

"But why would he have given a hundred and sixty thousand dollars of his program's money to the Rawlingses, then, when discovered, scrounge up the money from someplace else and repay it?"

Howe shrugged. "You're the one who works with those nuts. What super-secret study could those people have been fooling around with?"

"So secret that even Nelson's coworkers didn't know what it was? Like you told the lady, they don't work that way."

They sat quietly as the crowd applauded a guitar player's frantic riff.

Howe suddenly leaned closer. "Bailey, let me see the picture of the red-haired guy."

"Sure." Joe pulled the print out of his breast pocket and slapped it on the table between them.

Howe glanced at it. "Interesting."

"Interesting why?"

"If this was a hangout of Nelson's, he may have brought that guy here. Maybe the guy liked it."

"Yeah?"

Howe smiled and took a swig of his beer. "Because right now he's standing at the bar."

Joe turned and followed Howe's gaze. Christ. It *was* him. The red-haired man who had sat in on Jesse Randall's sessions. He was sipping a drink and swaying to the music.

"How do you want to play this?" Howe asked.

"I'm going to talk to him."

Howe slid out of the booth. "I'll cover the door."

"Good."

Joe turned back around. Red was staring right at him. Shit.

The man put down his drink and stepped away. Joe moved through the club, pushing past the happy-hour throngs who had wedged themselves onto the tiny dance floor. The man's fiery red hair appeared and disappeared through the crowd. He was heading toward the door.

Joe moved under the row of recessed blue lights near the bar. Where in the hell was Howe?

A woman screamed. Activity rippled around the door.

Joe reached into his jacket and gripped the handle of his revolver. He shouldered his way through the crowd and saw Howe on the floor.

"Give him room!" Joe yelled.

The crowd backed away only slightly as Joe crouched next to his partner. Howe's eyes fluttered.

"What happened?"

"I'm okay," Howe rasped. He pointed to the door. "Go!"

Joe could hear the bartender on the phone to 911. He jumped to his feet and ran out the door. It was dark outside, still and quiet.

A motorcycle kick-started in the lot next door. Joe turned as it roared over a small concrete barrier and hit the sidewalk. It was coming right for him.

He threw himself over the hood of a parked car. He rolled over it as the motorcycle's left handlebar clipped the passenger-side mirror. He yanked out his gun as he hit the pavement.

The bike whipped into a narrow alleyway, its ear-splitting roar reverberating off the tall brick buildings. Within seconds Joe could hear it racing down West Peachtree Street.

He instinctively turned toward his car, then stopped.

Who was he kidding? By the time he got on the road, Red and his motorcycle would have turned off West Peachtree and disappeared into one of the dark, anonymous corners of the city. Dammit.

"Are you okay?"

Howe had shuffled out of the club, his jacket off and tie loosened.

"Fine. What happened to you?"

"Jesus, he's good. The bastard chopped me across the throat and hit me in the solar plexus. I went down like a rock."

"Don't feel bad. He almost decorated my face with his tire tread."

Howe chuckled as he pulled out a pack of cigarettes and tapped one out. "Well, either you're on to something, Bailey, or our red-haired friend *really* doesn't want it known that he likes blues music."

8

hy can't we take the elevator?" Nikki asked as she and Joe started down the stairs to the atrium of their building. It was 8:15 A.M., and they were beginning their morning school-and-work run.

"Exercise is good for us. Plus the elevator's been acting up. I don't want you using it for a while." He hadn't told her about the accident the other night, explaining his bandaged fingers away with an offhand comment about getting them caught in the elevator doors. But he didn't want her riding the elevator until he had an idea how—

Wait a minute. He glanced back at the shaft. Maybe he *did* have an idea.

"Daddy?"

Not now. He'd look into it later. "Yeah?"

"I want to take judo lessons."

"Judo? What happened to ballet?"

"Judo's better."

"It won't get you in *The Nutcracker*."

They walked through the atrium and she pulled open the front door. "I don't want to do that anymore. I want to take judo."

He gazed searchingly at her. It wasn't like Nikki to change her mind so quickly. "Why judo? Is somebody bothering you at school, honey?"

"I didn't say—"

A microphone was suddenly thrust in Joe's face. "Do you believe Jesse Randall's powers are responsible for the unexplained attempts on your life, Detective?"

Joe instinctively pulled Nikki closer. Half a dozen reporters. Three media trucks. What the hell was happening?

"Tell us about the elevator, Joe."

Shit, Joe thought. Just what he needed.

"Are you afraid Jesse Randall might harm your daughter?"

"What does he mean?" Nikki whispered.

"Nothing, sweetheart." Joe walked to his 4Runner at the curb and opened the passenger-side door. "Get in the car."

"Daddy . . . ?"

"Please, honey." He boosted her into the passenger seat, slammed the door, and turned toward the journalists. "Not in front of my kid, okay?"

A chunky female radio reporter held a small DAT recorder in Joe's face. "Can you explain the incidents in the Landwyn library and your elevator?"

He pushed the recorder away. "Accidents happen."

A balding man with a thick mustache smiled. "Joe, my name's Gary Danton. I'm with *Nature Extreme*."

"And you admit it? So, how's the Loch Ness monster search going?"

"Not my beat."

"Aw, too bad. Look, I know you're working on a piece slamming me and the professor for trying to hold Nelson accountable for his results."

"Old news. What can you tell us about the attacks?"

Joe walked around to the driver-side door. "There have been no attacks. Who in the hell turned you people loose on me?"

"You know I can't reveal my sources."

"Of course. *Nature Extreme* is a bastion of journalistic integrity."

"Let's just say I heard it from someone a bit more open-minded than you."

Who would have done this? Joe wondered. Other than—

"Kellner," he said aloud. "He found out about this stuff and called you guys, right?"

"Let's get this straight," Danton said, ignoring the question. "We have two new unexplained occurrences, both while Jesse Randall slept. The elevator technician can't explain what happened to you in your building, and the Landwyn library staff tells me that you even brought in your instruments to try to figure out what happened to you there. Any explanations?"

Joe opened the door. "Nothing I can discuss. Don't stir things up now. This case is crazy enough already." ·

"Jesse Randall may be stirring things up," Danton said slyly. "Do you fear for your life, Detective?"

Joe snorted and climbed behind the wheel of the 4Runner. As he pulled away from the curb, he could see a few of the reporters scribbling in their notebooks. Damn. Whatever they were writing would probably be in the newspapers by the next morning.

Nikki spoke barely above a whisper. "What happened, Daddy?"

He flexed his bandaged fingers. "I told you about the elevator. It malfunctioned. And when I was at the library Saturday night, a few shelves fell over."

"Toward you?"

Joe shrugged.

"How did it happen?"

"They just fell. Sometimes things like that happen."

"Saturday was the day we went to see Jesse."

"Don't read anything into it, honey."

Nikki drew her jacket closer around her. "He was mad at you."

"He and his mother came to see me yesterday. Everything's okay now."

"Don't see him anymore, Daddy."

"Nikki . . ."

"Please, don't."

"Sweetheart, Jesse hasn't done anything. He didn't murder Dr. Nelson, and—"

"What if he did? What if his dreams caused it, just like everybody's saying? What if one of those dreams hurts you too?"

"You have to trust me, honey. I'll be all right."

"But what if you're wrong?"

"I'm not wrong."

Joe glanced at her. She was crying. Damn. He wanted to murder Kellner or whoever had tipped off those reporters. He pulled over to the side of the road, unbuckled his seat belt, and leaned closer. "Don't be upset, sweetie. Everything will be okay. Believe me."

"I do believe you. You never lie to me." She wiped her eyes with her sleeve. "Mommy's not really in jail, is she?"

He stared at her in bewilderment. "Where did *that* come from?"

"Amy and Monica said that Mommy's not really dead. They say we just tell people that because she's really in jail. Amy told me that lots of kids pretend that their mom or dad is dead because they're ashamed of them being in prison."

Joe shook his head in disbelief. Hateful little brats. "No, honey. Mommy's gone. I was with her."

Nikki gazed out the windshield. "That's what I thought. Amy and Monica never liked me. They're the liars, right, Daddy?"

"Right, honey."

"I wanted to fight them, but they're bigger than I am."

"Is that why you want judo lessons?"

She paused. "Yeah."

"That's not the answer. If Mommy was in jail, believe me, nothing on earth would stop me from breaking her out. Right?"

Nikki nodded.

"And I'm not going to leave you, ever. I'm going to watch you grow up, I'm going to scare the hell out of guys who dare to take you out on dates, and I'm going to walk you down the aisle on your wedding day. I'm going to spoil your kids like crazy, and then I'm going to spoil *their* kids."

She almost smiled. "If you live to be that old, *I'm* not going to be the one to change your diaper."

He laughed. "My diaper?"

"I've seen those commercials."

"You and I have very different ideas about old age, and for my sake, I hope *I'm* right."

She laid her head on his chest. "Be careful, Daddy."

"You didn't think this was enough of a circus?" Joe sighed as Kellner prepped the parapsychology lab for a telepathy test.

"You were holding out on us, Bailey. Why didn't you tell us about these incidents?"

"First of all, there's nothing to talk about. They were *accidents*. And second, I'm having a tough enough time on this case without being hounded by reporters. I'd barely climbed out of that elevator shaft when I thought of you guys going to town on this. It looks like I was right. How did you find out?"

"Everyone knows about the library shelves. The sixth floor was closed until Tuesday. After I heard about that, I remembered seeing you with bandages on your hands. Professor Reisman's secretary knew you had been in some kind of an elevator accident, so I called a few repair companies and found out about the problem in your building. Simple as that."

"So, rather than simply study the apparent phenomena, you felt compelled to run to the media."

Kellner's smile was full of malice. "The press hasn't been kind to this program, especially since the Spirit Basher came along. I thought this might help restore the balance."

"Right. At the expense of me and my daughter."

"Don't try to guilt me, Joe. You've cost this program tens of thousands of dollars in grants, and you've made sure that we're thought of as complete buffoons."

"*You've* made sure of that. My purpose is to protect your reputations and the reputation of this university. It's not my fault that you shoot off your mouths about every new 'discovery' before I've had a chance to show you they're complete frauds."

Kellner checked the seal on a fresh pack of test cards. "Enough already. I'm sure you didn't come here just to complain about a few reporters."

Joe let out a long breath. Let it go. "Okay, what can you tell me about Ted and Crystal Rawlings?"

"Who?"

He told Kellner about Ness's audit, the mysterious grant, and Nelson's subsequent return of the money.

Kellner claimed to have heard none of it before. He shook his head. "We occasionally investigate things on our own before we bring them to the attention of the group, but we're not in the business of giving out grants. We may pay travel expenses and put subjects up in a hotel room, but that's about it. A hundred and sixty thousand dollars? Are you sure?"

"Yes."

"I'd offer to look in Nelson's files, but you people have already taken them all."

"I checked them this morning. He had no record of the Rawlings family."

Kellner shrugged. "I'm sorry. I can't help you."

"Check with the rest of the spook squad, will you? Maybe he talked to one of them."

"I doubt it, but I'll ask."

Joe pulled out his notebook. "Okay, I have a question about one of the test sessions in Nelson's logs. Just a few days before they went to Dallas, Nelson tested Jesse in here. I can't find any video on it, and there are no results posted. There's just a notation that reads 'T.A.'"

"There you have it. 'T.A.' means 'test abandoned.'"

"Why would that happen?"

"Any one of a number of reasons. Do you know what the test involved?"

Joe checked his notebook. "It just says 'halo.'"

"Oh, that explains it. He was trying out a new piece of test equipment. It probably wasn't working correctly, so he canceled the rest of the session."

"Why is there no video?"

"Cassettes for T.A. sessions are usually put back into the pool and recorded over. It would serve no scholarly purpose to watch Nelson cuss out a piece of malfunctioning test equipment."

"If that's what really happened. What is this halo thing?"

"It's a cranial electrometer, but we call it the electric halo. It measures electrical activity emanating from the brain."

"Can I see it?"

Kellner glanced at his watch and frowned. "I guess so. It's here in the video booth."

He led Joe through a doorway into the small booth where the

testing center's sessions were transmitted by wireless video cameras to an array of receivers, monitors, and VCRs. He gestured toward the corner, where a bizarre-looking device was resting on a wig stand. It looked like a gold halo with dozens of long wires sprouting in every direction.

Joe placed it on his head and looked at himself in the reflection of a monitor. The wires drooped over his face and ears. "I hate to think how much the university paid for this thing. Does it actually work?"

Kellner removed it from Joe's head and put it back on the stand. "It does what it's supposed to do, but we've yet to establish a meaningful link between paranormal phenomena and electrical activity of the brain."

"After the abandoned session, was Jesse ever tested with this?"

Kellner thought for a moment. "No, I don't think so. And that's strange, because Nelson ran every other test on him."

The first broadcast news reporter called Joe at 11:45. The second called a few minutes after three. Four more called in the half hour after that. The "psychic attacks" story had broken wide open, and everyone wanted a quote. Was he afraid of becoming Jesse Randall's next victim?

Howe walked into the squad room and tossed down a copy of the newspaper. On the front page, just below the fold, was the headline: SPIRIT BASHER TARGETED BY REPUTED PSYCHIC? Howe smiled. "You didn't tell me you were a marked man, Bailey."

"*I* didn't know until the reporters started to stir things up."

"The boss wants to talk to you about it."

"Gerald?"

"Yep. Let's go."

Joe went with Howe to Lieutenant Gerald's office, where Joe

related the elevator and library incidents. Gerald had a peculiar look on his face.

Joe had seen that look before. A little fear, a dash of wonder . . . Gerald *believed*.

"I'm sure Jesse Randall and his supposed powers had nothing to do with it," Joe said emphatically.

Gerald nodded, but his expression didn't change.

The guy actually thought Jesse might be the real thing, even if he wouldn't admit it. Great.

"Watch yourself," Gerald said. "If anything else happens, I want to be the first call you make. Got it?"

"Yes."

"You're still convinced Jesse Randall's a fake?"

Joe flashed on the image of that flyer waving on the pole. "Yes."

"You said you'd be able to figure out his methods. Why hasn't that happened?"

"As with many so-called telekinetics, Jesse's demonstrations are brief and, at least when I'm around, he doesn't announce what he's going to do before he does it. That makes it difficult to analyze his technique."

"What's your next step?"

"Right now I'm going to see Jesse."

Gerald raised his eyebrows. "What good will that do?"

"For me, maybe no good at all. This one's for him."

As Joe approached the Randall home, he noticed that the gauntlet of reporters had grown larger, and the uniformed cop in front was now looking harried and even a little fearful.

Latisha let Joe inside, and he was startled to see a barrel-chested man standing in the living room.

"Detective Bailey!" the man's voice boomed. He thrust out his right hand.

As Joe shook hands, he suddenly recognized the man. Stewart Dunning. Defense lawyer extraordinaire.

Every cop's worst nightmare.

Joe had never crossed paths with him before, but Dunning had a reputation for making mincemeat of officers on the witness stand. He'd made a name for himself representing drug dealers, and he'd gradually expanded his client base to include white-collar criminals.

Arrested with a kilo of coke in the trunk? Call Stewart Dunning.

Got caught selling defective airline parts to the air force? Dunning's your man.

"What brings you here?" Joe asked, remembering that Dunning would gladly use any slip of the tongue against him.

"Jesse Randall is my client, Detective. No more unannounced visits. If you wish to speak to him, arrange it through me. I'll be present for any and all conversations you have with him."

Joe turned to Latisha.

"I'm sorry, but I have to protect my son," she said.

"With this guy? One of his clients was paying kids Jesse's age to carry bags of heroin. A little boy got killed for it last year."

Dunning glared at him. "That will be enough, Detective."

"Did you run over here to volunteer your services, Dunning? You saw all the attention and decided you wanted to grab a piece of it and get yourself on television?"

"I saw a child whose interests weren't being represented."

"I'm touched."

Latisha stepped forward. "Detective, I don't believe this man gives a damn about my son."

Dunning started to object, but Latisha held up her hand to silence him.

"It's not his job to give a damn," she said. "His job is to protect my boy, and I believe he'll do that. Not because he cares about

Jesse or me, but because he cares about himself and his reputation as a lawyer. I know what kind of man Mr. Dunning is, and whatever you think of him, he's one of the best."

Joe couldn't argue with that.

"I can't afford *any* lawyer, much less one like Mr. Dunning. So when he came to my door offering to help Jesse, what else was I going to do? What would you do if you and your daughter were in our position? I think you'd want her to have the best help she could get. Wouldn't you?"

He didn't answer. She was right, and he knew it.

"You've been decent to us," she said, "but I'm going to take Mr. Dunning's advice. In the future, I'd appreciate it if you would call him first if you want to ask Jesse any questions."

"I didn't come here to ask questions," Joe said. "The reporters have been blowing things out of proportion today."

"We've heard. Are you all right?"

"Yes. I know those accidents weren't Jesse's fault, but I thought he'd like to hear that from me."

Dunning motioned toward the front door. "Jesse is fine. If that's all, Detective . . ."

"What do you think, Ms. Randall?"

Latisha considered it, then nodded. "Jesse! Come in here, please."

Dunning shot her a disapproving glance.

Jesse appeared in the doorway, staring uneasily at Joe. "Hi, Mr. Bailey."

"Hi, Jesse. Crazy day, huh?"

"Yeah."

Joe moved closer. "People are trying to make this something it's not. They say that you're attacking me with your mind. I don't believe that, and I don't want you to believe it either. Okay?"

Jesse nodded.

"Now, are you *sure* there's nothing you want to tell me?"

Dunning stepped between them. "You promised not to ask questions, Detective."

"Jesse, please. This can all end with just a few words from you."

"We're finished!" Dunning said.

Joe studied Jesse. He looked troubled. Guilt, maybe? Or something else?

Dunning walked to the front door and opened it. "There's no physical evidence that links my client to the crime, Detective, and he has no idea how it happened. I can't see why you would have any cause to talk to Jesse anymore."

"Of course not. If it comes out that he has no powers, there's no story. The reporters will go away and your ride on the Hype Express will come to an end. Do you really want what's best for Jesse?"

Dunning forced a smile. "Good-bye."

Joe turned toward Latisha and Jesse. "Call me if you need anything. Anything at all."

He left the house and muttered a silent curse as he walked back to his car. Dunning's involvement would complicate things. He admired Latisha's ability to recognize the attorney's motives, but keeping Jesse cloistered away really wasn't in the boy's best interests.

Joe climbed into his car and drove north on I-75 toward Cartersville. He knew if he was going to get any more information out of the Rawlings family, it was going to be from Crystal. He would definitely pay her a return visit, but not yet.

Now he had to see a doctor.

The Columbia Cartersville Medical Center was a sterile complex of buildings on Joe Frank Harris Parkway, and it was easily the largest hospital within twenty-five miles. Sixteen-year-old Gaby Rawlings had died there.

Joe's questions to Crystal had clearly triggered some deep and disturbing memories about her daughter. He was pretty sure that in a town as small as Cartersville, someone at the hospital would remember Gaby Rawlings. He was right.

"It shouldn't have happened." Dr. Stanley Gelson shook his head. The surgical resident was an impossibly young-looking man with short, frizzy hair and round wire-rimmed glasses. He held Gaby Rawlings's patient file in his lap.

Joe was talking to him in the cramped waiting area of the hospital emergency room. *Mama's Family* was blaring from the television as a reminder of what a hellish experience those waiting rooms could be.

"Was there anything suspicious about her death?"

"Not suspicious, really, just needless. The kid's appendix ruptured. It's something we can fix these days."

"Why didn't you?"

"It was too late. Peritonitis had already set in. They should have brought her here hours or even days earlier."

"You think the parents were negligent?"

Gelson shrugged. "In this case, what's negligence? Driving your kid straight to the hospital when she has a tummyache, or waiting it out to avoid a two-thousand-dollar emergency room tab? It's happening more and more, I'm afraid. Without insurance, most people can't afford to be sick."

"The Rawlingses didn't have insurance?"

Gelson checked the file. "Nope. Tell me, are her parents still together?"

"Yes. Why do you ask?"

"I've seen a lot of these cases. In my experience, it's usually the husband who doesn't want to come in. If a child dies, everyone else in the family blames him. And he's usually even harder on himself. It rips families apart."

"Well, that hasn't happened to them yet."

"Hmm. Do her parents live on a farm?"

"No. Why?"

Gelson lowered his voice. "When they brought her in, she was wearing a pink pajama top. It looked like there were traces of blood on it."

"Blood? From where?"

"I don't know. She didn't have any external injuries. I asked her father about it, and he said she'd been using it as a painting smock."

"Did it look like paint?"

"No, and I *do* know what blood looks like. Anyway, it seemed strange to me, and afterward I decided to run a test on it."

"Did it match the girl's blood type?"

"No." He shook his head. "Detective, it was the blood of a pig."

Garrett Lyles strode into the First United Baptist Church, where he was one of the few Caucasians present. He'd always prided himself in his ability to blend in with his surroundings, but that clearly wasn't going to happen here. He was wearing a slightly dressier version of his TV cameraman disguise, so if any of the news crews outside happened to recognize him, it would appear that he was just following the story.

Six-fifteen P.M. The congregation was gathering for the Wednesday evening service, and he knew Latisha and Jesse Randall would soon be walking through the church's rear entrance. He'd followed them most of the trip from their house, peeling away only when it appeared their police motorcycle escort was taking notice of him.

Nice of the cops to put a man on Jesse. It helped Lyles feel a little more comfortable when he had to leave to grab a bite or catch a few Z's.

He watched the rear of the church, and finally he could see movement in the baby box, a small enclosed compartment where parents could watch the service with their screaming infants. Latisha and Jesse must have arrived. He'd been present last Sunday morning when the minister had asked them to sit there to avoid disruption of the service by journalists and photographers.

Tonight Lyles chose a seat in one of the rows that lined the side of the church. It offered him a good view of the baby box.

Yes, Jesse and Latisha had indeed arrived. They sat between two women holding infants.

Lyles reached in his pocket for his carved squares. He knew they were there, but it was good to feel their smooth finish and ever-so-precise markings. The church made him uncomfortable. One day soon, these houses of worship would be extinct, replaced with something far stronger than blind faith.

And the boy sitting in that little room would lead the way.

A high, raspy voice penetrated the din of the crowd, and the congregation quickly quieted. It was always the same: The minister would appear where the congregation least expected it, leaning against a doorway or seated in the back of the pews, speaking softly into his tie-clip battery microphone. Only after everyone had spotted him would he move through the church, speaking as if he were talking to guests in his living room. Very effective, Lyles thought. If his old pastor had been more like this guy, he might have ended up in another line of work.

After fifteen minutes or so, the minister nodded to his forty-member choir, and a beautiful female voice pierced the air:

Friends may fail me
Foes assail me

He, my Savior makes me whole
Hallelujah!

An organ and drumbeat kicked in, and the entire forty-member choir joined in.

Lyles had no particular liking for gospel tunes, but he couldn't help but be fascinated by the performers' energy and enthusiasm. He suspected this was the real reason for the church's high attendance; *his* religion would never need such a pathetic ploy to attract believers.

Jesus! What a friend for sinners!
Jesus! Lover of my soul
Friends may fail me
Foes assail me
He, my Savior makes me whole

Lyles smiled as the followers around him began clapping to the fast beat. He was sure that Jesse Randall wouldn't be taken in by this display. He glanced toward the baby box.

The room was dark.

Lyles stood, and the people around him took that as a cue to jump to their feet. It caused a ripple effect throughout the church, and within moments the entire congregation was standing, clapping and dancing to the music.

What the hell was going on in that booth?

Lyles slid down the side of the church, his eyes darting furiously, assessing the situation.

Friends may fail me
Foes assail me
He, my Savior makes me whole
Hallelujah!

A faint shaft of light appeared in the booth. It was the street-lamp from the parking lot, he realized. The baby box's outer door had opened and closed.

He moved closer. He could make out the booth's occupants, cloaked in the shadows. They were motionless, slumped in their seats. Latisha Randall was sprawled over the woman seated next to her.

Jesse . . .

Lyles peered through the plate-glass window, and by then the people nearby had noticed him and the dark baby box.

Jesse wasn't there.

Lyles bolted for the door. It wouldn't budge. Barricaded from the outside.

Without hesitation, he hurled himself through the baby box's plate-glass window. He quickly rolled clear, knowing that the real danger came from the large pieces of glass falling from the frame's upper edge. He pulled out his Lanchester as he scrambled over the inert bodies.

Latisha, the young mothers, the babies . . . How could this have happened in only a few seconds?

He threw open the door to the parking lot and crouched low. The uniformed cop was dead, flat on his back on the pavement, chest blown to hell, with a still-lit cigarette wedged between his index and middle fingers.

Fucking unbelievable.

Gunshots raining down around him.

Lyles rolled behind a rusty white church bus, squeezing off two bullets along the way. He hadn't seen the gunman, but he'd heard the shots; often that was all he needed, to zero in on the shooter and pick him off. Years of training with a little instinct thrown in.

A bullet whistled past his ear.

Too bad it didn't always work.

The bullets were hitting the wall and pavement with a dull ring that told him they were being fired from above. Lyles scoped out his surroundings.

Apartment buildings, but they were almost half a block away. Trees, but without leaves. No one there. A one-story school building on the other side of the parking lot. The shooter had to be there on the roof.

Another shot. People screamed inside the church.

Lyles looked around. Where was Jesse?

A high-pitched whine sounded behind him on the other side of the church. He knew the sound. A helicopter. Probably an Aerodyne 1400 series.

Here?

They must have trucked it in and set it up in the deserted office park across the street. Jesse was probably being boarded, they'd take off, and then . . .

Lyles ran back into the church. He held his gun high over his head as the crowd screamed and ducked in their seats. He didn't have to tell anyone to get out of his way. The gun did that for him.

He ran up the main aisle, leapt onto the pulpit, and charged through the doorway that he guessed would take him through the administrative offices. He ran through the dim, sparsely decorated rooms.

The chopper blades were rising into the air.

He burst into a dark room and ran toward the back. He threw open the door. Storage closet. But there, in faded white letters, were the words he was hoping to see: ROOF ACCESS.

He climbed the creaky wooden rungs as the chopper roared overhead. It was moving in to pick up the sniper. Stopping just short of the small trapdoor that opened onto the roof, Lyles listened for the gunman. Gotta plan this just right.

The door vibrated and shook from the chopper's downdraft.

Another few seconds . . . The chopper drew closer and the door shook harder.

Lyles struck the door full force, knocking it off its rusty hinges. The sniper, a small, wiry man, was climbing an aluminum chain ladder up to the helicopter's passenger compartment.

Lyles glanced up. Jesse was up there in the helicopter, unconscious. A bearded man was injecting him with a hypodermic needle.

No!

Lyles fired three quick shots into the sniper's back. The man dropped ten feet, stopping only when his left foot became entangled in the bottom rung. He hung upside down, facing Lyles, his face frozen in a death mask of excruciating pain.

The chopper pilot saw it all. The bird lifted off.

Lyles holstered his gun and leapt for the dead sniper's dangling arms. He gripped the man's nylon jacket, hanging on for his life as the helicopter rose into the sky.

For you, Jesse.

The chopper roared over the church steeple. Lyles climbed over the dead man, gripping his belt and using his chin as a toehold.

He grabbed the man's trouser cuffs and pulled himself up to the chain ladder. The chopper was swaying to and fro as the pilot tried to shake him loose.

Not a chance, buddy.

Lyles grabbed the lowest rung and hoisted himself up. The chopper roared over the nearby residential neighborhoods, its ladder violently swinging back and forth. The bearded guy was firing at him.

Lyles planted his feet on the ladder's bottom rung. He pulled out his gun, which served to get the bearded guy back into the passenger compartment.

Lyles cursed. Now what? He couldn't fire; if he shattered a

rotor, the chopper could crash. He couldn't risk it, especially with Jesse on board. And even if he did make it to the cockpit, he knew he'd have to kill the guys to take control. He was used to risky moves, but at the moment his options were severely limited. He couldn't take the chance of Jesse getting hurt.

The chopper dipped low as it neared the Coca-Cola headquarters building. Oh, shit. They were going to try to splatter him against the building.

The idiots. Helicopters were tricky machines even for the most skilled pilots. He'd worked with some of the best chopper jockeys in the business, and even they wouldn't try to skim six feet over a rooftop at full throttle. One gust of wind and the party's over.

Lyles climbed higher, higher, higher. . . . Because of these assholes, the boy could die right here, right now.

The helicopter lurched downward, almost causing him to lose his grip. He looked up, and his entire field of vision was filled with the building's white granite face.

Crack.

The sniper's body, still dangling from the bottom rung, slammed full force against the building. It tumbled from the ladder to the plaza below.

Lyles lifted his legs and tried to press himself against the chopper's underside as it roared over the building's rooftop plaza. He knew what he had to do. Dammit.

I'm sorry, Jesse. There's no other way.

Lyles let go of the ladder and dropped to the rooftop courtyard, rolling as he landed in a bed of exotic flowers. He turned and stared at the helicopter, now riding more smoothly as it cleared the building and headed west.

His left arm was bleeding. He clutched it with his right hand as he stood.

"Don't move!"

Lyles turned to see a security officer in his early twenties. The kid had a revolver leveled at him, and his hands were trembling. Probably the first time he'd ever drawn his gun, the poor bastard.

Lyles struck the guard's forearm, breaking his radius. The kid shrieked in pain, but only in the brief instant before Lyles drew his own gun and put a bullet into his heart. The guard fell face-down into a reflecting pool.

Lyles gazed up in agony at the helicopter as it disappeared into the night.

Hear me, Jesse. Do not be afraid. I am your soldier, your agent of destiny. I will bring you back to fulfill the prophecy.

And I promise you, anyone and everyone who stands in my way will die.

9

Joe ducked under the yellow police tape and stepped onto the blacktop parking lot of the First United Baptist Church. The place looked like a war zone. Large work lights illuminated the frantic scene, and cops and paramedics swarmed around with an air of confusion. Four infants, three women, and a man were spread out on the lot, only a few yards from the downed officer's covered body.

They were alive, but ill and woozy from whatever had knocked them out in the baby box. The children were crying, and two adults were curled up and vomiting.

Latisha Randall stood when she saw Joe, jerking free of a female paramedic. "Where's Jesse?"

"Ms. Randall—"

"Where is he?"

"I don't know. I came as soon as I heard."

Tears ran down her face. "You have to find him, Mr. Bailey. What the hell are you doing here, when my Jesse's out there somewhere?"

"We'll find him. What exactly happened?"

"I don't know. I was listening to the minister speak, and there was a strange smell, kind of like when you turn on your heater the first time in the winter. Then the woman beside me fell off her chair. The next thing I knew, I was lying here on the parking lot." Her lips trembled. "Without Jesse."

Joe nodded. It was pretty much as he'd heard it described by Lieutenant Gerald when he got the call.

"Dammit, the police were supposed to *protect* him," Latisha shouted.

"We did our best." Detective Howe walked over to them and motioned toward the covered corpse. "Maybe you'd like to discuss it with the officer. He's not quite cold yet."

"I'm sorry about that, but what are you going to do to find my boy?"

"The entire state will be looking for him," Joe said.

"Oh, great," Howe said as he looked past Latisha at someone coming toward them. "Just when you thought it was safe to go back in the water . . ."

"Ms. Randall, be careful what you say to these men," Stewart Dunning said.

Joe winced. The day was getting grimmer by the minute.

"What's *he* doing here?" Howe asked.

"Making our lives miserable," Joe said. "He's Jesse Randall's attorney."

Dunning put a comforting arm around Latisha. "I came as soon as I heard."

She shrugged him off. "Please, Mr. Dunning, I have enough to deal with right now."

"I should be here when you talk to the police."

"Your client has been kidnapped," Howe said. "Do you really think you're helping him by impeding our investigation?"

Dunning flashed him a tight-lipped smile. "I assume you fine people will bring him back, and when that happens, your investigation into Robert Nelson's murder will continue as before."

"It's continuing now," Joe said.

"Of course. Then you can appreciate my vigilance."

A police photographer pulled back the tarp and exposed the slain officer's corpse. Dunning tried to turn Latisha away, but she wouldn't budge. She stared at the officer's lifeless face.

She spoke in a whisper. "I didn't even know his name, but I know that he was a nice man. He came into the house to use the bathroom. He told me he had two little boys."

Howe nodded. "Twins."

She closed her eyes. "Why . . . ?"

Dunning once again put his arm around her and spoke to Joe and Howe. "What happened to that officer is a tragedy, but perhaps it could have been avoided if your department had assigned more officers to protect the boy."

Joe was incredulous. "You're saying it's the *department's* fault that he's dead?"

"Maybe. And some may also hold your department responsible for Jesse's abduction."

Howe leapt toward Dunning, ready to grab him by the throat, but Joe held him back. "That man died trying to protect Jesse!"

Before Dunning could respond, four unmarked Ford Explorers roared into the parking lot and stopped at the police line. Every cop on the scene knew what it meant.

The feds were involved.

Although technically the FBI had jurisdiction only on kidnapping cases in which the victim was taken across state lines, the bureau had a habit of horning in on high-profile abductions. The mere possibility of a border crossing was enough to involve the feds whenever they wanted a piece of the action.

"Hooray," Howe muttered as he shook free of Joe's grip. "The cavalry has arrived."

The first man out of the first vehicle was Raymond Fisher, a forty-five-year-old agent with whom Joe had once worked to break up an interstate telemarketing scam. Fisher's grim face and authoritative manner alienated him from most cops and probably even from his fellow FBI agents, but Joe liked him.

"Relax, guys," Fisher said in his gruff monotone. "We're just here to screw up your investigation and complicate an already confusing situation. You don't mind, do you?"

There was no smile, no glint in his eye, nothing to suggest that he was joking. That was Fisher.

"Agent Fisher, this is Latisha Randall, the kidnap victim's mother," Joe said.

Fisher shook her hand. "My apologies. I didn't mean to be glib. We're here to get your son back."

Latisha nodded.

"If you'll step to the last vehicle, there's someone there who will draw a sample of your blood."

"My blood?"

"Whatever knocked you out is still in your bloodstream. If we can determine what it is, it might help us trace the abductors. We'll be testing everyone who was affected."

Behind the last truck, an agent was already setting up a small table and a medical kit.

Latisha walked toward the table, closely followed by Dunning.

Fisher turned to Joe. "Has the church been sealed off?"

Howe stepped forward. "It's happening now. And we have guys checking the observation room vents for the knockout gas."

"I doubt you'll find anything. Any idea how many were involved?"

"Three, we think," Howe said. "One pilot to fly the helicopter, one sniper to pick off the officer and provide cover, one guy to make the grab. There may be a fourth involved, but we're not sure how."

This was news to Joe. "A fourth? What do you mean?"

"The people in the church saw a man running down the aisle with his gun drawn. He was in here for the entire service. Then a witness from an apartment building saw who we think is the same man on the roof. She said that this Rambo wanna-be shot one of the guys as they were making their escape in the chopper, then hitched a ride himself."

Joe glanced at the roof. "Who would do that?"

Fisher shrugged. "I guess it's too much to hope that it was one of your guys."

Before anyone could reply, a young uniformed officer approached with a walkie-talkie. "Gentlemen, I think you'll want to hear this."

HVKJ100A.

The helicopter license number was seared into Lyles's memory even though he knew it was probably bogus. But for now the chopper was the only real lead he had.

He rubbed his bruised and bloodied arms as he drove down the gravel road in Jonesboro, a small town just a few miles south of the Atlanta airport.

Please, please, please let the old man still live here.

A light up ahead. Could it be . . . ?

Yes. The old man's house. *Somebody* still lived there.

He stopped the car. He'd stolen the gold Camry just outside the Coca-Cola building; he didn't dare go back to his van, which was parked two blocks from the church. The entire neighborhood would be overrun with cops by now.

He reached into his pocket and felt the ivory squares.

Focus.

Direct your energy.

He had failed. He had failed Jesse.

No regrets.

That was the key. No regrets. The past did not exist. All that mattered was the present and the future that he could create. A future in which Jesse Randall would lead mankind from an age of pettiness and ignorance.

He cut the engine and looked at the white one-story house ahead. He'd been there only one other time, several years before.

He climbed out of the car and walked up the road. Loose gravel crunched beneath his feet, shattering the night's silence. He stopped as he heard a different sound. Metal against metal.

"Lester, don't shoot," he said. "It's me. Lyles."

Silence.

"I know it's you, Lester. Who else would be snapping in a nine-millimeter clip on some dirt road in the middle of East Bumble-fuck?"

A man rose from behind a tall clump of weeds. "*Eleven* millimeter. You're slipping. I heard you were in town."

"You're the third person who's told me that. Heard from who? It's not like I called a press conference."

Lester Post stepped forward and holstered his automatic. He wore a black jumpsuit similar to one that an auto mechanic might wear, and his scraggly gray-white beard waved in the chilly breeze. "What do you need, Lyles?"

Lyles stepped forward, but Lester suddenly took a guarded stance. Not unreasonable, Lyles thought. The guy was used to dealing with some pretty tough customers.

Lyles had met him over ten years before, when they had been part of a team sent in by a fringe animal rights group to hunt poachers on the African plateau. Lester had long since retired from the life of a mercenary, but he was now a major military supplies broker, outfitting militia groups and private security forces with weapons, vehicles, tents, and anything else a soldier of fortune could possibly need. If Lyles ever wanted to equip a small army, he knew Lester would be one of the top suppliers on his list.

"I need to locate a chopper," Lyles said. "I know it was in Atlanta earlier tonight. Can you help?"

"Is this gonna be one of those freebie 'do it for me for old times' sake' kind of deals, or do you have some cash to throw my way?"

"Cash. Lots of it."

"Good answer."

Lyles followed Lester inside his house, which was surprisingly well decorated for a man in his profession. Things were different downstairs, however; the basement was stocked with enough firepower to equip several platoons. Hundreds of rifles and handguns hung on brown pegboards that covered every inch of the walls. A long wooden workbench centered the area, where several more firearms rested in various stages of assembly. The place reeked of oil and gunpowder.

Lester walked to the back corner, where a monitor was surrounded by an array of loose computer components. He pushed a button on one of the circuit boards, and the monitor's screen flickered. "It's a mess," he said. "But every time I put everything all nice and neat in a case, I have to open it up to upgrade something. Technology's just moving too fast."

"I'm just glad you're here to keep up. I have a license number for the chopper, but it's probably fake."

"Give it to me. We'll see."

Lyles gave him the number, then waited a few minutes while Lester established a link to a database of aircraft licenses. Lester entered the number, and after a few moments the reply came back: LICENSE # NOT FOUND.

It didn't faze him at all. "Make and model?"

"Aerodyne Banshee. Mid-eighties model, maybe fourteen hundred series."

Lester rolled his chair to a shelf loaded with spiral notebooks. He selected one and began flying through the pages, glancing at hand-drawn sketches and chicken scrawls. Finally he found what he was looking for.

"The Banshee's rear rotor coupling is notorious for wearing out," Lester said. "And only Aerodyne makes 'em. For warranty purposes, the company keeps a good database of the parts they sell. If the password hasn't been changed, I can probably find out if that coupling has been shipped anywhere around here."

"How long will that take?"

Lester didn't reply as his fingers raced over the keyboard. After a few minutes he turned the monitor's screen in Lyles's direction.

"What is it?"

Lester smiled. "About four months ago that part was shipped to a mechanic who works out of the Charlie Brown airport in De Kalb County."

"Does it say who the chopper belonged to?"

"Nah, just the mechanic's name. A guy named Toby Cooper."

"You're a genius, Lester."

The Aerodyne Banshee 1490 helicopter stood in the middle of an open field, surrounded by a perimeter of police tape and work lights. Many of the police officers, FBI agents, and news crews from the church had quickly relocated to this new scene after the call came in. Several motorists had witnessed the chopper landing only a few hundred yards from the I-20 freeway, and they had flooded the 911 lines with reports of a helicopter in distress. It was now apparent, however, that there was nothing wrong with it, and that this was a carefully chosen rendezvous spot for Jesse's abductors to transfer to a less conspicuous mode of transportation.

"There are reports of a black Jeep entering the roadway shortly after the helicopter landed," Howe said as he joined Joe and Agent Fisher near the chopper's front windshield.

Fisher nodded. "I'm sure it's already been abandoned, probably within five miles of here. They knew the helicopter would attract a lot of attention, so they drove the Jeep to another location, probably some back road, and made the switch to a vehicle that would take them to the holding location."

Howe jammed his hands into his pockets. "I like the way you FBI guys talk like you're so sure how everything happened, like you were there."

Fisher shrugged. "I just play the odds." He turned to Joe, obviously weary of Howe's attitude. "You know Jesse Randall, right?"

Joe nodded. "Yes. We've spent some time together in the past week or so."

"So, is he a fraud, or what?"

"In my opinion, yes, but I still haven't been able to discover his techniques. I wasn't able to supervise any kind of formal experiment."

"Okay, has he ever demonstrated any ability, genuine or not, to transmit telepathic messages?"

Joe smiled. "I'm afraid not. I don't think we're going to be receiving any messages from him."

"Gotta cover all the bases. Tell me this: Do you think his tricks could actually help him in his situation?"

Joe watched the fingerprint team converge on the cockpit.

"That's hard to say, but he's very bright and he has an amazing ability to adapt to any situation."

"Let's hope he can adapt to this one."

Cold.

Dark.

Jesse's head hurt, and his mouth was dry. Was this another dream?

He couldn't see anything. Where was he? He was lying on what felt like a big pillow. He pulled himself up onto his hands and knees.

His stomach hurt in a way he'd never felt before. Oh, no . . .

He vomited.

He was still for a few moments, afraid that any movement would make him throw up again.

How had he gotten there?

"Mama?" he called out. "Mama?"

Nothing.

He crawled across the floor. It was padded. All of it. What kind of place was this? "Mama?"

A buzzing sound. Fluorescent lights flickered overhead. White, blinding light.

He squinted at his surroundings. It was a large room, maybe fifty by fifty feet, which was bigger than his entire house. Every inch of the floor and walls was covered with thick cream-colored padding. There was no furniture, no windows, and, as far as he could tell, no doors. Just row after row of fabric-covered panels.

He stood and pushed on the wall panel closest to him. It was soft, just like the floor.

It should've been a dream, but he knew it wasn't.

"Hello?" he shouted. "Can anybody hear me?"

There was a loud, sharp clanging sound.

One of the panels swung outward.

A thin, brown-haired woman stepped into the room, and the panel closed behind her. She was dressed in a strange outfit that resembled a surgical scrub suit. It looked like it was made from paper.

She gave Jesse an awkward smile and held out a large plastic tumbler. "You must be thirsty."

He nodded and took the tumbler. He drew it to his lips, then froze. He glared at the woman.

"Go ahead," she said. "It's only water."

He gulped it down and let the tumbler fall to the padded floor.

The woman nodded approvingly. "That's very good, Jesse."

"Where's my mama?"

"She's home. She's very worried about you."

"I want to go home."

"I wish I could get you out of here, Jesse, but I can't. There are some dangerous people involved in this."

"Who?"

She bit her lip. "I can't tell you that, but they want you to show them your powers. Can you do that?"

"I won't do it. Not until I can go home."

"It might make things easier, honey."

"I don't care. I want to go home."

She pointed at the cup. "Will you make the cup move for me, Jesse?"

"No."

"Please?"

Jesse reared back and kicked the plastic cup across the room. He folded his arms in front of him.

The woman backed away. "Maybe this isn't the best time. You probably need to be alone for a while."

Jesse fought back tears. He was trying to look tough, but he knew that his watery eyes were giving him away. "When can I go home?"

The woman also looked ready to cry. "I don't know, honey. I'm a prisoner here too."

He took a step forward. "You are?"

She nodded. "And unless we can give these people what they want, I'm afraid that they're going to hurt us both."

She turned away and walked toward the door panel.

10

yles pushed up the latch and swung open the gate to Toby Cooper's backyard. The aircraft mechanic lived in a modest ranch-style home in Smyrna, a working-class Atlanta suburb.

Three-fifteen A.M. He should have waited until later, but the cops might follow his trail, and he needed to stay ahead of them. They had already failed Jesse once.

Lyles pushed past the shrubbery growing on the side of the house. He stopped at the first bedroom window and pressed his ear against it. Silence. He stopped at the second window, which was cracked open an inch. He heard rapid, shallow breathing. A child, perhaps.

He entered the backyard and passed a rusty swingset and a long-neglected Jacuzzi. With only the moonlight to show the way, he glanced around for signs of a dog. There were none. Hallelujah.

He listened at the one remaining bedroom window, which was also cracked open. An adult was inside, he thought. Sleeping alone. Only one car was in the carport, so that made sense. Lyles usually compiled a complete profile of a house's occupants before venturing inside, but there just wasn't time in this case.

He walked back to the window of the empty bedroom and pulled a glass cutter from his pocket. Definitely the best way in. A quick inspection assured him that there was no hard-wired security system, but that didn't preclude funky motion detectors or doorknob sensors. The bedroom window was a safer route.

He cut a small wedge of glass near the latch and poked it through with his index finger. The wedge popped out and fell silently to the carpeted floor. He threw the latch, slid open the window, and climbed inside.

He glanced around, letting his eyes adjust to the darkness. He was in a kid's playroom, decorated with Sesame Street posters, a rainbow-colored table, and dozens of action figures.

He crept through the dark house, scoping it for occupants. As he'd suspected, a small boy was sleeping in the front bedroom. *Keep sleeping, son, and you may live through the night.*

There was no one in the living room or den, so that left only the back bedroom. He pushed open the door and looked inside. A chunky, fortyish man was framed in the moonlight, sleeping with his mouth wide open. Lyles leaned in and scanned the room until he saw a wallet resting on the chest of drawers only a few feet from the door. He picked it up and opened it. The driver's license confirmed that the mouth breather was indeed Toby Cooper. Lyles pocketed the wallet and opened his nine-inch Smetson knife as he stepped toward the bed.

His shadow moved across Cooper's face. The man woke with a start.

Lyles shoved the knife tip into his chest, just breaking the skin. A small stain of blood spread from the knifepoint across Cooper's white muscle shirt.

Lyles leaned close and whispered, "If you want your little boy to live, nod your head."

Cooper closed his eyes and nodded.

"If he wakes up while I'm here, I'll have to kill him, do you understand?"

Cooper nodded again.

"Good."

"I have a coin collection that's worth thousands," Cooper whimpered. "You can have it."

"I don't want your coins. I want information."

Cooper blinked several times as salty beads of perspiration ran into his eyes. "Fine. No problem."

"A few months ago you replaced a Banshee tail rotor. Do you remember?"

"Yes."

"Who owned the chopper?"

"I don't know."

Lyles applied pressure with the knife.

Cooper gasped. "Some guy I'd never met. And I haven't seen him since."

Lyles kept the pressure on. The bloodstain on Cooper's shirt spread faster.

"I promise!" Cooper said.

"Shh. Your son needs his sleep."

Cooper nodded. He was crying.

"Do you have a name? An address? License number?"

"Yes, but not here. I keep a little office—a closet—at the airfield. My records are in the desk."

"What airfield?"

"Charlie Brown. I can tell you exactly where my records are."

"You're going to *show* me."

"Please. Nobody's there until five. You can get them yourself. I won't tell anybody about this, I promise."

Lyles backed away, picked up a pair of slacks from a stool, and tossed them to Cooper. "We're walking out the front door in thirty seconds."

"What about my son?"

"He stays here and sleeps."

After Cooper dressed, Lyles guided him out to the stolen Camry. He bound Cooper's hands and feet in duct tape for the ride to Fulton County Airport's Brown Field, called Charlie Brown by the locals. It was a small airfield with three short runways and half a dozen small hangars.

The airport was quiet, but Lyles knew there must be a guard on duty somewhere. He pulled behind a hangar and cut the tape from Cooper's ankles.

"If you try to run, I'll kill you, then go back to your house and carve out your son's eyes. Do you have any doubt that I'm capable of that?"

Cooper shook his head. "No."

"Good."

"My office is through that door."

Lyles pulled him from the car and walked him into the dim hangar, where several prop planes were parked at grimy repair stations. They walked to a small office, which indeed was no larger than a closet. The mechanic opened a file drawer and looked through the mass of invoice copies and repair orders.

He picked up one and handed it to Lyles with trembling hands. "This was the guy."

Lyles looked at the handwritten name. "Rick Murphy?"

"Yes. I checked out his bird and saw that the rotor was about to go. I replaced it for him."

"How did he pay?"

"It's there on the invoice. Cash. I wrote down his driver's license number, and the helicopter's serial number is there too."

"What did he look like?"

"Jesus, this was like, three or four months ago."

"Think."

"Look, I could bullshit you and make up a description, but the honest truth is that I just don't remember. I'd tell you if I did. He didn't mean anything to me."

Lyles believed he was telling the truth. Shit.

Cooper's voice shook. "That paper is what you wanted, right? Take it."

Lyles folded the invoice copy and slid it into his jacket pocket. Cooper extended his wrists.

"What are you doing?" Lyles asked.

"Bind me with the tape again. Nobody will be here for another hour. That will give you more than enough time to make some tracks."

"That's very considerate."

He moistened his lips. "Unless there's . . . something else."

"I'm afraid there is."

Eight-twenty A.M. It was obvious to Joe that many of the sixteen detectives, uniformed officers, and forensics experts in Chief Davis's conference room hadn't slept. Tempers were frayed, and it was still too early for anyone to have a firm handle on what had happened to Jesse Randall the night before. Davis wanted answers, and when his personnel couldn't provide them, a lot of defensive posturing and finger pointing ensued.

No one had any idea who the kidnappers might be. Religious zealots on a mission to capture the Devil Child? Terrorists seeking the ultimate psychic weapon? Operatives from a mysterious government agency? Each explanation sounded more preposterous than the last.

The helicopter's license number was fake, and all serial numbers had been removed. A mechanic's inspection sticker had been found in the engine compartment, however, and a pair of officers were following up on it.

For Joe, it was merely the continuation of a bad day that had started when he woke early to tell Nikki about Jesse's abduction. She'd taken it hard.

There were no FBI agents present at Davis's task force meeting, although the chief had been promised cooperation from the agency. The feds had already provided the police crime lab with blood samples from the church knockout gas victims.

The discussion soon turned to Joe and his investigation. "He's a kid," Davis said. "If he's a fake, why haven't you been able to catch him?"

"I wasn't able to study him in a controlled environment. He hasn't been nearly as demonstrative with me as he was for Nelson and his team."

"There were a couple of attacks on your life, Bailey. No explanation for that either?"

"Not yet," Joe admitted. "I'm working on it. I sent samples of the bookcase base and the wooden floor to the lab. I think they may tell us something."

"Maybe it's time to get someone else on the case. A fresh perspective."

Joe leaned forward. "That would be a mistake."

Davis turned to Howe. "What do *you* think about it?"

Joe closed his eyes. Here it comes.

"He's right," Howe said. "It *would* be a mistake to reassign him."

Joe shot him a sideways glance, waiting for the kicker.

Davis looked surprised. "Only a few days ago you asked your lieutenant to remove him from the investigation."

"I've reevaluated my position."

Davis nodded. "Fine. The two of you continue your investigation into Robert Nelson's murder. Keep the lines of communication open with Lieutenant Powell, who will be heading up the investigation into Jesse Randall's abduction."

The meeting broke up at a quarter to eleven. Joe caught up with Howe in the elevator.

"Thanks," Joe said.

"For what?"

"The show of confidence."

"It was born of desperation. *I* sure as hell can't figure out how Nelson was whacked. How was Cartersville?"

In all the commotion with Jesse's kidnapping, Joe hadn't told Howe about his conversation with the emergency room doctor. He quickly filled him in.

"Pig's blood?" Howe said as they stepped out of the elevator and into the narrow hallway that led to the homicide squad room.

"That's what the man said."

"Had the girl just gotten off from a hard day at the slaughterhouse?"

"No, and her father lied about it. He told the attending physician that it was paint."

"This is getting more bizarre by the minute."

"Don't I know it."

"I'll dig a little deeper into the Rawlings family. I'll subpoena their phone records and see if I can get Internet usage reports from their access provider. Maybe you can talk to the lady again."

"You don't want to come with me?"

"She was a little scared of me. She liked you better, and she's more likely to give up more if you're there alone. I trust you."

"Why are you being so decent all of a sudden?"

"I've come to the conclusion that I'm going to get the shaft no matter what I do in this case. With that knowledge comes a certain freedom."

Jesse wasn't sure if it was day or night. There were no windows in the large padded room, and someone had taken his C-3PO watch. A big, bearded man dressed in the same strange paper uniform as the woman had silently come into the room and left a steak, a baked potato, and a glass of fruit juice near the door panel, then left. The empty dishes were still piled in a corner of the room. There were mirrors high on each wall, where he guessed that people were watching him. The way Dr. Nelson had during his experiments.

The door swung open. The woman again. Her eyes were bloodshot, her cheeks red. She looked as if she'd been crying. She walked over and knelt next to him.

"Hi, Jesse."

"Hi."

She squeezed a foam rubber ball in her right hand. "Did you like your food?"

"It was okay."

"Would you like something else?"

"Like what?"

"Ice cream?"

"No, thanks."

"I'm sorry about all this, honey. I really am. I wish we could get out of here."

"Are they really keeping you here too?"

"Yes."

"But why do they want *you*?"

She cast a quick glance at one of the mirrors. "I've worked with children before."

"Kids like me?"

She smiled warmly. "Oh, no. No one's quite like you, Jesse. I've seen what you can do. I guess they thought I could work with you and help you show them your abilities."

"If I do my stuff for 'em, what will happen then?"

"They'll watch you, maybe suggest a couple of other things for you to try, and that will be it. I'll go home to my kids, and you'll go home to your mother."

"You have kids?"

"A little boy and a little girl. The boy is just a little younger than you are. I really miss him. He probably doesn't know what happened to me."

Her frizzy blond hair fell over her forehead as she turned away from Jesse. She was crying. Her hands went limp, and the foam rubber ball dropped to the floor.

Jesse looked up at the mirror. Who was behind that glass? What did they want?

He turned back to the ball and stared at it. It rocked for a moment, then rolled a few feet away.

The woman took a sharp breath.

"There. That's what they want, isn't it?"

She nodded.

"That's what you wanted too. That's why you brought the ball."

"Thank you. Will you do some more for me?"

"Not now."

"When?"

"Maybe later. But I want my glasses back. I'm not doing anything else until I get my glasses."

"I'll see what I can do, Jesse."

"What's your name?"

"Myrna."

"Don't worry, Myrna."

. . .

"My husband told me not to let you in again," Crystal Rawlings said.

Joe stood facing Crystal on her front porch, and this time she seemed stronger and more confident. "That sounds like a guilty person talking," Joe said.

"I can't talk to you about Dr. Nelson."

"Guiltier still."

"I'm sorry."

"Then talk to me about your daughter."

She went white. "Gaby? Why do you want to talk about her?"

"She has something to do with this."

"You have no idea what you're talking about."

"When we were here asking about Dr. Nelson, you were think-ing about her."

"I always think about her."

"Especially then."

"There's nothing to say."

"I know you miss her," Joe said softly. "I lost my wife a couple of years ago, and it's hard to keep going sometimes. I'm sure Gaby meant a lot to you."

"Of course she did. She still does."

"Has anyone tried to reach her for you? Dr. Nelson, a spiritual-ist, anyone from the Landwyn parapsychology program?"

"No. I don't believe in that stuff. I don't believe in any of it."

"Tell me about her. Please."

Crystal's eyes were starting to mist.

Could he be any more of a schmuck? Joe thought. He was following the playbook, eliciting information by provoking a strong emotional response. He felt rotten, but it made him feel a little better to think that Crystal really wanted to talk about her daughter.

"Gaby would have turned seventeen tomorrow," she said.

"I didn't realize that. I'm sorry. This must be an especially difficult time for you and your husband."

She nodded.

"I know this is painful, but what exactly happened to her?"

"Her appendix ruptured."

"Was there anything suspicious about the way she died?"

"Suspicious?"

"Anything I should know about?"

"No. It was natural causes."

Joe spoke gently. "Ms. Rawlings, why was there pig's blood on your daughter's shirt when you brought her to the hospital that night?"

She closed her eyes and drew in a long breath. "Pig's blood?"

"Yes."

"That's ridiculous."

"How did that blood get on your daughter?"

"There must be a mistake."

"No mistake. Her doctor told me. He checked it out."

"Please leave us alone." Her voice shook. "We can't help you."

"I think you can. Did you know Dr. Nelson before your daughter died?"

Crystal hesitated. "Yes."

"Under what circumstances?"

Another pause. "We helped him with one of his projects."

"A paranormal studies project?"

"I can't discuss it."

"You can, and you must. This man was murdered, and we're evaluating everyone in his life as a possible suspect. The fact that you're being so secretive makes you and your husband look suspicious. Are you protecting your husband, Ms. Rawlings?"

Her eyes widened. "No!"

"Convince me. Tell me about Dr. Nelson. When did you first meet him?"

"A few months ago. I saw him only twice in my life."

"Two meetings, and he gave you a hundred and sixty thousand dollars?"

"I can't discuss this anymore."

"Nelson's dead, and if there's someone else involved, I need to know about it."

"That little black boy killed him, didn't he?"

"I think someone wants us to believe that. Dr. Nelson's killer is out there, and you may be shielding him even if you don't realize it. You could be putting yourself and your husband in a dangerous position. If the killer thinks you're holding information that may incriminate him, you could become a target."

"My husband told me that you guys might try to scare us."

"That's not why I'm here."

"Oh, no? In the past two minutes you've told me that I might be a murder suspect and a possible murder victim. What do you call that?"

"Pointing out some simple truths. Please. Talk to me. I don't want to bring you to the station, but I will."

"It won't do you any good."

"I want you to think about something. What would your daughter want you to do right now?"

She bit her lip. "What do you mean?"

"Exactly what I said. Is the memory of your daughter best served by your silence? Is that what *she* would have wanted?"

"You have no idea what Gaby would have wanted."

"That's why I'm asking you."

She thought about it. "Do you people look at phone records?"

"For who?"

"Anybody. Murder victims, the other people involved."

"Usually."

"So, you've probably looked at Dr. Nelson's calls."

"I can't comment on that."

"Have you looked at ours?"

He stiffened.

"You may already have your answer, Detective. You just don't realize it."

She slammed the door closed.

"I put in for the Rawlingses' phone records right after our chat with them the other night." Howe's voice crackled through the lousy connection. Joe was on his way back to town, talking to him on his portable phone.

"Damn, Howe, maybe you *are* a good cop."

"That'll be our little secret, okay? The phone records might be in already. If so, I'll do a cross-check with Nelson's records. I'll put the Little Bastard on it."

The Little Bastard was a processing unit that scanned a variety of standard documents, then searched for data matching designated parameters. The machine's colorful nickname stemmed from its infuriating tendency to malfunction whenever it was needed most.

Joe heard Howe's other line ringing. "Hold on, Bailey." After a minute, Howe returned. "Where are you?"

"I-75 and the Marietta Parkway. Why?"

"Get over to the Charlie Brown airport. I'll meet you there."

It was a few minutes past noon when Joe arrived at Charlie Brown's Hangar C. Howe, Fisher, and a group of police and FBI officers were already on the scene.

"What the hell happened?"

"Ask those guys." Howe pointed to Fisher and a pair of FBI agents. "They're the ones who sat on this for two hours before tipping us off."

Joe and Howe strode into the hangar and walked toward the repair station, where Fisher stood over Toby Cooper's corpse. The man's throat had been cut open.

Joe turned to Fisher. "This is the mechanic whose sticker was on that helicopter?"

Fisher nodded. "It happened early this morning sometime. His kid was home in bed and had no idea he was even gone. It looks like Jesse Randall's abductors were covering their tracks."

"Why would they wait?" Joe asked. "They planned everything else out to the nth degree. If they were afraid of this guy, they could have killed him days or even weeks ago."

"Who else would've done it?" Fisher's tone was mocking. "Jesse Randall? Yeah, maybe he used his psychic powers to strike at the mechanic who once serviced his kidnappers' helicopter."

Joe sighed. "Don't even say that as a joke, or it'll be on every newscast by dinnertime."

Lyles laid out his ivory squares on the car seat, waiting for the amphetamines to kick in. It had been almost twenty-four hours since Jesse Randall's abduction, and he hadn't even thought about sleeping. He couldn't. Not until he found Jesse and brought him back.

He'd tracked down the car license plate number that Toby Cooper had dutifully scribbled on the helicopter repair invoice. The info had cost Lyles $39.98 and a visit to a cyber café, where the data-x.com Web site kicked out the owner's name and address in a matter of minutes. Different from the name on the invoice, he noticed. Gino Lockwood of Roswell. Lockwood lived on the ground floor of a two-story apartment building. Lyles had found a spot at the curb that afforded him a view of Lockwood's parking space and apartment windows.

If only Bertram and Irene could see him now. Finally he was fighting for something that truly mattered.

He glanced down at the carved squares. Perhaps they could give him some guidance, some inspiration. He spread them out in a large grid of ten rows and ten columns.

Except he couldn't complete the pattern.

There weren't enough squares; he was one short. He checked his pockets. Empty. He searched the car seats and floorboards.

Shit. He'd lost it. But where? The church? Cooper's house? The airport?

He didn't believe there was any way it could be traced back to him, but it was still a loose end. He hated loose ends.

Unless this was meant to happen.

Unless the will of Alessandro was truly working through those squares. Then it would be all right.

He scanned the remaining squares, keeping a mental tally of the symbols present and accounted for. He realized which one was missing.

Vivida. Deception.

Was it a warning? A clue?

He glanced up, grabbed the squares, and jammed them into his pockets.

Gino Lockwood had just come home.

11

Deception?" Joe held the plastic evidence bag at eye level and squinted at the carved ivory square.

Raymond Fisher stared at him in surprise from the other side of the police conference room. He was flanked by two other FBI agents, who had been hastily introduced as Muñiz and Hill. Howe, Lieutenant Gerald, and Detectives Powell and Kessler, who were spearheading the abduction case, joined Joe in representing the Atlanta P.D.

"Very good," Fisher said to Joe. "It means lies or deception. Didn't anyone tell you that Latin is a dead language?"

"If they had, I wouldn't have wasted two years in high school studying it. So where did you guys find this?"

"Actually, one of your officers found it on the roof of the church schoolroom. It was clean, so it couldn't have been there long. At first, we thought it might be a piece from a language learning set."

"It's not," Joe said as he studied it. "It's called a reason square."

"You're familiar with it?" Fisher asked.

"One of the millennial cults uses them. They use these little squares like some people might use tarot cards—to predict the future, make sense of the past, give guidance, that sort of thing."

Muñiz, a bespectacled man in his early forties, stepped forward. "That's right. I'm a specialist in cults. I'm surprised you even know about this."

Joe shrugged. "I occasionally deal with cults in my work. A lot of them are fond of using tricks to convince people to join them and hand over their worldly possessions. I don't remember hearing anything negative about this one though."

"They call themselves the Millennial Prophets, and they're very secretive," Muñiz said. "Most millennial cults started springing up in the early nineties, and many have already disbanded. Their numbers peaked with the turn of the millennium, but it will probably take another decade or so for most of them to dwindle out. The Millennial Prophets go further back though. The religion was founded by an excommunicated Presbyterian minister, Alessandro Garr, in England, around the end of the nineteenth century." Muñiz took back the reason square. "There are one hundred words represented by the squares, and *vivida* is one of them."

"Is this cult dangerous?" Gerald asked.

"They're not reputed to be, but other than what I just told you, there's not a lot known about them. It's been a very secretive organization, even since Alessandro's time. They've never caused any problems we're aware of, and as a result, the bureau hasn't made it a priority to study their activities. We don't even know how many members they have."

Fisher stepped forward. "We know that there were two men on that rooftop: the sniper and the man who killed him. We're assuming the square was dropped by one of those two. A card-carrying Millennial Prophet."

Joe nodded. "Would I be wrong to assume that your agency is now compiling a phone book–size dossier on this group?"

Muñiz smiled. "Several phone books."

"Your tax dollars at work," Fisher said. "But would you gentlemen like to join us for a little more hands-on research?"

"Doing what?" Gerald asked.

"There's a former Millennial Prophet within fifty miles of here. His name is David Maxie. We're heading out to talk to him now."

"Are you sure he's home?" Howe asked.

"Positive. He resides in the state mental institution in Milledgeville."

Gino Lockwood crouched on the floor of his apartment, holding his sides and coughing up blood.

Lyles stood over him. "It'll heal. You won't even need to see a doctor for that. The next one won't be so gentle."

Lockwood stared up at him, trying to catch his breath. "Jesus," he wheezed. "Who the hell are you?"

"I'll ask the questions, unless you'd like another punch in the stomach."

"If you're looking for Sanchez, I don't know where he is. I don't work for him anymore."

"Who's Sanchez?"

Lockwood rolled over onto his side. He was a small man, around thirty, with a large mane of dirty blond hair. He'd opened his apartment door after Lyles knocked, and the flimsy security chain had been no match for a good solid shoulder blow. Lockwood wiped the blood from his mouth. "What do you want?"

"Tell me about the Banshee you took in for repairs a few weeks ago."

"The Banshee?"

"You took it to a mechanic at Charlie Brown airport. Your chopper?"

"No. I took it in, but it wasn't mine."

Lyles crouched near him. "Now, why would you have it repaired if it wasn't yours?"

"I'm a pilot, and I was up for a job. I did it as kind of a favor."

"A favor to who?"

"I don't know."

Lyles's gloved right fist flew underneath Lockwood's chin, pummeling his jaw. Lockwood covered his mouth and moaned.

"If the chopper wasn't yours, then whose was it?"

"Christ." He winced as he stroked his jaw. "Two guys wanted to hire me for a job."

"What kind of job?"

"A pickup." Lockwood suddenly sounded as if he had marbles in his mouth. "They weren't too clear."

"Picking up a person?"

"Look, they paid me a lot of money to keep my mouth shut about this."

"I'm offering you your life."

Lockwood nodded. "Yeah, I figured that out for myself. Could you get me some ice or something?"

"That depends on how helpful you are. What was the job?"

"Picking a guy up with a drop ladder. We practiced at an old rifle range in Cherokee County, out in the middle of nowhere."

"They didn't tell you what it was all about?"

"No. In my business, people usually operate on a need-to-know basis. I figured maybe they were looking to rip off one of the crystal meth labs in Florida. Look, I don't know who you work for, but—"

"I don't work for anybody. Who were these people?"

"Two men. They called themselves Smith and Johnson. They

never slipped up and called each other anything else. I was listening."

"Describe them."

"Johnson was kind of a plump guy, brown hair, with a beard."

Lyles nodded, remembering the man who had injected Jesse with a hypodermic needle in the helicopter cockpit. "And the other one?"

"He was a smaller guy. He was the one climbing the ladder."

The sniper, Lyles thought. "So why didn't you do the job for them?"

He shrugged. "They said their first choice had become available again. Plus I don't think they were too happy with our practice runs. They thought I was too cautious. I'm not going to take stupid chances for anybody, even for twenty-five grand."

"That's good money."

"I only get five for border jumps, so, yeah, it wasn't bad. They gave me the whole amount even though they didn't want me for the main event."

"You run coke from Mexico or South America?"

"You're fucking DEA, aren't you?"

"No. Where were you last night?"

"You sound like a cop."

"I'm no cop. Where were you?"

"Flying back from Guadalajara in my Cessna."

Lyles spied a black travel bag on the floor. He unzipped it, thinking he might find a time-stamped receipt that would either confirm or refute Lockwood's story. Instead, he found a copy of that morning's *Plano Times*.

"I refueled in Texas," Lockwood said.

Lyles tossed aside the newspaper. "Do you have a phone number for them?"

"No. They always called me."

Lyles shot him a skeptical glance.

"Honest. I'm not bullshitting you."

"How did they find you? Who put them in touch?"

"I have no idea. They just called me one day. I usually talked to Johnson. Or whatever his name really was."

"Any idea who they got to fly it?"

"I don't know. They kept saying that Nathan Schroeder or Michael Kahn wouldn't be afraid to do the moves they wanted. They fly for the big dealers here and the ones in Nashville and Birmingham."

"Good."

Lockwood swallowed hard. "You're gonna kill me, aren't you?"

Lyles thought for a moment. He'd assumed that the conversation would end with his murdering Lockwood, but there was really no need. Although he'd earned a reputation as a monster, he killed only when it was absolutely necessary. Lockwood, unlike the mechanic from that morning, represented no danger to him. This guy wasn't about to run to the cops.

Lyles shook his head. "You get to live. You're scum, but you're telling me the truth. And I know that you're not going to tell anyone about our little conversation. You don't know it yet, but you're an accessory to a very high-profile crime."

"What crime?"

"You'll know soon enough. Watch the eleven o'clock news. The fewer people who know about your involvement, the better off you'll be."

"Believe me, I won't say a word."

"Good. Just know that if you start talking, the authorities will be the least of your problems."

Night had fallen by the time Joe, his fellow officers, and the feds arrived at the Georgia state mental institution in Milledgeville.

Joe had expected an imposing Gothic structure, but the sprawling one-story complex looked more like a suburban high school. The institution's chief administrator, Dr. Barbara Camille, met them at the main entrance. She led them into an observation room with a large one-way glass, where they could look into a visiting area.

Joe and Muñiz had been chosen to speak to David Maxie—Muñiz because he was the cult specialist and Joe, presumably, because he was the only cop who'd recognized the reason square. They proceeded into the visiting area, and after a few minutes Maxie walked into the room with an orderly. Maxie was in his early forties. His head was shaved, and his jet-black eyebrows joined as one.

"Hello, David. How are you?" Muñiz said.

"Shitty," Maxie replied.

"Why's that?"

Maxie settled into the love seat while the orderly crossed his arms and leaned against the door. "It's cold, and I ain't got no hair. Should've kept my hair."

Joe smiled. "We can get you a cap."

"Don't want a cap. Want my hair."

"It'll grow back."

"By then it'll be summer. Don't need hair in the summer."

"We need to talk to you, David," Muñiz said.

"Is this about the president?"

Joe had glanced through Maxie's file on the way there. "We know about those letters you wrote the president. We're sure you didn't mean him any harm."

"I just wanted him to pay attention. He wasn't paying attention to me."

"We know," Joe said. "You're not in here because of that. Do you know why you're in the hospital?"

Maxie nodded. "My sisters think I'm sick. They think I might hurt myself."

"They obviously care about you very much."

"Bullshit."

"Who do you care about?" Muñiz asked.

Maxie glanced around the room as if the answer might be written on one of the walls.

Muñiz leaned forward. "Do you care about the Millennial Prophets?"

Maxie's eyes widened. "Of course."

"Alessandro Garr was a remarkable man, wasn't he?" Joe said.

"Alessandro," Maxie whispered reverently.

"If I want to become a Millennial Prophet, what should I do?"

"You gotta read the books."

"Alessandro's books?"

"Of course. So you'll be ready."

"Ready for what?"

"For the Child of Light."

"What?" Joe asked.

Maxie was clearly irritated. "The Child of Light. It's his time. I thought you knew the writings of Alessandro."

Joe bowed his head. "I have a tough time understanding them. Can you help me?"

Maxie straightened, obviously feeling superior. "The Child of Light will rise within a few years of the dawn of the new millennium."

"Rise from where?"

"From among us. He will eventually control all time and matter, then lead mankind into the new age. The age of Alessandro."

Joe inhaled sharply. "How will we know him when he arrives?"

Maxie smiled. "We will know. It's written in Alessandro's prophecy. He will be a darker-skinned boy of uncommon sensitivity. He was born under the ninth moon, on the anniversary of an apocalyptic event in his city's history. As the city rose, so will he. All matter changes to his will."

Joe shot a quick glance toward the observation window. It all made sense now.

"I'd like to know more about this," Muñiz said. "Can you put me in touch with other Prophets?"

"I belonged to the congregation in Honolulu. That was years ago. I don't know any others."

"Please think. It may be important."

"There's no one. I don't need a congregation to affirm my faith. My faith is in my heart and my head." He felt his bare scalp. "It's cold. I sure wish I had my hair."

Joe pushed open the door to the parking lot and walked with Howe, Muñiz, and Fisher. Muñiz was on his portable phone, relaying their findings.

"The Millennial Prophets think Jesse Randall is their goddamned messiah," Joe said. "We need to find out his birthday."

Muñiz covered his phone's mouthpiece. "I have someone on it. It's September first. He's running a check on the date now."

"That would explain that guy in the church, the one who shot one of the abductors," Fisher said. "He was protecting Jesse. A zealot playing bodyguard."

Joe suddenly made another connection. "He's been following Jesse for days."

"How do you know?" Howe asked.

"A few days ago, a man roughed up a little kid who was bullying Jesse."

"I read that in the report."

"I'll bet it was the same guy. He didn't just happen to be there. He was following Jesse. Just like he was following him last night. That time, the bullies had guns and a helicopter."

"If that is true, he's not exactly a knight in shining armor. He wasted that innocent guard on the Coca-Cola building."

"Small price to pay if the survival of your messiah is at stake."

Muñiz cut the connection on his phone. "September first is the anniversary of the first burning of Atlanta."

"An apocalyptic event in his city's history," Joe said. "Jesse has enough in common with the prophecy that they think it's him." Joe's mind raced. "We'll get the raw footage from those news cameras in front of Jesse's house. If this protector was hanging out there, maybe somebody caught him on tape."

"Subpoena unaired footage? That opens up some sticky First Amendment issues, Bailey."

"Not this time. Believe me, nobody's going to want his station to be known as the one that refused to help save the life of an eight-year-old boy."

Joe got home a few minutes before nine, and the first sight that greeted him was Suzanne Morrison sitting on his sofa with Nikki.

"Hi, Daddy!" Nikki said.

"Hi." He couldn't take his eyes off Suzanne. "What are you doing here?"

She smiled. "I came to see you."

"She got here about an hour ago." Vince came in from the kitchen. "I know you always tell me not to let strangers in, but she said she knew you."

"Anybody could say that, Vince."

"I know, but she—"

"She smiled at you, didn't she? And that's all it took."

"Well—" He sighed. "Yeah."

"Just what I thought. How are you, Suzanne?"

"Fine. Your daughter was just showing me some of her CDs. We have some of the same musical heroes."

Nikki was beaming. "Daddy, she writes music that orchestras play. She said she'd give me a CD!"

"That's great. I'd like to hear it too."

"Me too," Vince said enthusiastically.

Joe patted his shoulder. "That'll be enough from you tonight. Suzanne, what can I help you with?"

"Actually, I thought I might be able to help *you*."

"With what?"

"I've been reading about your psychic attacks."

"Don't believe everything you read."

"I don't. That's why I'm here. I'd like to take a look at your elevator."

"My elevator?"

"Psychic attack number one, right?"

Joe glanced at Nikki, but she didn't seem to be bothered by the discussion.

"Suzanne doesn't think Jesse's powers are real," Nikki said, perhaps sensing his concern.

"I've been saying that all along. Now that *she* says it, you believe it?"

"I don't know yet," Nikki said. "And neither will you until you know all the facts."

"You sound like me," Joe said. He turned to Suzanne. "Or is it *you*?"

"You have a smart daughter."

"Yes, I do."

"I thought we'd take a look at your elevator." Suzanne patted a black leather satchel. "I brought my examination equipment."

Joe cracked a smile. "Your spirit kit?"

"Yep."

Vince stood up. "Joe, if you don't want to check it out, I'll go with her." He turned to Suzanne. "I've been kind of helping Joe out on this case, watching the Jesse Randall test sessions, and—"

"Sit down, Vince."

Vince sat down.

"Stay here with Nikki. Suzanne and I are going to take a look at the elevator."

If his neighbors didn't think he was nuts already, they certainly would now, Joe thought. He and Suzanne were in the basement, wearing galoshes, latex gloves, and lighted goggles. They directed their flashlights up at the bottom of the elevator car, which was suspended six feet from the bottom of the shaft. They had pulled the emergency stop button and turned off the alarm bell.

"If this elevator was rigged, whoever did it could have removed all the evidence that night," Joe said.

"Why didn't you check it out?"

"I thought it was an accident. It wasn't until the library shelves fell that I thought it could be something else."

"Aren't you curious about how it happened?"

"Of course. I already know how *I* would have done it."

"How?"

"See if you can figure it out."

Suzanne aimed her flashlight around the edges of the car bottom. "It looks like six bolts hold the floor in place."

"Yes, but the floor rests on four solid steel-edge panels. The panels weren't bent. The repairman had no idea how the floor could have fallen past the edge panels. As you can see, it's a snug fit."

"Did you find the nuts and bolts?"

"The repairman found them here in the sludge the next morning. They were intact."

She bit her lip. "The only way that floor could have fallen through the panels . . . is if it didn't."

"Yes?"

"What if the elevator floor was removed and bolted to the *underside* of the panels?"

"Interesting . . ."

"You probably wouldn't have noticed it when you were stepping into the elevator. As far as the mechanical malfunction, I assume there is some way to take manual control from a remote panel."

Joe pointed to a gray box on the wall of the basement. "Right there."

"There's one thing I still can't figure out. How could they trigger the floor drop? It couldn't have been just a matter of loosening the nuts. Somebody else might have stepped into the elevator."

"Have you heard of blast caps?"

"No."

"Special-effects people use them in movies. Low-power plastic explosives that can be triggered to blow with a radio signal. They can be molded into almost any shape."

"Like a bolt?"

"Yes. Stunt drivers use them to blow lug nuts off speeding cars. I figure someone could do the same thing to an elevator floor."

"Wouldn't there be a residue?"

"Of course, but this oily sludge would help cover up a lot. And at the time I wasn't suspecting anything like this."

Suzanne shone her flashlight onto the floor of the elevator shaft. "The evidence would've been blown to bits. The pieces would be mixed into the oil with decades of debris."

"That's the way I figure it."

"Clever. You're good at your job, Joe."

"So are you. I still haven't figured out how you rig your séances."

"That's because they're not rigged."

"Give me a hint."

"No hints to give."

"Try."

"Okay, here's one: They're real."

"Do you use a push rig or a pull rig?"

"Neither."

"Do you hire a private detective or do the research yourself?"

"Daphne does the research."

"Your dead friend. Right."

"I didn't ask for this ability."

"But if you got it, flaunt it, huh?"

She pulled herself from the shaft and swung her legs over the cold, dirty floor of the basement. "You have no idea how many times I've wished I *didn't* have it."

"I wish I did."

"No, you don't," she said softly. "It's lonely."

Joe climbed out of the shaft and brushed himself off. "I'd think you'd be very popular."

She smiled sadly. "Do you know how hard it is to date a man, then try to tell him that I have regular conversations with my dead childhood friend?"

"I've met some guys who would be really into that."

"All the wrong ones. The men I like are creeped out by it. The men who aren't bothered by it, I don't like."

"Maybe you should look for another line of work."

"That wouldn't stop my conversations with Daphne."

"Is she always there, in your head?"

"She was when I was younger. I think she realized it was making me crazy. Now she comes only when I call for her."

Joe studied Suzanne. If it weren't for the elaborate physical effects in her séances, he would swear she believed everything she was telling him. Some palm readers, spiritualists, and dowsers actually believed in their imaginary abilities, but the obvious thought and preparation behind Suzanne's effects made that impossible in her case.

She drew her knees up to her chest. "Why do you think I spend so much time looking for people who can do the things I do? I know you think I'm just trying to find newer and better ways to rip off people, but I'm telling you, I do want to feel a little less alone."

"You're an extremely attractive, intelligent woman. You don't need to do this."

"It's not my choice. Look, I've seen so many fakers that I'm almost as skeptical about this stuff as you are. I doubt Jesse Randall is the real thing, but if he is, he probably feels the same way I do."

Joe shrugged.

"Let me help you figure this out. Even if you think I'm a fake, I'm the best damned fake you've ever seen. Who better to expose a bit of psychic trickery? Other than you, I've probably exposed more reputed psychics and mediums than anyone in the city."

"Kellner and his team offered to help me too."

"They're clowns. Any kid with half an hour and a magic book from the school library could fool them."

"Jesse Randall isn't an amateur. However he does it, he's amazing."

"I know. I'd love it if he were the real thing." She wrinkled her brow. "Would you?"

"It hasn't even occurred to me."

"Would you be happy if you discovered that my abilities were genuine? Or the powers of the other people you study?"

"I can't let myself think that way."

"Why the hell not?"

"I wouldn't be able to do my job. Why do you think Kellner

and the spook squad are so easily fooled? They want to believe. They want to believe it so badly that they don't let themselves see the truth. If I let myself feel that way, I might not be able to see it either."

"I want to believe, and it hasn't hurt me."

"For me this is just how it needs to be."

"That's too bad. You might enjoy your work more the other way."

"I'd be disappointed more."

"Maybe. But you'd live in a world where anything is possible, where there are no boundaries. That's a nice world to wake up to every day."

He turned to face her. It had been a long time since anyone except Nikki had talked to him about how he thought and felt about anything. Part of her con? Maybe, but he didn't think so.

"What do you say, Joe? Can you use a consultant?"

"I'll give you the same sketches that I've passed around to a few people in the magic community. If you come up with any ideas, you've got my ear."

It was the dream again, Jesse realized. *The dream.* The voices, the dogs barking, the hands pulling him underground . . .

Except this time he couldn't punch the shadowy figures floating around him. They were always just out of reach. Because he couldn't hit them, the hands' grip on his ankles never loosened. He couldn't kick free. He was being pulled deeper and deeper into the cold, hard ground. . . .

"Wake up, kid."

In an instant, he found himself jolted awake, in the waking nightmare that was no less terrifying than the one he had just left behind.

"Did you hear me, boy? You're not here to sleep. You've got work to do."

Jesse sat up and stared at the bearded man who was shouting at him. The same man who had been bringing him his meals. Until then the guy probably hadn't said ten words to him.

"When can I go home?" Jesse said.

"Never, if I have anything to say about it."

"The lady said I could go if I showed what I could do."

"You haven't shown us shit, kid."

"I made the ball move."

"We need more than that. When are you going to show us something else?"

"I can't always do it. Especially when I'm sad or scared."

"You whiny-ass little brat . . . Myrna may put up with your crap, but I won't. Enjoy your meal. It's the last one you're getting until I see something special."

"Okay."

"Okay what?"

Jesse crossed his arms. He hated this man. This must be all his fault. "Okay, I won't eat."

"Son of a bitch!" the man screamed, flipping over the tray of food. "You may think you're hot shit, but we don't need your sorry little ass. You'd better watch yourself."

Jesse scrambled back toward the wall, bracing himself for the slap or punch he knew was coming.

"Charles!" Myrna called out from the doorway. "Please leave Jesse alone. He'll help us. I promise."

"When?" Charles said, still glaring at him. "By the time he's ready to go to college?"

"Please. Let me work with him awhile longer. I promise he'll do what you want."

"He'd better."

"He will."

Charles stepped away. "If he doesn't, I swear I'll bury both of you in the same hole." He left through the passageway and slammed the panel closed behind him.

Myrna rushed toward Jesse and enfolded him in her arms.

"That man scares me," he whispered.

"Me too. We have to be very careful around him."

"We gotta find a way out of here."

"There's no way. Believe me, honey, I've looked. Unless . . ."

"What?"

She glanced at the observation windows. "Unless there's some way to use your powers to get us out of here."

He shook his head. "It doesn't always work."

"But if your life depends on it . . ."

"There has to be some other way."

"There isn't."

He dejectedly shook his head.

She was silent for a moment, then smiled. "Hey, I have a surprise for you."

"What?"

She reached into her baggy pocket and pulled out his eyeglasses.

"Thanks!"

He reached for the glasses, but she held them out of reach. "They told me that you have to show them something else before I can give them to you."

He stared bitterly at her, then sat cross-legged on the floor next to his spilled food.

"I'm sorry, honey."

In front of him, a paper napkin twitched a few times, then jumped a few feet away.

Myrna gasped.

A small piece of lettuce flipped over and bobbed up and down, almost as if it were waving to him. Then it stopped.

"May I please have my glasses now?"

She gingerly opened her hand, and he took his glasses and put them on.

"They're never gonna let me out of here, are they?"

"Of course they will."

"I don't believe it. They're never gonna let me go."

"Maybe you can bargain with them, Jesse. You obviously have something they want."

"I'm not gonna bargain."

"It may be our best hope."

"No." He glared at her. "I hate them. And if they don't let me out of here, they're gonna be sorry."

12

"I think the Little Bastard came through for us, Bailey." Howe walked toward Joe's desk at 9:02 A.M., holding several crumpled pieces of paper.

"Looks like it was a struggle."

"We wouldn't call the machine the Little Bastard if it were easy. The damned thing almost shredded the output, but I managed to wrench it free. There was one phone number that Nelson and the Rawlingses each called several times. And get this: It was the week before Gaby Rawlings's death."

"Are you serious?"

"Yep. It came back to a guy named Andrei Yashin. Was he someone Nelson worked with?"

"I don't think so. I know almost everyone on the parapsychology team, and that name doesn't sound familiar."

"I have an address."

"Let's go."

. . .

Within half an hour, Joe and Howe were standing in front of the weather-beaten door of an apartment in Garden Hills. It was a complex of ten units, all in a one-story strip facing a pothole-ridden tar parking lot. A sign next to the door read DR. ANDREI YASHIN—WELLNESS SPECIALIST.

A woman in her early sixties answered Joe's knock. "Come in, gentlemen. You're early, but Dr. Yashin can see you."

Joe put his hand on Howe's forearm to keep him from producing his badge. "Thank you."

"This way, please."

As she turned around, Howe gave Joe a questioning glance.

"Play along," Joe whispered.

They followed her through the sparsely decorated apartment to the dining room, which looked somewhat like a doctor's office. A large massage table was in the middle of the room, next to a table of gleaming chrome instruments unlike anything Joe had ever seen.

"My name is Eve. Which one of you will the doctor be seeing?"

"Him," Joe said quickly, pointing to Howe.

Howe shot him an annoyed glance.

"Very good." She handed Howe a flimsy hospital gown. "Take your clothes off and put this on, please."

"You've got to be kidding," Howe said to Joe as much as to her.

"You heard the woman." Joe turned to Eve. "That's why he brought me along, to keep himself from chickening out. This won't hurt, will it?"

"Of course not."

Joe turned back to Howe. "See? You've got nothing to worry about. I'll hold your clothes for you if you'd like."

Howe was still glaring at him.

The woman pulled Joe out of the room as she drew a pale green curtain over the entranceway.

"Would you like to wait in the other—"

"He stays here," Howe said from behind the curtain.

"He's useless without me." Joe smiled. "Is Dr. Yashin around?"

"He's meditating."

"Ah."

"While he changes, perhaps I can get some information from you." She picked up a clipboard hanging next to the dining room entrance. "He hasn't eaten in the last twelve hours, has he?"

He remembered the chocolate chip bagel Howe had devoured in the car. "No."

"Have his headaches persisted?"

"If anything, they've gotten worse."

"Well, I promise that he'll feel better almost immediately after the session today."

"You hear that?" Joe called out to Howe.

"Yeah." Howe spoke sourly from behind the curtain.

"There's the matter of payment. Dr. Yashin agreed to accept two hundred dollars now, plus another two hundred Friday."

"Of course." Joe opened his wallet, but all he had was sixty. He was about to call out to Howe, when a fistful of twenties was suddenly thrust from behind the curtain.

"Two hundred dollars," Howe said.

Eve took the money and fastened it to the clipboard. "Dr. Yashin will be out in a moment." She walked into the back bedroom.

Howe pulled aside the curtain, revealing himself in the shorter-than-short hospital gown and a pair of black dress socks. "Not a word," he said.

"Shh." Joe pulled him from the room and guided him toward the kitchen. "The room may be bugged."

"Bugged?"

"I'm not sure what this guy is all about," Joe whispered. "He's some kind of healer. He may have listening devices in that room so he can pick up patients' conversations, then amaze them with what their bodies tell him about their lives."

"Let's just take the son of a bitch in."

"Not yet. We can buy ourselves some leverage."

"But why do I have to go on the table?"

"Your vision may be blocked by a towel or something. I need to be able to watch him."

"I could have watched him."

"You wouldn't know what to look for."

Howe pulled down the hem of the small gown. "Just be careful where you look."

The bedroom door creaked open. They walked back toward the massage table, where a thin, long-faced man in his late forties was arranging the instruments.

"Dr. Yashin?" Joe said.

"Yes. Good morning." The man spoke with a trace of a Russian accent. "I would offer to shake hands, but I don't want to contaminate the instruments."

"Of course."

Yashin spoke to Howe as if he were a sick child. "How are you feeling, my boy?"

"Worse by the minute."

"I'll take care of that. Please lie on the table faceup."

Howe gave Joe a wary glance as he slid onto the table and lay back.

Yashin motioned to a frayed couch in the next room. "You may wait in there."

Joe cast a glance at the waiting area, which featured a coffee table with stacks of New Age medical magazines and issues of *Fate, Nature Extreme,* and other periodicals. "I'd rather stay in here," he said.

"It would probably be best if you would just go into the next room and—"

"He's staying," Howe said. "It's the only way I'm going through with this."

"As you wish."

Eve returned to the room, carrying another pair of instruments. They looked like scalpels but with thick chrome handles that spiraled down to dull blades.

"Why are we here?" Joe asked. "Why not in a real office?"

"Society is always slow to accept advances in medicine," Yashin said in the well-rehearsed manner of a man who had answered the question a hundred times before. "Those of us on the frontier are subjected to harsh scrutiny, and this helps us be a little less conspicuous."

"Are you licensed?"

Yashin waved at a diploma on the wall. It was in Russian. "Of course. I studied at the Odessa Homeopathic Institute."

"That's where you got your doctorate?"

"No. I received my doctorate at the university in St. Petersburg." He turned from Joe. "Now, if you please, we must begin."

"Of course."

Yashin ran his hands over Howe's skull, feeling every contour. Twice he paused and made clicking sounds with his tongue.

"Am I all right?" Howe asked.

"There's a buildup here of humors. I'm surprised you can even function. You came here just in time."

"What are you going to do?"

"Take them out, of course." He held up his hand. "Number twenty scalpel, please."

Howe's eyes widened.

Eve handed Yashin a thick-handled scalpel. Joe watched carefully as he applied it to Howe's forehead.

"Just relax, young man." Yashin swiped across the forehead, leaving behind a thin line of blood.

"Bailey . . ." Howe whispered urgently.

Joe gave his arm a reassuring pat.

Yashin swiped his scalpel again, and this time small pieces of organic matter appeared in the streaks of blood. "Excellent," he said. "The humors are coming right out."

Eve picked up the fleshy matter and placed it into a beaker. Yashin put down the scalpel and squeezed Howe's forehead, producing even more bloody, pulpy matter.

"Very toxic," he said. "You should feel better soon."

Howe appeared to be dazed.

"Will there be scarring?" Joe asked.

"No scarring. His body will heal itself completely by the time he gets up from the table. You'd never know he had surgery."

Joe whipped out his badge. "Atlanta police. Put down the scalpel."

Eve quickly lifted the beaker to her lips.

Howe bolted upright and grabbed her wrist. "Those are *my* humors you're trying to swallow."

Eve cut loose with a string of obscenities, some in English, some in Russian. She spit in Howe's face.

"That's not the best way to earn goodwill," Joe said as he snapped a pair of handcuffs on Yashin.

"What is this? What's going on here?" Yashin's accent was suddenly thicker.

"You're under arrest for fraud and practicing medicine without a license."

Yashin motioned toward his diploma and started to object, but Joe cut him off.

"A *local* license." Joe used a hand towel to pick up the scalpel. "I haven't seen one of these before. The blood and pulpy matter is stored in the handle. When you run it across your patient's skin, you squeeze the handle and the blood and guts run down the underside of the blade and appear to be coming out of an incision."

Howe reached for his jacket, pulled out his cuffs from the pocket and fastened them onto Eve's wrists. "How were you so sure this weirdo wasn't going to cut me?"

"I saw a tiny drop of blood forming at the end of the scalpel even before he got near you with it. Plus the blade looked too dull to penetrate the skin. I told you I knew what to look for." Joe lifted the beaker and held it up at eye level. "This is pig's blood, isn't it?"

"I want a lawyer."

Joe shook his head. "I wouldn't if I were you."

"You are not me."

"No, but if I were, I'd know that there's only one thing I could do to stay out of jail tonight, and it doesn't involve calling a lawyer."

Joe and Howe ran Yashin and Eve in to the station and put them in two different interview rooms. They left Eve alone while they concentrated on Yashin.

"Tell us about Gaby Rawlings," Joe said.

"I don't know who you're talking about." Yashin folded his hands in front of him.

"You operated on her without a license. She died. That opens you up for manslaughter at least. Maybe even murder."

"Murder?"

Howe sat across from Yashin. "You killed her. Is there another way we should look at this? If so, you'd better start talking."

Yashin held his head in his hands and muttered something in Russian.

"Come again?" Howe said.

"I didn't kill her!"

"But you did operate on her."

Yashin paused, then answered carefully. "If I did see this woman, I did not harm her."

"She was a sixteen-year-old girl," Joe said, leaning into his face. "What the hell happened?"

"I cannot help you."

"You'd better start," Joe said. "And you'd also better tell us how Robert Nelson was involved."

"Dr. Nelson?"

"Yes. Did you meet him before or after you met the Rawlings family?"

Yashin ran his hand over his jaw. "Before," he finally answered.

"How did you meet him?"

"First I need some assurances from you."

Howe slapped the tabletop. "You're not getting any. How did you meet Nelson?"

Yashin sighed. "He came to see me. He wished to see me work. Around the same time, Mrs. Rawlings contacted me. Her daughter was very ill, and she wanted me to help her. Dr. Nelson and I went to their house, and I operated on her."

"You scammed her."

"No. What I do is convince the mind that the body has been healed. If the mind believes that, good health will follow."

"Like it did with Gaby Rawlings?"

"That was unfortunate. I spent the entire night with her. Several times her father wanted to take her to the hospital. Dr. Nelson persuaded him to wait."

Joe felt ill. "And the whole time you were waving your scalpel over her, doing your stupid sleight-of-hand tricks? Couldn't you see she was in trouble?"

"Of course. But she was so young. . . . I was sure it would pass. And I suppose I wanted to convince Dr. Nelson of my abilities.

He kept saying that he thought she was getting better. We had no idea what was really happening."

"Until she died?"

"Before that. In the morning I knew there was something terribly wrong. I told them there was no more I could do, and that they should get her to a hospital. Even then Dr. Nelson resisted the idea."

"Nice guy," Howe said.

"Her parents took her to the emergency room, but it was too late. A few days later Mr. Rawlings threatened both me and Dr. Nelson. Somehow he knew how I worked. He knew about the scalpels, everything."

"How did he know?" Howe asked.

"I don't know. He even knew about my past. I worked under another name in Belgium a few years ago, and he knew about that too. He said he'd have me and Dr. Nelson arrested and brought up on charges. It scared us both."

"So Nelson paid off Mr. and Mrs. Rawlings."

"Yes. It was the only way. Dr. Nelson was afraid the publicity would destroy his program. He gave them a large grant in exchange for their silence."

"When the university caught on, how did he repay the money?"

Yashin wrinkled his brow. "I'm sorry?"

"Nelson had to repay the money out of his own pocket. Did you help him with that?"

"No. I don't know anything about this."

"Are you sure?"

"Yes. We ceased all communication with each other. He said he was going to destroy all his records having anything to do with me or the Rawlings family. I never heard from him again."

Joe felt sick. "How can you still do this? After watching that girl's life slip away while you scammed her and her family . . ."

"I help a lot of people. I unlock the healing powers of the mind. It may look like a trick to you, but to those who believe, it gives them hope. Oftentimes, that hope is the one thing that makes the difference between life and death."

"Is that what you tell yourself?" Howe said.

"I know it to be true."

"We're going to let you go for now," Joe said. "But this isn't over. And whatever happens, this part of your life is finished. If I ever hear you're still in business, I guarantee that we're going to revisit these manslaughter charges. Do you understand?"

"Yes. Completely."

"One last question. Do you really have a doctorate?"

"Yes," he said, shifting uncomfortably. "In art history."

Joe and Howe tracked down Ted Rawlings at a Cartersville nursery school, where he and his crew were steam-cleaning the carpets.

"We did nothing wrong," Rawlings insisted, checking to make sure he was out of earshot of his crew. "We trusted those two men."

"Dr. Nelson and Dr. Yashin?" Joe asked.

"Yeah. The Russian guy was so sure he could help Gaby. He charged us a lot less than it would've cost to take her to the hospital. I swear to God, I didn't know he was a cheat. I never would've let him near Gaby if I'd known."

"Do you think Dr. Nelson knew?"

"No. He was egging the Russian guy on. It really seemed important to Nelson that they prove the guy's stuff was real. The Russian wanted to quit, but Nelson told him to keep trying." Rawlings's lips tightened. "That son of a bitch."

"How did you find out that Dr. Yashin was using trickery?" Joe said.

"I watched him."

"There's got to be more to it than that," Howe said. "You suddenly knew all about his past in Belgium. How did you find out?"

Rawlings took a rag out of his back pocket and nervously wiped his brow. "A fella told me."

"Who?" Joe asked.

"I don't know. He came to see me a few days after Gaby passed on. He told me what he knew about Dr. Yashin, and I told him what had happened to Gaby. He thought my wife and I should get something for our pain and suffering."

"It was his idea to take money from Dr. Nelson?"

"Yeah, but I thought it was a good idea too. My wife wasn't so crazy about it though. She thought maybe we were betraying our daughter." He cleared his throat. "I don't know, maybe we were. I haven't been able to make sense of anything since Gaby left us."

"So you blackmailed Dr. Nelson?" Howe asked.

"Blackmailed? Hell, no. I told him that we should be entitled to some kind of settlement. He gave us some research money."

Joe smiled incredulously. "A hundred and sixty thousand dollars in research money?"

"A hundred and sixty thousand dollars for what he did to my family. He made us promise that we'd never talk about it to anyone. He said that people might accuse me and my wife of neglect. I didn't believe that, but it scared Crystal pretty bad. I think she's still feeling guilty."

"And you aren't?" Joe said.

Rawlings swallowed hard and looked away. "Are we almost through here?"

"What about this man who came and told you about Dr. Yashin?" Howe said. "What did he look like?"

"He was a red-haired fella."

Joe and Howe shared a quick glance. "What kind of car did he drive?" Joe asked.

"He didn't drive a car. He rode a motorcycle."

13

Natalie Simone rolled over in bed and looked at the clock: 3:37 P.M. Shit. She'd meant to get up earlier and go to an ammo bazaar at the Alabama border, but she'd been partying with friends until six that morning. Gotta keep that from happening too often, she told herself. If she couldn't continue to supply the best guns and ammo, a lot of other people in town would.

She shuffled into her living room. All she needed was caffeine and maybe a little—

She screamed.

Garrett Lyles was sprawled across her sofa.

He chuckled. "A lot of women look like hell when they first wake up. Glad to see you're not one of them."

She could feel her heart pounding in her throat. Keep it together, she told herself. "What the hell are you doing in here?"

"Relaxing. I haven't gotten much rest lately."

"Don't you have someplace else you can do that?"

"Sure. But I wouldn't be able to talk to you afterward. I could have knocked, but you might not have been eager to see me. I could hear you snoring from outside your window, so I decided to come in and kick back for a while."

She glanced at the door. "How?"

"Don't worry. Your booby trap works fine. I just happen to be extraordinarily good. If I weren't, I'd be lying on the floor with a nine-millimeter shell in my chest."

"That's what it was designed to do. With the clients I have, I can't take chances."

"I can relate."

"I'm sure you didn't come in here just to take a load off."

"No, I didn't. I need you to put me in touch with Jules Cavasos's organization."

"Jules Cavasos? Why?"

"It's not necessary for you to know that."

"He runs the city's biggest drug syndicate. What makes you think I could help you?"

"I'm sure that your business puts you in contact with his people on occasion. That's all I want. Contact. The higher up, the better. I'll handle the rest."

"Handle what?"

"Again, not necessary for you to know."

She took a deep breath. Why did this guy unnerve her so much? He was still lying on her couch, his right hand behind his head, tucked underneath the cushion.

She smiled. "Tell me, am I holding artillery now?"

"Doubtful. I don't think you strapped your Berettas under the sleeves of that nightshirt."

"If I did, and tried to draw on you, I'd be dead in less than a second, wouldn't I?"

He didn't respond.

She nodded. "Because underneath that pillow, I'm sure you're holding that Lanchester I sold you. If you're as good as I hear you are, you could probably shoot me dead right through the pillow."

"How did we get off on such an unpleasant tangent?"

"Okay, maybe I can get you close to one of Cavasos's boys. What's in it for me?"

"Two thousand."

"Five."

"Time is of the essence. This needs to happen today."

"Today? Are you crazy?"

He pulled the Lanchester out from under the pillow and put it on the coffee table. "If I had time to waste, I wouldn't need your help, Natalie. Get busy."

Joe and Howe returned to the station to find Fisher and three of his FBI colleagues heading toward the fourth floor.

"Bailey, it looks like you were right," Fisher said. "Your fellow officers got an ID off one of the news tapes. They think the guy who shot the sniper was on the press line in front of Jesse Randall's house."

"They *think*?" Howe said.

"We're on our way to meet Detectives Powell and Reinertson at your A/V center. There's a witness from the church on her way. Care to join us?"

They went to the fourth floor audiovisual room, a facility that was destined to grow in size and importance as more uniformed officers were miked and patrol cars were outfitted with video cameras. When Joe sprained an ankle the year before, he had spent a tedious two weeks in the center, logging tapes of routine traffic stops. He'd had more fun during his last root canal.

Powell, Reinertson, and a middle-aged woman were already hunched over a monitor. Powell introduced her. "Gentlemen, this is Leonora Madison. She's a member of the church choir."

"First soprano," she said proudly.

Powell gestured toward the monitor. "We spotted a man on the press line who matches the description of the guy who stormed through the church. We were just about to show Mrs. Madison the tape and see what she thinks."

"Anytime you're ready," Leonora said. "I got grandchildren coming to my house in an hour."

Powell brought up the footage of the press line.

"My God, that's him," Leonora gasped.

"Who?" Joe asked.

She pointed to a tall man with long hair, wire-rimmed glasses, and a droopy mustache. "He wasn't wearing the glasses, but I'm positive that's him."

Powell turned to Joe and Fisher. "Exactly who we thought. He matches the description given to us by several witnesses."

"He was watching Jesse," Joe said. "You should talk to Alan Whatley. He's the bully who got roughed up last week. He might be able to tell us if this is the same guy."

"His mother is bringing him after school."

"Good," Joe said. "I'll talk to the journalists working the press line and see if anybody knows anything about him. I'm heading over to the Randall home anyway."

"Why?" Howe asked.

"To find out if Ms. Randall knows anything about our red-haired friend."

"Were you giving interviews out there?" Latisha Randall asked after she opened her front door for Joe to enter. Her face was drawn and tired, and she looked as if she'd aged ten years since he last saw her. "Why were you talking to those reporters?"

He stepped inside the house. There were several large flower arrangements around the room, probably from friends and well-wishers. The flowers made him uncomfortable; they seemed too much like funeral bouquets. He hoped they didn't give Latisha the same feeling.

"We think one of the men at the church was posing as a reporter," Joe said. "I was asking the people on the line if they knew anything about him."

"He was one of the kidnappers?"

"We don't think so. He may have been trying to protect your son. It's possible he's the same man who roughed up the boy who was picking on Jesse." Joe showed her a printout from the news videotape. "Look familiar?"

She studied it. "Afraid not."

He showed her the picture of the red-haired man. "How about this one?"

She squinted at the photo. "I've seen him. He was at some of Jesse's tests."

"Did you ever talk to him?"

"No. I had no idea who he was. There were a lot of people hovering around those sessions."

The doorbell rang. Latisha opened the door, and Stewart Dunning walked into the house.

"What's he doing here?" Joe asked.

Dunning smiled. "I could ask the same question about you, Detective."

"I saw you outside," Latisha said. "Mr. Dunning told me to call him if the police ever showed up here, so I did."

The attorney crossed his arms. "I instructed her not to let you in until I got here. She's too accommodating for her own good."

"Maybe she recognizes that I'm trying to help her son."

"So am I, Mr. Bailey."

Joe turned to Latisha. "All the videotaped test sessions I've seen were recorded several weeks after Jesse began to demonstrate his abilities. Do you have any home videos of your own, recorded earlier?"

"No. We don't have a camcorder."

"Why do you ask?" Dunning spoke sharply.

"By the time those sessions were conducted, he'd had time to refine his technique. If I could see earlier tapes of him, recorded right after he started doing this stuff, it might be helpful to me."

She shook her head. "I'm sorry, I can't help you."

"Just thought I'd check. How have you been doing?"

"How do you *think* she's doing?" Dunning snapped. "I think that will be all, Detective."

"Don't be rude," Latisha said in the same tone she used to scold her son. "I didn't call you to come over and insult him."

Dunning's tight-lipped smile oozed condescension. "It's best that we limit our contact with Detective Bailey. Every minute a police officer is talking to you, that's one minute he could be out there trying to find Jesse."

"I assure you, there are many, many people out there looking for your son," Joe said.

"It's just that I'm so worried."

"Of course you are."

"I'm worried for another reason. Jesse has a respiratory condition, and he uses an inhaler twice a day. It helps him breathe."

"Did he have it with him?"

"No, it was in my purse."

Dunning soothingly patted her arm. "I'm sure he'll be fine."

"Did you tell any of the other officers about this?"

"Of course."

"Who?"

"One of the first officers I saw after I woke up. He was in a uniform."

Joe pulled out his notebook. "He may not have passed it on to anybody. Is it a prescription?"

"Yes. It's called a Pulmicort Turbuhaler. It's corticosteroid powder."

"Can I have his doctor's name?"

"Why?" Dunning interjected.

"The investigating officers may wish to contact him. It'll give them a better idea what Jesse's up against."

"Dr. Andrew Hearn," she said. "His offices are in Midtown."

Joe jotted down the name. "Is there anything else?"

"Like what?" Dunning said. "Be specific."

Joe had had enough. "Anything that might help us find her son. Anything that might help me figure out how he does what he does. Anything that might help her get rid of the bloodsuckers on the sidewalk, and in here, Mr. Dunning, before she goes insane. Is that specific enough for you?"

Dunning stared at him for a moment. "May I speak to you outside, Detective?"

"Now?"

"Yes. I suggest the backyard rather than the front, unless you want to hear our conversation on the evening news."

"This is my boy we're talking about," Latisha said. "If you have anything to say to each other, you can say it right here."

"I'm sorry," Dunning said. "I need to talk to him outside. We'll be right back."

"Don't bother," she snapped. "You can let yourself out the back gate." She turned on her heel and walked down the hallway.

"Ms. Randall . . ." Joe said.

She was gone.

Dunning and Joe stepped outside and walked along the flower garden that framed the backyard. "Emotional times," Dunning said. "It's taking its toll on everyone."

"You seem to be holding up all right."

"I know you think I'm some kind of bloodsucker, but I really do want what's best for Jesse. I know what it's like to grow up without money. I don't know if you've noticed, but I've been refusing all interview requests and keeping a low profile. This isn't a PR gambit for me."

"Maybe I misjudged you."

"You don't really think that, do you?"

"What do you want to talk to me about, Dunning?"

"I'd like this to be off the record."

"In my business there's no such thing. What do you want?"

Dunning gazed at a bed of zinnias. "Do you have one solitary scrap of proof that Jesse Randall is not what he appears to be?"

"My investigation is ongoing."

"I'll take that as a no."

"Take it any way you like."

"Detective, I've never believed in this stuff. Not at all."

"That puts you in the minority. Most people have at least some belief in the paranormal."

"I've read the accounts of his test sessions, but most of his tricks—the metal bending, the sealed-box card readings, reproducing drawings that others have made—are easily duplicated by magicians. But now . . . I'm sure he's still alive."

"I hope so."

"You don't understand. I'm *sure*."

Dunning was trembling.

"How are you sure?"

His lower lip quivered. "In my house, during the last couple of days, there've been . . . occurrences. Objects moving by themselves. Strange noises. It began the night Jesse and I first met. I could tell he didn't care for me."

Joe stepped closer. "Are you positive?"

"Yes. I've seen some of these things with my own eyes. My

television lifted off its stand and smashed against the wall of my bedroom. Every pen and pencil in my den is now sticking in the wall behind my desk. I think they were shadow storms."

"Why didn't you say anything before?"

"It didn't exactly bolster my client's case. It's been terrifying. I haven't slept in two days."

"Did your wife see any of these things?"

"Yes, but after the first night she went to her sister's in Miami. She couldn't take it anymore."

"I'd like to see your house."

"I was hoping you'd say that."

Joe followed Dunning back to his two-story brick home near the posh Atlanta Country Club Estates. Towering over the other neighborhood residences, Dunning's home was as showy and excessive as the man who owned it.

Joe grabbed his spirit kit and entered the house with Dunning. The place was, as he expected, spectacular. Water was a major motif throughout the house, with artificial streams, waterfalls, and indoor koi ponds in almost every room.

"Beautiful house," Joe said.

"Thank you. I helped design it. I studied architecture before I went into law."

"A lot of my coworkers probably wish you had pursued that instead."

"I'll take that as a compliment." Dunning pointed to a large empty pond in the living room. "Look."

"What about it?"

"When I went to bed the other night, it was full. About three A.M. I heard a strange noise. I came downstairs and realized that it was the sound of water splashing all over the room. It was coming from this pond."

Joe knelt beside it. The pond was two feet deep, nine feet long, four feet wide, and bone dry. "Did you get a close look while it was happening?"

"Yes. At first I thought my dog might have fallen in, but when I turned on the light, I saw there was nothing in there. The water continued to splash over the side like waves crashing on a beach. It didn't stop until the pond was dry."

"Were you here the whole time?"

"Yes. It took only a few minutes. I was in here mopping and getting my rugs off the floor. As soon as it was over, I climbed inside and looked around. There wasn't anything there. Thank God we didn't have any fish in this one. Those koi cost me a fortune."

Joe rubbed his hands over the pond's inner wall. Smooth. "What else?"

"Come this way." Dunning led him into his den, where about thirty pens and pencils were sticking into the hardwood paneling. "I was downstairs, looking over some briefs, when I heard what I thought was a knocking sound. I came in here and found this."

Joe gripped one of the pencils and pulled it from the wall. "The lead isn't even broken."

"I know. How could this have happened?"

Joe opened his spirit kit and pulled out a digital camera. He took photos from several angles, then put away the camera and picked up a tiny brass measuring pin. He inserted it into the hole and jotted down the measurement.

"What good does that do?" Dunning asked.

Joe pulled out three more pencils and measured the hole depths. "This will tell me what type of force we're dealing with. I should be able to calculate the pounds per square inch exerted on these pencils, which may narrow the field of possibilities."

"I think the field is pretty narrow already," he said dryly.

"Let me see the television."

They climbed the stairs and walked into the master bedroom. It was a mess. Piles of broken plaques, picture frames, and ceramic objects littered the floor in front of a wall that was now entirely bare.

Joe pointed to the broken objects. "Were you in the room when this happened?"

"Yes, I was sleeping. I think everything came off the wall at once. Before I could turn on a light, I heard a huge crash next to me."

Joe looked down next to the bed, where a television was in pieces.

Dunning pointed to the bare wall across the room. "It came from over there."

Joe pulled a can of fingerprint powder from his kit and brushed the television.

"You think someone came in here and just threw it at me?"

"In cases such as this, the simplest solution is often the correct one." Joe squinted at the broken casing. "But even if there were prints, it would be tough to get them off this. How's your security system here?"

"About as good as it gets. In my line of work, I need it. Between outraged citizens and disgruntled clients, I can't be too careful."

"Sensors on every door and window?" Joe asked.

"Upstairs *and* downstairs. Plus motion detectors covering every square inch of the house except this room. There's no way someone could have gotten in without my knowing about it."

Joe looked up at the bedroom's vaulted ceiling. "No attic over this room, right?"

"Right."

Joe took more pictures with his digital camera, then paced around the room. How in the hell could this have happened?

"I've been torn about whether or not to tell Latisha Randall about this. On one hand, it might give her hope that her son's still alive."

"But if this gets out, it could also feed hysteria. We have no idea who has Jesse, or why. There's no telling what effect this news would have on them."

"I see your point."

"Keep this quiet for now, and please leave everything as it is. I may need to come back here."

"Don't worry, my bags are already packed. I'm going to a hotel. I feel like I'm risking my life by staying one more minute."

Joe half smiled. "If it's this stuff you're afraid of, you might want to stay away from the ritzy hotels you're used to."

"Why?"

"They don't bolt their furniture down."

Jesse stared at the Styrofoam maze that Charles had carried into the room in two sections. It had taken the man ten minutes and fourteen curse words to put it together, and when he was finished, he left without any explanation of why he'd brought it in. The maze was about the size of a doorframe, with a confusing array of two-inch-wide passageways. It rested on two cardboard sawhorses in the middle of the room.

Myrna strode through the entranceway. "Ready to have some fun, Jesse?"

"Fun?" He shook his head. "Not in here."

"This is very important, Jesse. If you cooperate with them, it could make things easier for you."

"Easier how? Will they let me go?"

"Maybe."

"Please don't lie to me."

"I'm not lying, Jesse. I don't have all the answers, but I do know that they can make things very unpleasant for both of us. Believe me."

He nodded toward the maze. "What's this for?"

She held up a small plastic ball. "It's for a little game."

"You mean a test."

She placed the ball into the maze. "This will be easy for you, Jesse. Try to have fun with it."

"What am I supposed to do?"

"Do you see the blue line on top of some of those maze walls?"

"Yeah?"

"They want you to make the ball roll along that line and move through the maze. Do you think you can do that?"

"I need my music to concentrate."

She smiled. "We're ready for that. We have some of your favorites here. What would you like to hear?"

"You got some Grandmaster Flash?"

She looked up at the mirrored window. In a few seconds, the throbbing beat of "Showdown" echoed in the room.

"Is that okay?" she shouted above the music.

He nodded, took off his glasses, and leaned over the maze. He stared at the ball for a long while.

It was still.

He looked away, took a deep breath, then turned back.

The ball began to rock.

Jesse tilted his head, and the ball finally began to roll through the maze.

Myrna smiled. She said something, but Jesse couldn't hear her over the thunderous music.

The ball slowed as it reached an intersection, then turned right, following the blue line. Jesse stepped around the maze.

The ball turned again, then rolled almost the entire length of the maze. Jesse followed along, keeping his eyes glued to the ball.

It turned again.

Halfway there.

Jesse rolled his shoulders to the beat. He could do this. . . .

The ball turned three more times, then picked up speed as it neared the end. It finally dropped to the floor just as Grandmaster Flash's chorus kicked in.

He saw Myrna's lips form one word: "Incredible."

He felt a rush of excitement. He'd shown them.

The music faded out.

"That was amazing, Jesse. You did that so well."

"Thank you."

"We have one more thing we'd like you to try for us."

"I'm kind of tired."

"Just give it a try. This will be something new for you. Have you ever tried to use your talents to affect living things?"

"What do you mean?"

"You're amazing at moving small objects around, but can you influence the movements of actual living beings?"

He wrinkled his forehead. "I never tried that. I never *wanted* to try that."

Charles reentered the room with a small box.

Myrna took Jesse's hands in her own. "I want you to try something for me, honey. Please keep an open mind."

Charles opened the box and picked up a small brown mouse by the tail. He dropped it into the maze.

Jesse looked at the mouse. "What do you want me to do?"

"Don't you know already?"

"You want me to steer the mouse?"

"Just try, Jesse. Concentrate."

"I can't make the mouse go where he doesn't want to go."

"See?" Charles said. "We're wasting our time with this little prick."

"Quiet, Charles." Myrna squeezed Jesse's hand. "Please, honey. Try."

He walked back to the maze. "You want this mouse to walk the blue line?"

"That would be fine."

"I need my music."

"Can you try it without?"

"No. I've never done this before. I need it."

Before she could reply, Grandmaster Flash came back over the P.A. system.

Jesse leaned over the maze and stared at the mouse. "Does he have a name?"

Charles snickered. "Whatever you want it to be, kid."

Jesse faced the mouse head-on as it meandered down a passageway. Suddenly it stopped.

The smile left Charles's face.

The mouse hesitated, took another step, then turned around and walked toward a blue passageway.

Jesse stepped around to the other side, his eyes never leaving the mouse. It was coming to the blue passageway.

Jesse opened his eyes wider.

The mouse stopped, then turned down the narrow blue passage.

It was working.

The mouse passed the next blue turn but suddenly recoiled as if it had been struck in the head. It turned back and found its way to the blue passage.

"That *didn't* happen," Charles said in amazement.

Myrna smiled. "Keep it up, Jesse."

Jesse stepped around the maze as the mouse neared the end of its journey. Every time it missed a blue turn, it suddenly froze, then retreated to the appropriate passageway.

"What exactly are you doing?" Myrna asked.

"Persuading him."

"But how?"

Jesse paused while the mouse approached yet another intersection. It turned on its own. "I'm making it unpleasant for him if he doesn't do what I want him to do."

"Unpleasant?" Charles asked. "You're actually hurting him?"

Jesse didn't answer. One turn to go. The mouse passed it, then stopped, once again reacting as if it had received a blow to the head.

This time it didn't turn back.

Jesse leaned closer and opened his eyes wider. The rodent winced once, twice, then three times, as if struggling against some unseen force. Charles and Myrna shot nervous glances at the observation window.

"What the hell are you doing to it?" Charles said.

Jesse almost smiled. Charles sounded good and scared. "I'm telling him where he needs to go."

"And if he doesn't listen, what will happen to him?" Myrna asked.

"You don't want to know," Jesse said, glancing up to catch their reactions.

Nervous. Maybe even panicky. Good.

He was tired of being the scared one. Let them see how it felt.

The mouse finally turned. Jesse followed him around the maze until he chose the correct passageway.

"He had no choice," Jesse said.

The mouse finished the maze, and Charles grabbed it and held it at eye level. "He looks okay."

"He's fine," Jesse said.

"I'll get this stuff out right away," Charles said, nodding toward the maze and sawhorses. He spoke to Myrna. "Will you be okay while I take the mouse away?"

She hesitated.

They were afraid of him.

"I—I'll be fine," she stammered.

Jesse glanced around at the padded floor and walls, suddenly realizing why the room was set up this way.

They were afraid he would use his powers to hurt them.

That also explained the paper uniforms and Styrofoam maze. They didn't want anything around that could be used as a weapon.

He stepped closer to Myrna. She backed away slightly.

Before, he'd hated to have people afraid of him. But here, trapped in this awful place, maybe it was just what he needed.

14

Natalie Simone's cell phone rang with a spirited rendition of Beethoven's "Ode to Joy." She picked it up from her dining room table. "Natalie here."

She listened for a moment, then cut the connection.

Lyles joined her at the table. "Short conversation."

"That was one of Cavasos's people. He wanted to make sure I was near my phone so that my contact doesn't waste his time."

"Who's the contact?"

"Ryland."

"Ryland who?"

"Just Ryland. He picks up an occasional piece from me."

"Is he high in the organization?"

"High enough for you, I'm sure. What do you want with these guys? You're not into drug trafficking."

"I'm into whatever pays the bills. Like you, I suppose."

She shot him an ice-cold glance. "I sell guns, and that's it. I don't deal drugs and I've never killed anybody, which is more than I can say for you."

He chuckled. "I'm surprised no one's killed *you* yet, with that smart mouth of yours."

"People have tried."

"So that's what the Berettas up the sleeves are for."

"They've saved my life more than once." She leaned back in the chair. For the first time, she was actually feeling comfortable around Lyles. She'd heard from the other suppliers that he was some kind of killing machine, and although that could be true, they neglected to tell her that he was also a funny, personable, and good-looking man.

He sat next to her. "Do you see yourself still hiding guns up your sleeves in twenty-five years?"

"Hell, no. I'll be retired and living on a dolphin ranch in Hawaii."

"Ride 'em, Flipper."

"I haven't been able to save much yet, but I will. You must have a lot socked away."

"Sure. But when you've got all the money you'll ever need, you start looking for other things to make life worth living."

"Like what?"

"Spiritual things."

She laughed.

"What's so funny?"

"You and I both are going to hell. You know that, don't you?"

"No."

"Surely you don't think you're heading for heaven."

"No. Heaven is coming here. Sooner than you realize."

The cell phone rang again, and she answered it. "Natalie here." She listened. "Hi, Ryland. I got in more of those German automatics you like. If you wanna take a look, it'll have to be tonight. They'll be gone by tomorrow morning."

She gave Lyles an encouraging glance, then wrote down an address. "See you at eleven."

She cut the connection and smiled. "We're in business."

"A corti-what?" Howe asked.

"A pulmicort corticosteroid inhaler," Joe replied. "Its trade name is Turbuhaler. Jesse Randall uses it twice a day for a respiratory condition."

They were in Lieutenant Gerald's office, keeping him posted on their progress. Joe handed Howe a memo page on which he'd jotted the inhaler name. "If Jesse's abductors have any interest in keeping him alive and well, they may try to get some of this soon, if they haven't already."

"Good work," Gerald said. "I trust there have been no more unexplained attacks on your person."

"Not on *my* person," Joe said. "But I should tell you about my afternoon with Stewart Dunning."

"Vince, you're missing it!" Nikki yelled from her spot in front of the television. She was watching *Titanic* for the fiftieth time.

"How many times do I really need to see Leonardo drown?" Vince said, drawing furiously on a large sketch pad.

"It's more exciting than watching you draw pictures all night."

"I'm still trying to help your father figure out some things. Like those shadow storms at Nelson's house before he was killed. I have some ideas that I'm going to run by him when he gets home."

"Yeah, and he'll shoot those down just like all your other ideas."

"Not this time."

The phone rang.

Nikki answered it. "Hello?"

A strong male voice spoke. "Hello, is this Nikki Bailey?"

"Yes. Who is this, please?"

"I'm Detective Mark Howe. I'm working with your father on a case right now."

"He told me about you."

He chuckled. "I won't even ask about that."

"My dad's not here right now, but if you want me to take a message—"

"No, I have a message for *you*. The battery died on your dad's cell phone, and he radioed in to ask if someone here would tell you to wait outside for him. You guys are going out to dinner."

"Aw, man. He said I could help him cook tonight."

"Don't look a gift horse in the mouth. I wish someone were taking *me* out to dinner."

She sighed. "Okay. Thank you."

"Sure thing."

She hung up and turned to Vince. "Dad wants me to meet him outside so he doesn't have to find a parking space. We're going out to eat. You wanna come with us?"

"Nah. I gotta meet someone a little later."

"Who?"

"A friend."

"A woman friend?"

"Yes, if it's any of your business."

"Oh." The corners of her mouth drooped.

He closed his sketch pad and playfully bopped her on the head with it. "She's a *friend*. Come on, let's get downstairs."

They were outside the building in less than two minutes, standing under a streetlight near the building's main entrance. A car approached from down the street, but Nikki and Vince saw that it was not her father's SUV.

"I'm charging your dad double time for this," Vince said. "It's cold out here."

Nikki zipped up her jacket. "Stop being such a baby."

"A baby? You think that I— Ow!" Vince clutched the side of his leg.

"What?"

Vince began to sway. "I feel . . . weird."

"Vince . . ." Nikki grabbed his arms to keep him from falling over. Even under the dim streetlight she could see the color draining from his face.

"It's hard to breathe," he whispered.

Something whistled past her ear.

She turned toward the street. The car had stopped, the driver's window was rolled down, and the shadowy figure behind the wheel was aiming a pistol at her.

Before she could react, Vince pulled her closer and angled his body between her and the car. "Run," he said.

"Not without you."

"Go!"

"We'll cut between the buildings."

The car door swung open.

Nikki yanked Vince's hands. "Come on."

She pulled him along with her, running toward the narrow walkway that separated her building from the abandoned shoe factory next door.

Something else whistled past her head. She turned and saw a small gleaming projectile about an inch long embedded in the wood molding of her building.

"Tranquilizer," Vince said, slurring the word slightly. "Hurry."

He pushed Nikki forward as he heard the car door close. They ran into the shadows of the narrow walkway and jumped over dozens of copper pipes that were strewn about. Footsteps followed behind them.

"He's coming," Nikki said. "Faster!"

Vince's eyes fluttered as he stumbled forward. "I can't do it. . . ."

"You have to!"

"Keep going, Nikki. Find someplace to hide."

"No!"

"He's after you. Not me. I have a surprise for him. Go!"

Nikki turned. The man, who was wearing jeans and a dark hooded sweater, was gaining on them.

"Go!" Vince said again.

She sprinted ahead. Almost immediately, she heard Vince fall. The pipes rolled and rattled as he hit the ground. But she didn't look back.

She emerged in the back courtyard of the old factory, where she'd played dozens of times even though her father had told her not to. The grass was overgrown, cropping up over and around abandoned industrial machinery.

She crawled inside a half-buried corrugated pipe, invisible to anyone who hadn't explored every inch of the cluttered old courtyard. She heard a scuffle in the dark walkway.

Vince.

Pipes rattled. She huddled in the darkness, eyes closed, praying that Vince would be all right.

The noise stopped. Silence. Then footsteps. Coming closer.

Someone moved through the tall grass of the courtyard. "Nikki," a familiar voice whispered.

Vince!

Nikki poked her head up. Vince was staggering through the courtyard, holding a three-foot section of copper pipe.

She crawled out of her hiding place and ran toward him. "I'm here!"

He hugged her.

"What happened?"

"I pretended to pass out, then grabbed this pipe and let him have it when he tried to get by me." He squinted in the darkness. "Is there another way out of here?"

"This way."

Nikki led him to a jagged hole in the back gate. They squeezed past the splinters and found themselves on a dark stretch of Ridley Avenue.

Nikki nervously glanced back at the courtyard. "Who was it?"

"I don't know. But he was definitely after you."

"Why?"

"Maybe your dad can tell us."

A pair of headlights speared them from the end of the block.

"Shit." Vince grabbed Nikki's hand.

"It's him!" Nikki said.

The car suddenly picked up speed.

Nikki tugged at Vince's arm. "Hurry!"

The sound of the car's engine filled her ears. She turned and saw it roaring toward them, kicking up a gray cloud of concrete dust.

Vince picked her up and staggered to a tall graffiti-marked concrete wall surrounding an industrial complex. He strained to lift her. "Pull yourself up, honey."

"But how will you—?"

"Do it!"

She gripped the top of the wall and swung her right leg over. She looked back. The car was only yards away. "Vince!"

He looked up at her with his now-heavy lids.

No . . .

Then, as she watched, the car roared straight into him and struck the wall. Nikki screamed. She fought to hold on as the wall shook from the impact.

A bus turned onto the block.

"Help me!" Nikki shouted. "Please!"

The car pulled back, then squealed away, leaving Vince's twisted body on the sidewalk. Nikki closed her eyes, trying to block out the horrible sight below her.

It didn't work.

Joe grabbed the clipboard out of the emergency room receptionist's hands. "Where's my daughter?"

"Sir, if you'll wait a minute—"

"I can't do that." He scanned the list and spotted Nikki's name. "E-Six. Where is that?"

"Sir—"

"Tell me now, or I'm going to barge through every one of those doors."

Joe heard a calm voice behind him. "It's okay. I'll take him back."

He turned to see the tall Latino doctor who had tended to Cy Gavin the other night. "How is she?"

"A few cuts, some minor bruises. Physically, she's fine. Emotionally, well . . ."

"Take me to her."

"This way." The doctor led him down the busy corridor. "It would be best not to make her relive the experience just yet."

"I'm not here as a cop," Joe said.

"I didn't think you were." He gestured toward an open door.

Joe ran into the room. Nikki was lying on the bed, staring up at the ceiling. She didn't seem to realize that he was in the room.

"Honey?"

She still didn't look at him. "Vince is dead, isn't he?"

Joe brushed the hair off her forehead. "Yes," he whispered.

"The man was after *me*."

"Shh."

She sobbed. "I thought I was gonna die. . . ."

"It'll be okay."

"No. It won't be okay for Vince."

He sat on the edge of the bed and held her. "I know, honey."

"I saw it happen. I *saw* it."

"Shh. Try to relax."

"Why did it happen?"

"I don't know, honey."

She buried her head in his chest, and he held her closer. There would be time later to get the whole story from her. The bus driver had given a good description of the car that had hit Vince, and the officers on the scene had already taken what little description of the suspect Nikki could give them.

Now she just needed her father.

An hour and forty-five minutes later, Joe left the room and walked past the reception desk.

Howe stood up in the waiting area. "How is she?"

"What are you doing here?"

"The lieutenant told me. I came right away."

"Someone identifying himself as you told my daughter to go outside."

"I heard. It wasn't me, Bailey."

"Where were you around six?"

"Are you serious?"

Joe stepped closer. "Where were you?"

"I was either with you talking to the lieutenant or in the conference room having my powwow with the FBI guys."

"Whoever did this probably got worked over with a metal pipe. There should be bruises."

Howe glared at him. "You want me to take off my goddamned shirt? Is that it?"

Joe held his glance a moment longer, then turned away. "No. I'm sorry. It's just—this is my *kid.*"

"I know. I have two girls. I'd go crazy if anyone tried to hurt them."

Joe sat in the waiting area. "She's sleeping now."

"Best thing for her."

"I just don't get it. Why her?"

Howe sat next to him. "Three possibilities: It was a random attack, somebody you've busted before is looking for payback, or someone wants to impede your present investigation."

"*Now* look who's quoting old academy lectures."

"Nope. This one's all mine."

"Which do you think it is?"

"It was too calculated to be random. He knew who you were, who I was, your schedule, all that. I've already asked Karen to run a check on the prison releases of your collars, but I'd guess most of them aren't the violent type."

"You're right."

"That leaves the third possibility. Maybe you're doing something right in this case, and it scares somebody."

"They think this will derail my investigation?"

"If they'd taken your daughter, would you even be thinking about Jesse Randall and Robert Nelson?"

"No."

"Even now is there anything you'd rather do than pack up the car and take her away from all this?"

Joe stared at him. "I guess some people *can* read minds."

"The question is, what now?"

"She needs me."

"You and only you?"

"She's been through a lot."

"Then you have a choice to make."

Joe pressed his temples with his fingertips. He hated Howe for making it all seem so clear-cut, so black and white.

Especially when it was anything but.

On a dark stretch of Monroe Drive, Natalie flipped up the hatchback of her Range Rover. "Anything catch your eye?"

Ryland peered into the carpeted hatch, where eight automatic handguns were displayed. He was a plump, round-faced man with beady black eyes and unnaturally white teeth. "Nice toys, gorgeous."

"Flattery will get you a break only if you want to buy all of them. Otherwise, I don't negotiate."

Ryland's smile practically blinded her. "All of them? Business has been good, but not *that* good. How much for the Glock?"

Two sharp whistles sounded from across the street. Natalie and Ryland glanced up to see Lyles, hands clasped behind his head, being pushed from the shadows by two men with guns.

Ryland turned toward Natalie. "Friend of yours?"

Natalie didn't respond.

"We found him hiding in the doorway," one of the men said to Ryland, holding up Lyles's Lanchester. "He had this on him."

Ryland glared at Lyles. "Who the hell are you?"

"Someone who can help you make some cash."

"I make plenty on my own."

"Not this easy."

Ryland whirled on Natalie. "What's the matter with you? You know the drill. You're supposed to be here alone."

"Just like you are."

"These guys are here for my protection. It looks like I needed it."

Lyles smiled. "Nonsense. I just want a business reference from you."

"That's why you're out here on a dark street at eleven o'clock at night?"

"That's pretty much it."

Ryland turned to Natalie. "Is this guy for real?"

"Listen to him."

"Okay." He gave her a suave smile. "For you, Natalie, I'll listen."

"Ugh. Please don't say that."

Lyles slowly took his hands down. "I'm looking for a chopper jockey to do a job."

"What makes you think I know one?"

"His name's Michael Kahn. I hear he's one of the best."

"Why would I ever need the services of a . . ." He feigned confusion. "Chopper jock?"

"Jockey. Can we stop being coy? Everyone in the Southeast knows your organization."

Ryland grinned. "Only in the Southeast?"

"And it's common knowledge that Kahn does some flying for you."

"So what do you want me to do about it?"

"Introduce me. It's the only way I can meet him. You know these guys, living out of their suitcases wherever their plane or chopper happens to be. They're nearly impossible to track down."

"Not for me," Ryland said.

"Which is why I'll give you ten thousand dollars to arrange a face-to-face meeting with this guy."

"Cash?"

"Nah, I'll cut you a check. And in the 'memo' section, I'll write 'For personal introduction to interstate drug trafficker.' Of course it'll be cash."

Ryland turned to one of his men. "Check him for a wire."

The man patted Lyles down, paying special attention to his chest and collar. Satisfied that he was clean, the man nodded to Ryland.

Lyles chuckled. "FYI, Ryland, listening devices have gotten very, very small. If I wanted to record you, I could be wearing a mike disguised as a shirt button. That pat-down was absolutely worthless, unless, of course, your guy was doing it for his own enjoyment."

The man glared at Lyles.

Ryland closed Natalie's hatchback. "There are other pilots, you know."

"Not like Michael Kahn."

"What are you planning? It must be pretty big."

"Big to me."

"Maybe I should just cut myself in for a piece of it."

"I'm already cutting you in. Ten thousand dollars' worth."

"Make it twenty-five, and I'll take you to see him within twenty-four hours."

"He's in town?"

Ryland checked his watch. "Not yet, but he soon will be."

Joe glanced around Nikki's bedroom, trying not to look dazed. In the past few hours he'd lost one of his best friends and almost lost his daughter. It didn't seem real.

Hold it together, man. Keep moving.

He picked up a stuffed bear and held it over Nikki's open suitcase. "Should I pack Mr. Cuddles?"

She shook her head. "I'm not five."

"Sorry."

She sat on her bed. "I wish you could come with me."

Joe caressed her cheek. Her face was still red from crying. "I'm sorry, honey. You said you were okay with this."

"I know."

"You'll have fun with Grandpa. He'll let you sit in the projection booth and eat yourself sick on Milk Duds and Jujubes. I forgot to ask what the movie is this week. If he'd known you were coming, I'm sure he would have booked *Breakfast at Tiffany's*."

She didn't look at him. "That's okay. I've seen the tape a million times."

He sat next to her. "You know why we're doing this, don't you?"

"Yeah."

"Until we know what's going on, you're not safe with me. I'll worry about you, and I won't be able to do my job."

"I know."

There was a sharp knock at the front door. Joe and Nikki walked into the living room, and before he could check the peephole, a voice called out: "It's Carla!"

He threw open the door, and Detective Carla Fisk rushed inside and hugged Nikki. "Oh, baby. I'm sorry."

Nikki squeezed her. "Hi, Carla."

Joe hadn't seen Carla since that night at Nelson's murder scene, but when he called and asked her for a last-minute favor, she didn't hesitate before agreeing.

She flashed Nikki a smile that was crooked, yellow, and wonderful. "Don't you worry about anything, hon."

Joe walked back to Nikki's room. "She's packed up and ready to go. My dad will be expecting you. I can't tell you how much this means to me."

"My pleasure," Carla drawled. "I have the next three days off, and I'm going to visit my sister. She lives in Savannah too. You're sure there's nothing else I can do?"

Joe came out with Nikki's suitcase and knapsack. "You're doing enough by taking her away from here. My dad was on the force, and he's one tough hombre. He can take good care of her."

"Yeah, I've heard stories about your old man." Carla subtly moved her jacket to the side just enough to show him her shoulder holster. "I can take good care of her too."

"Thanks, Carla."

They left the apartment, walked downstairs, and loaded the luggage into Carla's Chevy Nova.

Nikki hugged him. "When can I come back?"

"Soon, I promise."

"When?"

"I'm not sure, sweetheart. When we know it's safe."

"I'm gonna miss you."

"Nowhere near as much as I'm gonna miss you, honey." Joe raised her chin. "Don't give Grandpa too hard a time, okay? No matter how much you ask, there's no way he's going to run a week-long Leonardo DiCaprio film festival."

Carla opened her door. "That does it. Nikki and I are going to Florida instead. Did you bring your sunscreen, hon?"

Nikki smiled and got into the car. "Be careful, Daddy."

"You know I will. I'll call you tomorrow."

Carla started the car, and Nikki's gaze clung to Joe's until they drove out of sight.

Joe let out a long breath. He felt like bawling like a baby. He felt like crying for Nikki, for Vince . . .

Vince.

The poor kid. He'd always been there for anybody who needed him, eager to prove himself. Even though he had nothing to prove, at least in Joe's eyes.

Dammit. Anyone who thought there was any order or meaning in the universe needed only to look at deaths like Vince's. There was no meaning there.

Joe knew there was someone he still had to tell about Vince's death. Sam Brewster, who'd taken a chance and given Vince the job at his magic shop. He'd also given Vince more love and respect than anyone had ever given him in his life. Sam would take it hard.

Joe checked his watch: 11:45. Sam would be asleep, but it didn't matter. He'd want to know right away.

Joe pulled out his keys and walked toward his car.

15

Y ou're late," Kellner said as Joe strode into his classroom at 9:15 the next morning.

"Late for what?" Joe's head was throbbing. He'd spent most of the night at Sam's, looking through pictures and programs of Vince and his performances. It had been a long, sad night.

"You missed Suzanne Morrison's demonstration. It was in the testing room, just as you requested."

Joe turned away. Shit. He'd forgotten all about it. He was supposed to meet the team at eight.

"It was spectacular," Kellner said. "I was just about to watch her tape. Would you like to see?"

"Sure."

Kellner inserted the cassette into the classroom's video player. A shadowy infrared-enhanced image of the testing room appeared on-screen. Suzanne, Kellner, and three other members of the team were seated in the room. An empty chair tumbled across the floor, hit the wall, then rolled up to the ceiling.

It bounced off the ceiling twice, then fell to the floor.

Joe stepped back from the monitor. What the hell was that?

The entire table shook. An old spiritualist's trick, but Suzanne was nowhere near it. One by one, the members of Kellner's team backed away. Its vibrations became more and more intense until it abruptly flipped over with a sharp crack.

"How long ago was this?" Joe asked.

"We just finished fifteen minutes ago."

Joe flew out of the room and ran down the hallway. He gripped the testing room's doorknob. Locked.

He glanced up the corridor. Kellner was walking toward him. "Let me in there," Joe said. *"Now."*

Kellner pulled his keys from a retractable wire cord at his waist. "What do you think you're going to find?"

"I'll know when I see it."

Kellner unlocked the door, and Joe pushed past him. The table was still upside down, and the chair was lying against the wall.

Joe's eyes darted around the room. "Were you the last one in here?"

"We all left together. I locked the door myself."

Joe ran back into the hallway and grabbed a coat rack from a nearby classroom. He raced back into the testing room and rammed the rack through the suspended ceiling, knocking one of the panels out of place.

Kellner gasped. "What are you doing?"

Joe squinted at the opening, then knocked away several other ceiling panels with the rack. One of the panels almost struck Kellner on the head.

"You can't do this!" Kellner shouted.

"Watch me."

Within a minute Joe had knocked away every panel. He jumped on a chair and peered through the ceiling rails.

Nothing.

Other than an air duct and wiring for the light fixtures, the area was clear. He jumped off the chair.

"Satisfied?" Kellner asked caustically.

Joe picked up a chair and tossed it into the corridor.

"What was *that* for?"

Joe's only response was to pick up another chair and toss it out.

"Jesus, Bailey!"

Three of Kellner's students gathered in the doorway to watch.

"Get out of the way!" Joe said as he tossed a chair between the startled students. He gestured toward the table. "Can you guys give me a hand with this? I want to move it out."

The students stepped into the room but were stopped by Kellner's glare.

Seeing that no help was forthcoming, Joe gripped one of the table legs, slid it across the carpeted room, and pulled it through the door.

He gathered the remaining chairs and tossed them into the corridor. The room was empty.

"What now?" Kellner snapped.

Joe glanced around the room, sweat covering his face. He furiously kicked the metal carpet guard in the doorway. It finally came loose. He gripped the carpet's exposed edge and ripped it from the floor.

"Are you nuts?" Kellner shouted.

Joe pulled up the carpeting all the way to the far end of the room, pushing and kicking until it separated from the concrete slab beneath.

More students had gathered in the hallway, craning their necks to witness the Spirit Basher's meltdown.

Kellner pointed a pudgy finger at Joe. "If you don't stop this right now, I'm calling security."

Joe cut his hand on a carpet staple. Blood ran down his

fingers, but he couldn't feel it. He pressed the wound against his shirt. "Don't call security, call Professor Reisman. He'll back me up."

"Don't be so sure. He has a weird prejudice against the destruction of school property."

"Call him." Joe looked up to see that Kellner and the kids were staring at him with morbid fascination, the same way they might look at a man who was setting himself on fire.

He turned away and ripped up another section of carpet. There was an answer in there somewhere. There had to be.

Kellner backed away. "I'm calling Reisman right now. If he's not in, my next call will be to security. You can't do this."

"Looks like he's already done it," one of the students cracked.

Kellner shoved the kids back. "Everyone, get out of here now. You hear me? Go."

There was some reluctance on the part of the students, but they scattered. Kellner hurried back toward his office.

Joe pulled up the last of the carpet, pushing it all into a large clump in a corner of the room. There was nothing there. Just a big concrete slab and glue stains. How could that be?

He beat on the walls, listening for any hollow cavities. He knew he should sweep them with his sonar reader, but at the moment his car seemed so far away. And even without the reader he could tell there was nothing behind the damned walls.

Exhausted, he sat on the cement floor and nursed his bloody finger. His gaze wandered around the room. Christ, what a mess. Had he lost his mind?

"Are you all right?"

He looked up to see Suzanne Morrison in the corridor, carefully stepping over the ceiling panels. "What happened here?"

"Just looking for a lost contact lens," he deadpanned. "Don't you hate that?"

"Missed you this morning."

"Yeah." He let out a long breath. "This room was unattended a full fifteen minutes after your session. You could have removed your rigs."

"Without anyone seeing me?"

"The test was over. No one was looking."

"I didn't come here to argue with you."

"Then why did you come here?"

"I ran into some of the kids outside, and they told me you were in here. I wanted to invite you to a concert. One of my chamber pieces is being performed at Kennesaw State University. I thought you and your daughter might like to come."

He stared at her in bemusement. "Do you realize how weird that invitation is under the circumstances? I just tore apart this test facility because of you, and now you're inviting me to a concert."

She smiled. "You can't help being stubborn. Do you want to come or not?"

"Nikki can't make it. She's out of town."

"What about you?"

"I really don't know."

"If it's crowds you're worried about, believe me, it won't be an issue."

Joe managed a smile.

She knelt next to him. "You look tired, Joe. Really tired. Are you sure you're okay?"

He closed his eyes. He still hadn't absorbed it all: Vince's death, the thought of almost losing Nikki, and his complete inability to explain Jesse's and Suzanne's tricks. He had never felt so weak, so powerless.

"Just tell me how you do it," he said.

"You know how I do it, Joe. Even if you don't want to admit it to yourself yet."

"I *don't* know. I wish I did."

"I wish you did too." She stood and moved toward the door. "There will be a ticket for you at the box office tonight. I hope you can make it."

He nodded.

"Get some rest, okay?"

He didn't reply. His eyes were fixed on one of the ceiling panels lying on the floor of the hallway. He walked over and picked it up.

"What is it?" she asked.

He held the panel up to the light. There were four circular indentations in its soft upper surface, forming the corners of a square. "Something was resting on this."

"My hydraulic crane," Suzanne said sarcastically. "You caught me."

Joe shook his head. He dragged a chair back into the room, jumped on it, and peered through the ceiling. A shaft of light appeared about thirty yards away, poking through another dislodged ceiling tile in another room.

He jumped off the chair and quickly walked down the hallway. Suzanne followed him as he measured his paces to a storage closet. He tried the knob. Locked.

"What did you see?" she asked.

Joe pulled out two rigid pieces of wire from his wallet and began working on the lock. "Maybe nothing."

There was a sharp click, and he turned the knob and opened the door.

Suzanne nodded her approval. "I'm impressed."

"Don't be," Joe said. "I used to be able to do this submerged upside down in a tank of water."

He walked into the janitor's closet and glanced up at the ceiling. One of the tiles was slightly askew over a high shelf. He turned over a bucket and stood on it, peering at the top shelf. There were four marks on the dusty surface.

"I'm telling you," Suzanne said, "I've never been in here."

Joe stepped off the bucket. "I believe you. You'd have no reason to put a VCR in here."

"A VCR?"

Joe walked back toward the testing center, and she followed. "I think so. Something the size of a VCR was sitting up there until recently. If that's the case, I have a pretty good idea what was sitting on that panel above the testing center."

They walked into the testing center's observation booth and he lifted a small receiver unit that picked up signals from the array of wireless video cameras. He placed the receiver on the ceiling tile, and the feet perfectly matched the size and layout of the indentations.

"We have a winner," Suzanne said.

"I think somebody was using a receiver unit to intercept the tests done here and record them on a VCR in the closet down the hall. They probably strung a video cable from here to there."

"Someone else was recording my test sessions?"

"Yours, Jesse Randall's, everyone's."

"Who would do that?"

"Good question."

Joe went to headquarters, where almost every cop he met asked about Nikki. He knew they weren't just paying him lip service; they cared. That spirit was one of the things that had brought him to the force in the first place.

He bypassed the third floor and went straight to the A/V lab, where a technician helped him grab a frame from one of Jesse's test sessions. The video printer spit out the enlarged picture, and Joe took it down to Jennifer Li, a sergeant in the special investigations unit. Jennifer cracked most of her cases seated at a large computer workstation, where she pieced together paper trails with blazing speed. She also possessed a memory that rivaled the array of hard drives at her fingertips. A glance at a tire tread was usually all she needed to reel off the make and manufacturer, and a tiny piece of a receipt was often enough for her to pinpoint the retailer that had issued it.

She looked up from her monitor. "How's your girl, Joe?"

"Shaken up pretty bad, but she'll be okay. I need your help."

"Anything."

He handed her the print, a zoomed-in image of the red-haired man at one of the test sessions. "I'm trying to figure out who this guy is."

Her eyes zeroed in on the keys clipped to the man's belt loop. "You want me to look at the key chain?"

"Yes. See that bar-code card attached to it? Is that a supermarket discount card?"

She picked up a magnifying glass and examined the picture closely. "I don't think so. It's a little too large. It could be a health club membership tag or . . ."

"Or?"

She moved her mouse over the pad and brought up a page of bar-code key tags on her monitor. She scrolled down the collection, comparing the low-resolution print to the images on her screen.

"What are those?"

"Security cards. You wave them at a scanner to get into building garages, elevators, offices, those kinds of places."

"There must be thousands of buildings in this city that use cards like that."

"Yes, but there are only a few dozen security companies that service those buildings." She clicked on one of the cards to en-large it, then held the picture next to the monitor.

"It's a match!"

"Same shape, same color, same lettering position," she said. "It belongs to Apex Security. They're pretty small. I don't think they service many properties."

"Looks like I win."

"What do you mean?"

"Howe thought it would take you at least thirty minutes to run this down. I bet him you could do it in less than five."

As Lyles and Natalie drove into the tiny Acworth airstrip, the last traces of sunlight disappeared behind a nearby row of pines. Ryland was already there, flanked by his two bodyguards.

"He's not expecting me," Natalie said. "You should have come alone."

"I need to know you're not working with him to set me up."

"So if he tries to kill you and take your money, you'll use me as a shield?"

"Something like that."

"You don't know who you're dealing with. If that's what he wants, he wouldn't hesitate to blast right through me to get to you."

"I don't know. Seems like he has a crush on you."

"Doesn't matter. He'd kill his own mother if it meant more money in his pocket."

They pulled alongside Ryland's car and climbed out. Lyles glanced around the deserted airstrip. "Where's Kahn?"

Ryland crossed his arms. "On his way. You hear that?"

Lyles cocked his head, and he could hear the staccato rhythm of a helicopter engine in the distance.

"You got my money?" Ryland asked.

Lyles tossed him a banded stack of fifty-dollar bills.

Ryland looked at it with disgust. "This is bullshit. We agreed on twenty thousand. There's not more than two or three here."

"It's three. I'll get you the rest after I've met Kahn."

"That wasn't part of the deal."

"It is now."

The bodyguards moved into alert mode as the chopper's engine grew louder.

Ryland stared at Lyles. "If I don't get the rest of it, you're not going to live through the night."

"I wouldn't expect anything different. I just need some assurance I'm going to get what I want out of this transaction."

The rotor suddenly grew louder, and the helicopter roared over the treetops. It was a red and white Crown Windrider, better suited for corporate charters than drug runs, Lyles thought. It hovered over the tarmac and slowly came down for a smooth, beautifully controlled landing.

Lyles's gaze narrowed on the pilot.

Was it you? Did you take him from us?

The rotor powered down. The pilot kicked open the cockpit door and ambled toward them with a shit-eating grin on his face. What a piece of work, Lyles thought. Michael Kahn was a thin, long-haired man who wore silver-painted cowboy boots and a plaid flannel shirt that covered a tie-dyed T-shirt. A ridiculously long walrus mustache covered half his face. He looked like the result of a bizarre cowboy-hippie gene-splicing experiment.

Ryland playfully pounded fists with Kahn. "I heard you made the delivery this morning. Good work."

"Easyville, big man." Kahn's southern accent was about as thick as it could get without being completely unintelligible.

Ryland pointed at Lyles. "Here's the guy I was telling you about."

Kahn smiled even more broadly. "Hey there, friend. I hear you got some work for me!"

"Maybe," Lyles said. "Ryland tells me you're pretty good."

"Pretty good? Was Jimi Hendrix a *pretty good* guitar player? Is Jack Nicholson a *pretty good* actor? Is—"

Lyles cut him off. "Okay, I get it. I do have a job, but I'm not sure if you have experience in this kind of thing."

"Friend, I have experience in pret' near every kind of thing."

"Kidnapping?"

Kahn's smile vanished.

It was him.

"Kidnapping?" Kahn said it as if he'd never heard the word before.

"Yeah. Me and another guy make the grab, you airlift the three of us out. Easyville?"

Kahn nervously scratched his cheek. "Uh—I don't do that shit, friend. You'd better look somewhere else."

"No, I think you're just the man I'm looking for."

"Bullshit." Kahn turned toward Ryland. "What the hell's going on here? Do you even know who this guy is?"

Ryland obviously didn't understand his anger. "He wants to throw some work your way, man. Listen to him."

"Fuck you." Kahn walked back to his helicopter.

Ryland nodded to his bodyguards, and they advanced on Lyles.

In one smooth motion Lyles reached into his holster, gripped the handle of his Lanchester, and squeezed off five quick shots through the back of his jacket as he spun around. One bodyguard fell dead and the other lay twitching on the ground.

As Lyles whirled toward Ryland, he caught sight of Natalie holding her Berettas. Who was she siding with? Before he could decide, two shots rang out and Natalie fell to the ground.

Ryland had put two bullets into her with his snub-nosed .38 revolver.

Funny. Lyles had him figured for an automatic.

He killed Ryland with one clean shot through the mouth. The bullet broke his front left tooth in half before demolishing the entire back of his head.

Lyles spun toward the helicopter. "Don't move, Kahn."

Kahn stood at the open cockpit door, again wearing that idiot grin.

"What's so funny?"

"I was starting to think you were a cop. Shows what I know."

"Get on the ground, arms and legs spread to the four corners. Don't even think of reaching for the handgun you're carrying."

"Whatever you say, friend."

As Kahn spread out on the ground, he was still grinning. Crazy bastard.

Lyles knelt beside Natalie. She'd taken hits in the arm and right torso. She was still conscious. "Goddamn, it hurts. What's your expert opinion?"

He examined the wounds. "The arm's nothing. I can't tell about your side. Too much . . ." His voice trailed off.

"Too much blood?"

He nodded.

"Great. And the one person who can help me will be five thousand dollars richer if he lets me die."

He applied pressure to the chest wound. "I pay my debts. If it comes to that, is there anyone I should give the money to?"

She closed her eyes. "No. No one. Pretty pathetic, huh?"

"Just relax."

"Jesus, I sold Ryland that gun."

"Are you having trouble breathing?"

"Not really. It just kind of . . . burns."

After glancing up to make sure Kahn was behaving himself, Lyles shed his jacket and tied it snugly around Natalie's chest. "That should slow the flow of bleeding. You could come out of this okay."

"Get me to a hospital."

"No. Too many questions. Surely you know someone who can fix you up."

"Yeah, but he charges a fortune. He'll eat up all my profits."

"But he'll give you your life. We're going there."

"What about your friend?"

Lyles stood and walked to where Kahn was lying on the ground. He struck him three times on the base of the skull, knocking him unconscious.

Lyles turned to Natalie. "He'll come with us."

Joe walked through the underground parking garage at Woodlake Downs, an exclusive Lenox Road high-rise condominium building. A phone call to Apex Security had told him that six buildings in the metro Atlanta area were using their card system. Four were downtown office buildings, one was a hair-care-product depot in Mableton, and one was this pricey residence that was a favorite of high-powered young executives and Hollywood actors shooting films in the city. He and Howe would check the businesses tomorrow, but Joe decided to swing by Woodlake Downs on his way home from work, when there would be a greater chance of catching the residents at home. He wasn't in a hurry to get back to his apartment. He knew it would be difficult to find both Nikki and Vince gone.

He walked through the garage's aisles of cars. His head hurt; it hadn't stopped throbbing since he first found out about Vince. He'd just spoken to Professor Reisman, who was understandably concerned about Joe's destruction of the parapsychology testing center. Reisman knew what had happened the previous night, and he'd diplomatically suggested that Joe take a few days off from his university work. Reisman clearly thought he was crazy.

Joe rounded a corner in the garage. There it was. A black BMW motorcycle, the same one that had almost run him over outside Blues Junction.

He'd found the red-haired guy.

Joe pulled out his notebook and jotted down the license plate number. He'd have somebody on the evening watch run it through, and—

"So you found me, Mr. Bailey."

Joe glanced up.

The red-haired man stepped from the shadows of the garage, wearing a bemused smile.

Joe dropped the pen and paper. "Keep your hands where I can see them."

The man spread his palms outward.

"Step closer."

The man slowly walked toward Joe. "I'm here in the spirit of cooperation," he said in a middle-European accent. "I've done nothing wrong."

Joe pulled out his handcuffs. "You assaulted a police officer."

"I was not yet prepared to speak candidly." He nodded toward the cuffs. "Are those really necessary?"

"Afraid so." Joe yanked the man's hands behind him and clasped the cuffs around his wrists. "Tell me, are you prepared to speak candidly now?"

"I wouldn't have let you see me if I wasn't. My name is Claude Zurcher. My employer has authorized me to be completely forthcoming."

Joe turned Zurcher around to face him. "Your employer?"

"The Lindstrom Institute for Paranormal Studies in Bern, Switzerland."

"What do you do?"

"I'm a researcher. It's my job to travel the world, searching for subjects worthy of my institute's attention."

"Subjects like Jesse Randall?"

"Precisely."

"I suppose your institute was where Robert Nelson wanted to take Jesse."

"Yes."

"Why did Nelson need you? Jesse was the best thing that ever happened to his career. Did you offer him a job?"

Zurcher hesitated. "Am I under arrest, Mr. Bailey?"

"At the moment, yes. Depending what you tell me, you may improve your position."

Zurcher leaned against a parked Mercedes while Joe read him his Miranda rights. "I waive my right to counsel," he said. "I didn't offer Dr. Nelson a job, but I did give him something he needed very much."

"Money?"

"Yes. Mr. Bailey, you of all people can appreciate just how difficult it is to find instances of genuine paranormal phenomena. My institute is extraordinarily well supported by public and private funds, but that support will come to an end without results. My job has been to bring in subjects who will provide those results."

"Even if you have to resort to bribery?"

"Incentives."

"Whatever you want to call it, Nelson took your money to influence Ms. Randall to let Jesse go to Switzerland for your institute to study."

"Yes, but to Dr. Nelson's credit, he turned me down when I

first approached him. He wasn't interested in my offer. Then he made a mistake with that Rawlings girl. He stood there, doing nothing, while that faker worked on her. I was watching his activities closely at the time, so it was a simple matter to piece together what had happened."

"You spoke to the girl's parents and persuaded them to press Nelson for a settlement."

Zurcher raised an eyebrow. "You've done your homework. Yes, I convinced them that they were entitled to some measure of compensation. There's nothing wrong with that. I thought it might encourage Dr. Nelson to take me up on my offer. To my disappointment, he merely channeled the money through his program."

Joe nodded. "Until Roland Ness's audit, when he suddenly found himself in the position of having to repay a hundred and sixty thousand dollars to the coffers. Your offer must have looked pretty good to him then."

"Very. Suddenly he was most eager to take our money. I was allowed to participate in the sessions, and he began to put pressure on Jesse to join us at our institute."

Joe looked away. Christ. Jesse never could have imagined the trouble his tricks would stir up. "Why didn't you just offer the money to Jesse and his mother? They're not wealthy people. They might have taken you up on it."

"It's against the institute's policy to offer payment to our subjects."

"Because it's not ethical?" Joe said caustically.

"Because we don't want to give the subjects a financial motivation to cheat. We provide food, lodging, and some incidental expenses. Nothing more."

"Except to Nelson, who made out like a bandit."

Zurcher shrugged.

"Did your institute abduct Jesse?"

"No, we don't operate that way. For one thing, we would be unable to publicize our studies, which is precisely why we want him. And if we did have Jesse, I would have no reason to remain here. I would be in Bern, enjoying what's left of the opera season."

"Why *are* you still here?"

"I'm hoping the boy will soon be found. Mr. Bailey, I know how suspicious I must seem to you. That's why my institute gave me permission to cooperate with you in every way possible. We're willing to do anything we can to help you."

"Then tell me, did you plant a video receiver above the testing lab to intercept Jesse's sessions?"

Zurcher looked puzzled. "No. Someone did that?"

Joe grabbed Zurcher's arm and pulled him toward the garage entrance. "You got anything else for me?"

"No. Judging from our trajectory, I suppose I haven't sufficiently improved my position."

"We're going to the police station. We'll contact the Lindstrom Institute in Switzerland, and if what you say checks out, then we can talk about where you stand."

Lyles drove to the side entrance of Natalie Simone's apartment building. It was 10:16 P.M., and he and Natalie had spent the evening in Cat Morgan's basement operating room in Midtown. Cat specialized in emergency procedures on gang members, thieves, and other criminals who could not afford to have their gunshots and other injuries reported to the police. Lyles wasn't sure of his qualifications, but Cat performed his operation on Natalie with the skill and confidence of an expert surgeon. His fee was one of Natalie's choice semiautomatic handguns, payable in advance. Before the procedure, he'd given Lyles a syringe loaded with enough sedatives to keep Michael Kahn safely knocked out in the trunk. Kahn was still there, but Lyles knew it was almost wake-up time.

Natalie gripped the car door handle. "Thank you. You could have left me to die out there."

"Yes, I could have."

"Why didn't you? You got everything from me that you needed."

He stared at the dashboard for a moment. "Today. But the only way to stay alive in my business is to have a large network of people you can count on, in every corner of the world. Someday I may need you again."

"That's why you saved me?"

"Yes."

"I don't believe you. You don't need me."

"Then why'd I do it?"

"I don't know. But I hope the guy in the trunk helps you find what you're looking for."

"I hope so too."

"It must be really important to you. More important than money."

"It is."

"What if you don't find it? What then?"

"I can't even consider that possibility. I can't go back."

"Back to where?"

He finally looked up from the dashboard. "You'd better go inside and get some rest."

"I guess this is good-bye."

He handed her a thick fold of bills. "Here's your money. Thank you, Natalie. Do you need help up to your place?"

She opened her door. "No. Good luck."

"Good-bye."

She held her arm and gingerly walked up the stairs to her apartment.

. . .

Joe sat in his car on a dark street in Morningside, letting the engine idle. It had begun to rain, but he still didn't want to go home.

Claude Zurcher's story had checked out. The director of the Lindstrom Institute had backed up everything he said and promised to keep Zurcher in Atlanta while the case was still being investigated. Joe had just gotten off the phone with Howe, bringing him up to speed. Howe had seemed a little upset that Zurcher was allowed to go home, but of course he was the one who'd taken the punch to the stomach at the club.

After Joe had left the station, he called Nikki. She was still upset, of course, but it sounded as if her grandpa was doing his best to keep her occupied. She didn't want to talk about Vince. The feelings were too raw, too painful. Joe felt the same way.

Joe glanced at the small house on the other side of the sidewalk. Why was he here? Before he could come up with an answer, he cut the engine and climbed out of the car. It was one of those cold, miserable winter rains, but he could barely feel it. He walked to the house's front door and rang the doorbell.

Suzanne Morrison answered, wearing sweat pants, socks, and a worn *South Park* T-shirt. She squinted at him. "Joe?"

His hair was soaked, and water droplets ran down his face. "Hi."

"Hi."

"Sorry I didn't make it to your concert."

"I really didn't think you would. After I saw you today, I heard on the news what happened with your daughter and Vince. I'm sorry."

"Thanks."

A gust of wind sprayed him with a sheet of cold rain.

She opened the door wide. "I'm sorry, come in."

He stomped on the mat and walked inside.

"Take your coat off and I'll hang it over the radiator."

He shed his jacket and handed it to her.

"I'm glad you came over," she said as she left the room. "I was worried about you this morning."

He smiled ruefully. "And you're not now?"

She laughed in the other room.

"It's been an insane couple of days," he said. "I guess I was just going along for the ride."

She came out and tossed him a towel. "Dry your hair. Would you like some decaf?"

"That would be great."

He followed her to the kitchen, and they made small talk while she brewed a pot. They sat at her table, and she warmed her hands on the mug. "What brings you here?"

He looked down into his coffee. "I guess I didn't want to go home, and I felt like talking. I remembered that we did that pretty well."

"I thought so."

"I'm sorry you had to see me like that this morning. I went a little crazy. When I couldn't figure out how you did it, I guess it brought back the frustration I've been feeling over Jesse Randall and Nelson's murder. If I'd been able to figure out how Jesse does his tricks, he might not have been abducted."

"You can't blame yourself."

"Sure I can. And if what happened to Vince and Nikki had anything to do with this case, I—"

"Don't beat yourself up, Joe."

He shook his head. "A little boy has been kidnapped and one of my best friends is dead because I haven't been able to do my job. I think that's pretty good cause for beating myself up."

"You'll do your job."

"It's this goddamned helpless feeling. I haven't felt this helpless since—"

"Since your wife died?"

He nodded.

"Did you come here tonight to talk to her?"

He stared at her in shock. "No," he said sharply. "I told you—"

"I'm sorry. Forget I mentioned it. I guess I misread you."

Some of the tension left him. "I may be acting crazy, but I'm not about to go off that particular deep end."

"Joe, what do you think happens to us when we die?"

"Nothing."

"Just like that? We cease to exist?"

"Do you have any evidence to the contrary?"

"Yes. I've shown it to you."

"We won't get into *that* right now. I've seen nothing that convinces me that human existence continues when our bodies fail."

"Even if it wasn't for Daphne, I could never believe that. You think that all of our thoughts, emotions, dreams, and desires are just . . . biology?"

"Yes."

"What about all those people with near death experiences and the tunnel of light they see?"

"First of all, only a small percentage actually report that. And there's a lot of evidence to suggest that it's just the effect of overstimulated neurons in the brain. A few G's in a flight simulator will give you the same effect."

"More biology."

"That's the way it looks."

She studied him. "Feeling the way you do . . . it must have been especially horrible to lose your wife."

"It would have been horrible no matter what."

"A lot of people take comfort in the thought of a hereafter, Joe."

"A lot of people get taken advantage of."

"You would never let that happen to yourself."

"Damn right."

She smiled. "You're not investigating me in your capacity as a police detective, are you?"

"No. Purely as a consultant to the Landwyn parapsychology department. Roland Ness may get a little upset that all the money he's sunk into the program still hasn't produced any results, but what the hell. He's a billionaire."

Joe took a sip of his coffee. "So, if you'd care to enlighten me as to how you pull off your séances, there will be no legal repercussions."

She laughed, a full-bodied laugh he found enormously appealing. "Thank you, but no. Even if there was something to tell, you didn't come here for that."

"What did I come here for?"

"Hmm. Aside from the obvious, I think that tonight, after losing your friend and being reminded of your wife, you wanted to be with the one person who might make you believe that there could be an afterlife."

He stood up. "That's ridiculous."

"I don't make you feel that way? Not even one-hundredth of one percent?"

"No."

She stood and moved toward him. "I think you're lying. To me and to yourself."

"Think what you want. And what did you mean by 'aside from the obvious'?"

"The obvious. You show up at my door after midnight on a rainy night. . . ."

"I had no intention of—"

She placed two fingers over his lips, silencing him. "You're lying to yourself again."

She was right, he realized. At least about this.

He slowly, carefully drew her close. God, she felt good, filling the emptiness, banishing the loneliness. . . . "Is this okay with you?"

She slid her arms around him and pulled him closer. "It's more than okay."

He kissed her, oblivious of everything but her smooth, warm lips and the sound of the pounding rain outside.

Michael Kahn's eyes bulged and his tears and snot ran onto the duct tape plastered over his mouth.

Lyles had been working on him for twenty minutes, even though he suspected that Kahn had been willing to talk after five. By laying the groundwork with twenty minutes of excruciating pain, Kahn would be all the more cooperative and less likely to want to return to his agony. They were in a densely wooded area in Cherokee County, not unlike the area where he'd laid that television reporter to rest. That seemed like a lifetime ago, Lyles thought.

He had been performing a variety of techniques on Kahn, ranging from pressure-point manipulation to simple slugs across the jaw. Different people responded to different stimuli, so there was no telling what would work best with Kahn.

Lyles peeled the tape off Kahn's mouth. "It *was* you who flew away with Jesse Randall."

Kahn wiped his sore mouth on Kahn's shirtsleeve. "What the hell do you want, friend?"

"In case you hadn't noticed, I'm not your friend. I was on that helicopter ride too."

Kahn's eyes widened. "You're him?"

Lyles nodded. "You could have killed the boy that night."

"No way. I knew what I was doing."

"Where is he?"

"How the hell should I know? I was strictly a pilot for hire."

"You'll have to do better than that."

"Look, I don't know who hired me, why they wanted him, or where they took him. It was none of my business, and I just plain didn't care."

"You'd better start caring . . . friend." Lyles pressed his thumb into the base of Kahn's throat. When Kahn began to turn a pale shade of blue, Lyles pulled away.

Kahn coughed a good thirty seconds before speaking. "Look, man. I only talked to three guys. The guys I was supposed to pick up in the chopper. I got a phone number for one of them. It went to a voice-mail system. Maybe that'll help you."

"Anyone can hire a voice-mail service anonymously."

"It's all I got."

Lyles thought about it. "Okay. It may be enough."

"If you kill me, you're gonna have a price on your head so big that every contract killer from Boston to Miami will come looking for you."

Lyles smiled. "You think a lot of yourself, don't you?"

"Some very powerful people depend on my services."

"You're going to call that number, and I'm going to tell you exactly what to say."

The shadows had stolen his breath.

Jesse was underground again, trying to kick and claw his way to the surface, but he wasn't moving. The shadows were swirling around him, laughing, taunting, teasing. . . .

They had his breath, and they weren't giving it back.

He was suffocating.

Jesse . . . Jesse . . . Jesse . . .

This voice sounded different.

Jesse . . .

His eyes snapped open.

Myrna was leaning over him. "Jesse . . . honey, are you okay?"

It took him a moment to realize where he was. The room's lighting had been dimmed, as it always was when he was expected to sleep.

"Hard to breathe," he wheezed.

"You've just been having a bad dream. Sit up and have some water."

Jesse pulled himself up and took the plastic cup from her. He gulped the water but coughed it up before he could finish. "I'm sorry."

She wiped the water off her gauze blouse. "Are you okay?"

He leaned against the wall. "Still hard to breathe. I think I need my inhaler."

"You use an inhaler?"

"My mama makes me use it."

Myrna quickly glanced at the observation window. "What kind? What's it called?"

Jesse took a few quick breaths and swallowed hard. "It's a prescription my doctor gives me. My mama has to go to the drugstore to get it. I think it's called a Turbuhaler."

The door swung open. It would be Charles lumbering into the room, angry because he'd been stirred from a sound sleep.

But it wasn't Charles.

Myrna's eyes widened in shock. "What are you doing here?"

Jesse couldn't believe what he was seeing. It was the hotshot lawyer who'd come to his house.

Jesse sat up as hope surged through him. "Did you come to take me home?"

"I'm afraid not, Jesse," Stewart Dunning said.

16

As Joe lay in Suzanne's bed, listening to the gentle rain outside, he tried to understand how it had happened.

He never would have imagined his day could end this way. Lying nude with Suzanne, holding her close. Smelling her thick, shiny hair.

There had been no one since Angela. Until just seconds before he kissed Suzanne, he couldn't have even considered himself with anyone else. Least of all with a spiritualist he was supposed to debunk.

He checked his watch: 2:15.

"Regrets?" Suzanne asked.

"No."

"Give it a few hours." She smiled.

"I don't suppose you were so incredibly overwhelmed with my technique that you're now willing to explain to me how you perform your séances."

She laughed. "So *that's* how the Spirit Basher gets results."

"If I depended on that, I'd be reading parking meters by now."

"I beg to differ."

He leaned closer. "You realize that I will find out how you do those things."

"You're wasting your time, but everybody's entitled to a hobby."

"You've just been lucky. I've been distracted."

"I know." She stroked the hair on his chest. "You probably didn't notice that I was attracted to you the first minute we met."

"No, but when it comes to that kind of thing, I've always had the worst radar in the world." He paused. "I liked you too."

"I thought so. My radar is pretty accurate."

He smiled. "And Nikki's crazy about you. She would have loved to see your concert."

"There will be others. Hopefully." Her tone suddenly sobered. "Anything on Jesse Randall?"

"No. I have a feeling my department is getting squeezed out of the investigation. The FBI is all over it, and they're not known for being the most cooperative bunch."

"That's too bad."

"I can't do anything about it. My assignment is to concentrate on Nelson's murder."

She picked up a sketch pad from her night table.

He smiled. "You're going to draw my picture?"

"Only if you want to see yourself as a stick figure. I've been sketching some ideas about the levitation effects at Nelson's house before he died."

"I have some ideas about that too."

"Me first. Would you like to see?"

"Sure."

She showed Joe her drawings. "I've never actually been to his place, but almost all the shadow storm activity took place on the first floor, right?"

"Right. How did you know?"

"Nelson's girlfriend has been talking about it on every TV news show in town, and one of the newspapers printed pictures of the kitchen. I'm surprised you'd let journalists traipse through a crime scene."

"We didn't. Those shots were taken last year, when Nelson hosted a fund-raising dinner."

"Well, this morning, when I saw that you'd knocked out all the ceiling panels in the parapsychology testing lab, it gave me an idea."

Joe smiled. "Other than the possibility that I'd lost my mind?"

"Yes. Nelson had a suspended ceiling on the first floor. Is it possible that there's framing above the panels strong enough to support someone's weight?"

"Not only possible, but definite. I've seen it."

Her face lit up. "Really?"

"There's a space of about twenty inches before you hit the true ceiling. More than enough room for someone to crawl."

Suzanne noted the height on her sketch pad. "The newspaper wasn't clear on this, but by any chance were all the levitating objects on high shelves, within a few feet of the ceiling?"

"Every single one. They were either on upper shelves or, in the case of the pots and pans, hanging on a ceiling-mounted rack."

"What about access?"

"There's an entrance in the laundry room just off the kitchen. It could have been possible to gain entry from there and move through the ceiling to the kitchen and den. The only barrier is a load-bearing wall on the far side of the den."

"Ten'll get you twenty the phenomenon didn't go beyond that wall."

"You got it. And Nelson and his girlfriend never actually saw the objects rise off the shelves. They came flying out of rooms.

Whoever was in the ceiling could have reached down, picked up the objects, and tossed them. By the time Nelson went into the room to check things out, the ceiling panel could have been replaced and the person would be safely out of sight."

"What about the pots and pans? Didn't they actually see them swaying back and forth, clattering into each other?"

"My guess would be fishing line. A length could have been tied to the handle of just one pan, then pulled from the ceiling, around the edge of a panel. If it was tied to a pan in the middle, the line would've been tough to spot. As the pan swayed back and forth, it would create a domino effect. Pretty soon all the pans would be moving and clanging."

She let the sketchbook fall into her lap. "Dammit, and I hoped *I'd* be telling *you* something."

"I actually got some help from Vince. Nikki showed me some sketches he'd made last night, just before . . ." Joe looked away.

"Vince really admired you."

"I admired him. He'd really pulled his life together." Joe sighed. "If you really want to help me, come up with an explanation for Nelson's murder."

"That was upstairs. I haven't figured it out yet."

"That makes two of us."

Suzanne shot him a sideways glance. "How are you so sure *I* didn't do it? I knew Nelson, and I have a pretty good idea how to do this stuff."

"You have an alibi. Members of the spook squad observed you doing two back-to-back séances that night."

"You checked me out?"

"Howe did. We checked out all of Nelson's so-called discoveries who might have had the skill to pull this off."

She pulled away slightly. "I don't know how I feel about that."

"If you were in our position, wouldn't you do the same thing?"

She thought about it. "You're right. You'd have to eliminate all of us from consideration."

"Which we have. Believe me, I wouldn't be here tonight if I thought there was any chance you did it, Suzanne."

She snuggled closer. "Well, as long as you don't think I'm a killer, I guess it's okay that you think I'm a fraud."

Stewart Dunning sat on the padded floor beside Jesse. "How are you feeling? Better?"

"Yeah." He pulled his blankets around him. Myrna had given him a hot, salty liquid to drink, and it no longer hurt to breathe.

"Good. We'll see about getting you that inhaler. You should have asked for it before. We want you to be comfortable."

Jesse scowled. "It's your fault that I'm here."

"It's not just me. And it's for your own protection."

"Protection from what?"

"From everyone and everything that could hurt you. There's only so much we can do for you out there. People fear what they don't understand. We were content to watch you from afar until Dr. Nelson's death brought you so much attention. We can't risk losing you."

"You and who else? Myrna and Charles?"

"There are thousands of us all over the world. We're the Millennial Prophets, Jesse. You're one of us, even if you don't realize it."

"Are you crazy?"

"We wish we could let you go home, but that's impossible right now."

"I want to see my mama."

"I'm sorry. Maybe later."

Jesse felt a surge of anger. "Don't you make me mad."

Dunning wasn't fazed. "You frighten Myrna and Charles, but

you don't scare me, Jesse. Nelson's death was a good example of what you're capable of, but you were asleep at the time. You can't consciously produce phenomena of that magnitude yet. Otherwise you would have broken Charles in two by now, and this room would no longer be standing."

"How do you know? Maybe I was holding back."

"For what reason? You'd do anything to get out of here, wouldn't you?"

"Maybe, maybe not."

Dunning smiled faintly. "Then I guess I'm taking my life into my hands. It's worth the risk to help ensure your place in the world. We want only what's best for you, Jesse."

"Going home would be best for me."

"Not now."

"When?"

"When the Vicar says you can."

"The Vicar?"

"The leader of our sect. You're important to him too. He's been watching you here, and he'll chart your course."

The door swung open, and another man entered the room. He had gray hair and a white beard, and he looked familiar. Jesse remembered seeing him on TV.

"Here he is," Dunning said. "He's been very eager to meet you."

The man, smiling uneasily, leaned over and extended his right hand. "Hello, Jesse. My name is Roland Ness."

Roland Ness. Here. Jesse wasn't sure what Ness did, but he knew that he was a billionaire. He'd once seen Roland Ness high-five the president. Jesse remembered it because both men seemed so clumsy, and they came close to missing each other's hands.

He and Mama had laughed and laughed about that.

Ness leaned down and whispered, "It's a pleasure to meet you, Jesse."

Jesse shuddered. Ness's voice almost sounded like one of the whispering shadows in his dreams.

"I know who you are," Jesse said. "My mama says you have more money than God."

Ness chuckled. "That may be true, but, of course, I'm sure he doesn't operate on a cash basis."

"I don't want to stay here anymore."

"This is only temporary, dear boy. We're constructing a new home for you as we speak. It will be a beautiful complex in the Caribbean. Lots of land for you to play on. But you have much to learn, and much to teach."

Jesse thrust out his chin. "I want to see my mom."

A flicker of fear crossed Ness's face. Fierce satisfaction soared through Jesse as he realized Ness was scared. Just as Myrna and Charles had been.

Dunning was still calm. "Control yourself, Jesse. If you behave, we'll consider letting you see your mother."

"You're lying."

Ness shook his head. "No. We would have preferred that you stay with your mother awhile longer, but it was getting too dangerous for you. We know that you were being sent death threats every day. I'm sure no one told you that."

"No one had to. People were screaming at me in front of my house."

"Animals," Ness muttered. "And there's an even more dangerous man out there. His name is Lyles. I believe you met him last week."

"He helped me."

"He's insane. He was once a member of our sect, but we had a disagreement over his methods. His intentions are good, but he sees himself as a soldier fighting a holy war in which any and all enemies are to be exterminated. I'm afraid he's gone over the edge, and he could have hurt you, Jesse."

"You don't believe in hurting people?"

"No, but I'm afraid a police officer was hurt at your church. That wasn't supposed to happen, but your safety is more important than anyone else's."

Jesse felt his chest tightening again.

Ness gently held him by the shoulders. "We've been looking for you. I funded the Landwyn parapsychology program for you, Jesse, even before I knew who you were. The prophecy of our founder, Alessandro, gave us reason to believe that the Child of Light would be found sometime within the next few years."

"The Child of Light?"

"You, my boy. I fund several first-rate university paranormal studies programs around the world, hoping that either they would find you or you would find your way to them. Happily, that's exactly what happened."

Jesse stared at Ness in bewilderment. "Why do you think I'm him?"

Ness lifted a tattered hardcover volume and opened it to one of several bookmarked pages. "It's all here, Jesse."

Joe turned the corner and drove down Avenue K, thankful the journalists had abandoned their sidewalk vigil in front of the Randall home. It was only 6:30 A.M. though; they would undoubtedly be back for live stand-ups for the noon and evening newscasts. He parked in front of the house and knocked on the door.

Latisha answered, dressed in a red and white Target cashier's uniform. "Come in. Thank you for coming."

She had called his pager-activated voice mail less than an hour before. He'd come straight from Suzanne's and hoped he didn't appear as rumpled as he felt.

"Why did you call?"

"When you asked if I had any home videos of Jesse, it started me thinking. I don't have any, but I thought my brother in Macon might. That's where Jesse was when he first started doing this stuff. Well, I called Derek—that's my brother—and he says he did shoot some video. I wrote his address out for you here." She handed him a page torn from a memo pad. "It probably won't help you though."

Joe glanced at the address. "Thank you. We can use all the information we can get."

"That's what I figured." She furrowed her brow. "Is your little girl all right? I heard what happened on TV."

"She's fine. I sent her away for a few days. I sure miss her."

"Like I miss Jesse." She reached out and took his hand.

He squeezed hers, unsure whether he was giving comfort or taking it. Both, he realized.

He let go and held up the address. "Thank you. Does your attorney know that you called me?"

"No."

"What would he say about that?"

"I don't give a damn anymore. I just want Jesse back."

Kahn's voice cracked as he talked into the gas station's pay phone. "We need to renegotiate, friend. I didn't know the heat was going to come down on me this hard."

Lyles nodded his approval, angling the Lanchester at Kahn's chest.

"It'd be in your best interests to talk to me," Kahn said. *"Immediately."* He used his sleeve to wipe the sweat from his face.

That should do the trick, Lyles thought. Whoever had hired Kahn wouldn't want him blabbering to anyone about it.

After what seemed like an eternity, Kahn smiled. "Great. I'll see you there."

He hung up.

. . .

Charles stared at the phone in his hand before putting it on the cradle. Shit. That wacko helicopter pilot was trying to blackmail him.

He stood in front of the pay phone in a convenience store parking lot. He hadn't dared to call from Ness's house or his cell phone. Couldn't have any connection between him and this guy.

They all knew that Michael Kahn was the one weak link in their abduction of Jesse. Everyone else involved was a trusted Millennial Prophets follower, but no one in the group had the piloting skills they needed. They'd thought that a drug pilot would be discreet and would want to steer clear of any contact with the law.

Charles's first thought was to call Ness.

No, he'd take care of this himself.

Lyles crouched near a gravel road less than a mile from Turner Field. In only a few hours, local teenagers would be selling parking spaces on the road for five bucks a pop, even though they didn't own the land or have any rights to it. For now, however, the area was deserted. Lyles was hiding in the tall grass that bordered the road, keeping a close watch on Michael Kahn.

Kahn called out from the road. "Are you sure this is a good idea? The guy sounded pretty pissed off."

"Don't worry about him."

Kahn cocked his head. "Somebody's coming!"

Lyles had already heard the approaching car. "Stay cool. If you try to tip him off, you'll be dead before you know what happened."

"All you need is one clean shot at him, right? Then I can go?"

"Right."

"I'd feel better if I had a gun."

"You're not going to need it. I'm a better shot than you'll ever be."

"I hope so."

Lyles checked his Lanchester's ammo cartridge and snapped it into place.

A late-model Cutlass appeared from around the bend, kicking up dirt and gravel. It stopped twenty yards from Kahn.

With the engine still running, the driver sat in the vehicle for a long while, almost as if sizing up Kahn. He finally cut the ignition and climbed out.

"Greetings and salutations, Kahn," the man said.

Lyles recognized him instantly. The bearded man from the helicopter.

"Howdy, friend."

"Friend, huh? Do you always blackmail your friends? Call me Charles."

"The game has changed," Kahn said. "I got cops and feds breathing down my neck like you wouldn't believe."

"Part of the bargain. If it wasn't, we would have hired a chopper jockey from Pilots-R-Us."

"I didn't bargain for this, friend. There aren't many people who can fly the way I can, and it's only a matter of time before the cops take a long, hard look at me."

"So get out of town."

"That's my plan, but it's going to cost me a lot of work. I figure you owe me a little something extra for my trouble."

"You've already been well paid."

"I need another fifty thousand."

Silence. Then the man spoke. "That shouldn't be a problem. How do you want to do this?"

"What do you mean?"

"Do you want to meet later, or do you want to go with me to get the money now?"

"Uh—" Kahn's eyes darted to Lyles's hiding place. Lyles could almost read his mind: *Shoot him. What the hell are you waiting for?*

"Well, we can meet later," Kahn said. *You've got a clean shot. Take it.*

"Fine. I'll give you an address." The man reached into his jacket.

"You better not stand me up, friend. Because if you do—"

Three gunshots. A thin stream of blood ran out of the corner of Kahn's mouth. He stumbled backward and collapsed onto the ground.

Charles was holding a revolver. He jammed it back into his shoulder holster and walked to his car.

About damned time, Lyles thought. He was surprised Charles had let Kahn live as long as he had.

Charles started his car and pulled away.

Lyles turned and made his way down a grassy embankment. His car was waiting on the muddy lot below, perfectly positioned for him to drive to the main road and follow.

He could've just grabbed the guy, but this required a bit more finesse. There was a trail to be followed, and Lyles knew that it could only lead to the Child of Light.

Derek Adams sat across from Joe, tapping a videocassette against his palm. They were in his modest, well-lit home in Macon. Joe had driven there straight from Latisha's house, a ninety-minute trip that had taken over two hours due to an accident on I-75.

Derek was a heavy man, and he puffed when he talked. "I could have sold this tape, you know."

"Why didn't you?"

"Didn't seem right, making money off the boy. But I bet some of those news shows would give me good money for it."

"You're probably right."

"The first time Jesse showed us what he could do, he was sitting right where you are now. He leaned over that coffee table and used his mind to push checkers around the board. Then he moved balls of paper, toy cars, you name it."

"How did the rest of the family react? Did you treat him differently after that?"

"Differently?"

"Did you make him feel he was special?"

Derek considered the question. "Well, he *was* special, so I guess the answer would be yes."

"Did Jesse get a lot of attention from your neighbors and friends?"

"Of course. We showed him around quite a bit. We were proud of him, you know?"

Joe nodded. "Is there anybody who could have taught him to do these things?"

Derek laughed. "No way. Latisha told me that you still didn't believe in his powers, but it's the real deal. He scared my wife to death when he first started doing this stuff. She even took him to Janey Clary to check him out."

"Who?"

"An old Creole woman who lives near the paint factory. Practically everybody on this side of town grew up with her. She was the cafeteria lady at the high school. A lot of people think she uses white magic, and they go to her for love potions and stuff like that. Silly, if you ask me. But after Jesse showed us his powers, Tonia, my wife, took him to see Janey, to see if his powers were white or black." He grinned. "Janey spent some time with him and then she told us that not only were Jesse's powers real, but that he was good through and through."

"He met her only after he'd already started showing you his powers?"

"Yes."

Joe pointed to the videocassette. "May I see it?"

Derek pried himself out of the chair, turned on his television, and slid the cassette into his VCR.

The screen flickered and Jesse appeared. He was in the same room where Joe was now, surrounded by balls of paper, small toys, and tokens from board games.

Derek's voice boomed through the television speakers. He was obviously the cameraman. "Do the game pieces, Jesse."

Jesse stared at four Trivial Pursuit plastic pie pieces. They shook, then scooted across the floor as Jesse leaned over and followed them with his gaze.

There was applause and delighted squeals. The camera panned to show eight or nine people watching from the doorway. The rest of the family, Joe guessed.

The camera whipped back to Jesse. "How about the fire truck?" Derek asked.

Jesse leaned over a plastic fire truck. It was larger than his other toys and seemed to require more concentration. His chin dropped to his chest, but his eyes never left the truck.

The truck shuddered. Jesse leaned closer. It shuddered even more.

The camera zoomed in for a tight close-up on his face. Joe studied him. He'd never seen Jesse hold his head that way. Joe walked to the television screen and crouched in front of it. There was something different this time, different from all the taped test sessions he'd seen.

"Give me the remote," Joe said. Did he just see what he thought he saw?

Derek handed him the remote control. Joe scanned back the tape and watched again.

"Holy shit," he said under his breath. It wasn't just his imagination.

Derek crouched next to him and squinted at the screen. "What do you see?"

"Exactly what I've been looking for."

17

A ny friend of Jesse's is a friend of mine. You *are* a friend, aren't you?" Janey Clary opened the steel-barred security door and motioned for Joe to enter. She was probably in her eighties, but her dark golden skin was still smooth. She spoke with a slight Creole accent.

"I like to think of Jesse as a friend," Joe said as he walked into the small, musty house. "I'm trying to help him."

She smiled. "You won't find him here, Mr. Bailey. You won't find anything here except a lonely old lady."

"You can't be that lonely. I hear that you help a lot of people with your white magic."

She made a raspberry sound. "People want reassurance, that's all. I just dress it up a little."

"Like you did with Tonia Adams when she brought Jesse here?"

Janey sat in a large easy chair. "Oh, lordy . . . Poor woman thought he might be the son of Satan." Janey cackled. "Wouldn't surprise me if she was checking his scalp while he slept, looking for those three sixes!"

"Jesse showed you his powers?"

"Oh, yes. Such a sweet, sweet boy. All summer long he'd come a couple of times a week. I sure missed him when he went back home."

Joe sat across from her. "You never met him before he started showing his powers?"

"Never. Only afterward, when his aunt wanted me to tell her that he wasn't the demon spawn. Which I did, gladly."

"So what did you think of Jesse's powers?"

She grinned, flashing a set of perfect teeth that had to be false. "Verrrry interesting."

Joe cocked his head. "You knew, didn't you?"

"Knew what?"

"You *knew*."

She was still smiling. "I don't know what you're talking about, Mr. Bailey."

"Sure you do. I'm trying to help Jesse, and I hope that you will too. You knew he wasn't what he seemed to be, didn't you?"

She hesitated. "I don't want any trouble."

"Ms. Clary, I'm not here to make trouble for you. This is about Jesse. Please, for his sake, be honest with me."

"I haven't talked to anybody about this."

"It's a good time to start. Please."

She sat in silence, then nodded. "Of course I knew."

"When?"

She shrugged. "Right away. I showed him what he was doing wrong. He wouldn't have gotten very far otherwise."

"Why didn't you tell his aunt?"

"Because that's not what she wanted to hear, and if there's one thing I've gotten good at in this job, it's telling people what they like to hear. Jesse didn't want to make his family a part of it. This was his game, and if he got caught, he didn't want any of them to get any of the blame." She sighed. "I'm not sure how this is going to help you find him."

"You never can tell. So you taught him the other tricks. The telepathic drawings, the spoon bending . . ."

"Are you sure I'm not going to get into trouble for this?"

"Positive."

"Well, every time he came over, I taught him a new trick. It kept him coming, and I guess I liked the company. He was such a nice boy."

"I was impressed with his ability to reproduce drawings. Magicians often use a confederate, but I don't think he had one."

She shook her head. "He didn't need one."

"I watched the tapes, and the camera was always on Jesse. I couldn't see the other people in the room, but Jesse was watching them very carefully."

"That's the key, Mr. Bailey. You get more than fifteen or twenty people in a room and ask them to imagine drawing a simple shape, a few of 'em are going to tell you what to draw whether they realize it or not."

He smiled. "Did you teach him to read head and eye movements?"

"Ain't you the clever one? Yeah, if you tell a group of people to imagine drawing a circle, someone's head might move around, or their eyes may do a little loop-the-loop. If it's a triangle, you might see three sharp strokes of the chin or nose. It's not a sure thing, but the more people there are in the room thinking about drawing the shape, the better your chances are. And if you limit it to simple geometric shapes, well, how many simple shapes are there?"

"He was very good at it."

"He wasn't enjoying it. Maybe he was at first, when he was entertaining his family, but the bigger it got, the more upset he became. And that was last summer. I can only imagine how it was for him these past few months."

"Then why did he do it?"

"That uncle of his kept telling him how much money he could make. Jesse wanted to buy his mother a house and make it so she wouldn't have to work so hard. That's the only reason he did all this, I guarantee it. He's a good boy."

"It turned out to be very dangerous for him."

"He'll be all right."

"How do you know?"

"Faith. It's one kind of magic I *do* believe in."

Jesse paced around the room, pounding the padded walls. If he didn't get out of there soon, he was going to go crazy.

Roland Ness had kept him awake all night with his weird talk about the Millennial Prophets. *"You're the Child of Light, Jesse. Our new prophet. Our guide to a new age of enlightenment."*

He wanted to scream at the old man: *I don't have any powers! Leave me alone!*

But he didn't dare.

If they found out he was a faker, they might kill him. His tricks might be the only thing keeping him alive. What kind of test would they think up next?

He'd just wanted to help Mama. If he could've done that, he would have stopped doing those awful demonstrations.

He'd thought about telling the truth when Dr. Nelson was killed, but then he would never have gotten that house. He was going to tell only if the police arrested him.

Now he'd be lucky to stay alive.

The door opened, and Ness walked in with Myrna and Dunning. "Hello, Jesse," Ness said. "I hope you've had time to think about what I told you."

"What's to think about?"

"Your importance to all of us."

"If I'm so important, why won't you listen to me? I want to go home."

"I know you do, son, but there's a bigger picture to consider. We don't expect you to understand that right now, but you will."

Jesse nodded at Myrna. "Why does she have to stay here? She didn't do anything to you."

Myrna smiled. "Jesse, no one was forcing me to stay here. I'm a follower of the Millennial Prophets too."

"You told me—"

"We told her to tell you that," Dunning cut in. "We thought you might use your powers against us, so we gave you a friend you wouldn't hurt."

Jesse looked at her in bewilderment. "You lied to me?"

Dunning continued before she could respond. "Charles volunteered to play the bad guy. It wasn't easy for him, because he cares for you, Jesse. It was a test—we wanted to give you someone to focus your anger against. We took every precaution, with the clothing, the padding in the room, everything. Considering what happened to Dr. Nelson, it was quite a risk for Charles."

"Maybe it still is." Jesse tried to sound threatening. "Maybe it's a risk for all of you."

Ness recoiled slightly, but Dunning remained calm. "If you could have hurt any of us, you would have done it by now," Dunning said. "You still need to harness your abilities, Jesse. We can help you with that."

Dunning wasn't afraid of him, Jesse realized with despair.

Ness patted Jesse on the shoulder. "This isn't forever. It's just for now."

Fear was no longer a weapon. He had to find another way to fight them.

He settled back on his cushions. "I'm having trouble breathing again."

"Rest," Ness said. "Treat this like an experiment. Concentrate and try to make yourself well. Myrna will stay with you."

Jesse eyed her coldly. "No, thanks."

Ness shrugged. "We'll be keeping an eye on you from the booth. If there's anything you need, just call out."

"I won't need anything."

"The sooner you decide to work with us and open your heart, Jesse, the easier this will be."

"Then it's not gonna be easy."

Ness stood, and Dunning and Myrna followed his lead. "We'll talk after you've had some rest. You've had a lot of information thrown at you today."

Ness, Dunning, and Myrna walked out of the room.

\

"You never should have taken him," Dunning said as he and Ness walked down the long corridor outside the containment area.

Ness pursed his lips. "Someone could have hurt him, Dunning. People are terrified of the boy."

"They're in awe of him."

"All it would have taken is one insane person." Ness suddenly had a pained expression.

"You mean Lyles. He didn't hurt Jesse," Dunning said. "The only one he hurt was you."

"Expunging him was the hardest decision I ever had to make."

"It was the right decision. He's dangerous. Psychotic."

"That's exactly why I had to bring Jesse in."

Dunning chose his words carefully. "But out there in the world, Jesse is an ambassador for our cause. Maybe that's how he will lead us into the new era, instead of being poked and prodded in this bunker of yours."

"You're questioning my leadership?"

Dunning lowered his eyes. "No, Vicar, I am not. But you must admit—"

"What?"

"There's been a surge of interest in the Millennial Prophets since Jesse stepped forward. The news media was starting to pick up on it, and Alessandro's hundred-year-old writings suddenly have meaning for people all over the world. Isn't that what we wanted? If it ever got out that we kidnapped him—"

"It won't get out."

"Your thugs killed a police officer, and you're pretty sure Lyles murdered the two men you sent after him. Is this what the Millennial Prophets are really about?"

"I know you disagree with my decision, but you must learn to trust me. I know what I'm doing."

Dunning sighed. "For all of our sakes, I certainly hope so."

Joe leaned into the doorway with his portable phone, trying to escape the sounds of the Pryor Street traffic behind him.

Suzanne answered. "Hello?"

"It's me. Joe."

"It's a good thing I have a sense of my own worth. You sure rushed out of here in a hurry this morning."

"I know. Sorry about that. The case is starting to break."

A car honked behind him.

"Where are you?"

"In front of the Fulton County Government Center. Listen, are you free tonight?"

"I can be."

"I need your help with something."

"What?"

"I'll give you a call in a little while to explain, okay?"

"That's all you're going to tell me? I'm supposed to rearrange my evening for that?"

"It'll be worth it. I promise."

Lyles squinted at the car in front of him as it turned off West Paces Ferry Road onto Piedmont. One of the keys to surveillance was knowing just how much one could get away with. For some people, it might mean hanging back a quarter mile and ripping off another car each time the guy stopped someplace. Charles, however, was clueless. Idiot. Anyone who'd just murdered a man and participated in a high-profile kidnapping should have been looking over his shoulder every moment of every day.

Lyles looked at the man's lightbulb-shaped head. He'd love to shatter the bastard's skull all over the front windshield.

Patience.

There would be a time for that later.

Bertram and Irene Setzer had tried to teach him the virtue of patience, but by that time he'd already lost respect for them. The complacent fools. Under their leadership, the Millennial Prophet movement in Great Britain had almost collapsed. He'd been in the U.S. for several months, serving Vicar Roland Ness, when Bertram and Irene had come to Atlanta for a summit meeting to discuss Jesse Randall. Millennial Prophet leaders from all over the world had come for the event, and only the Setzers refused to believe that Jesse Randall was the Child of Light. There were some similarities between Jesse and the prophecies of Alessandro, they admitted, but that was merely a coincidence.

The fools were afraid of the truth, and by then he'd had enough of their ignorance. He killed them on their way to the airport.

He thought Ness would have been happy to see them removed so cleanly, but instead he was enraged. He refused to listen to reason and excommunicated him from the sect. The old man probably would have had him arrested if it wouldn't have brought the secretive Millennial Prophets under such intense scrutiny.

That stupid bastard.

Lyles accelerated to keep Charles in sight. They were now near Ansley Mall, a large strip center, and traffic was thinning out.

The guy suddenly swerved into the parking lot of a four-story office building. Lyles drove past. He couldn't risk letting the guy see him.

He turned into a convenience store lot, parked, and ran back toward the building just in time to see the bearded man walking through the main entrance.

What was in there? Surely not Jesse; he couldn't be so lucky.

Lyles dashed to the entrance and peered inside. A set of elevator doors slid shut. He entered the lobby. There was something instantly familiar about it even though he was sure he had never been there before. It was in the architecture, the decoration, and even the gold and white rectangular ashtrays near the doors.

He stared at the digital readout over the elevator. It stopped only once, at the fourth floor, before heading down again.

He turned toward the building directory. This, too, was familiar; he remembered seeing that funky italicized lettering. The fourth floor had only one tenant: Paltak Innovations.

Of course.

He ran from the building.

Six thirty-one P.M.

Joe had called a meeting of the task force and feds, and they were crowded into the headquarters' small conference room. It had been a long day for everyone, and Joe sensed an undercurrent of tension in the room.

"This had better be good, Bailey," Fisher said.

"I think it'll be worth your time." He addressed the group. "Thanks for coming. Most of you have seen the videos of Jesse Randall's test sessions. Those were recorded months after he first began to demonstrate his supposedly telekinetic powers, but this morning I was given a tape that was made just a day or two after they began."

Joe inserted the tape into the conference room VCR and pushed play. Jesse appeared on the television monitor.

"You called us here to look at another Jesse Randall video?" Howe asked.

"You'll want to see this one. Notice the position of his head."

Jesse tilted his head downward and stared at the objects. Joe froze the picture. "Shortly after this session, he changed his angle."

"Why?" Fisher asked.

"See for yourself."

Joe resumed the tape, and objects were now moving across the floor of Jesse's uncle's living room. The lens zoomed in for its close-up of Jesse.

Joe pointed at the screen. "Did you see that?"

No one had seen it.

Joe scanned the tape back and replayed it in slow motion. This time there was a response. Lieutenant Gerald stepped forward. "Did I just see that?"

"Look again." Joe scanned the tape back again and replayed Jesse's close-up in slow motion.

Jesse's face and eyelids were perfectly still, but his left eyelash was flapping.

Joe froze the image. "In several of the Landwyn University tests, Jesse's nose and mouth were covered to make sure he wasn't merely blowing on the objects. But no one ever covered his eyes."

"His eyes?" Fisher asked.

"Yes. Specifically, his left eye. That was his secret: Jesse was blowing on the objects through his eye socket."

The group stared at him in astonishment. "That's impossible," Howe said.

"Rare, but not impossible. It's called periorbital respiration. There's a perforation in the membrane behind his eyeball that allows him to expel air from the socket. I spoke to his doctor, and he had no idea Jesse had this condition. But he did say that Jesse has had respiratory problems his entire life. It might be related."

Fisher shook his head. "How can this happen?"

"There's no way to tell. He could have been born with it, or it could have been caused by an infection."

Howe stared at Jesse's face on the video monitor. "This is bizarre. It was almost easier to believe he had telekinetic powers."

"Which is why no one thought of it," Joe said. "This afternoon I checked with my old mentor in the magic business, and he told me that there was a nineteenth-century sideshow performer who could blow up balloons through his eye. That would've taken the same kind of air pressure Jesse Randall needed for his tricks."

He smiled grimly as he saw everyone's stunned expressions. "Watch it again."

He scanned back the tape, and as the camera went in for its close-up, everyone saw the flapping eyelash. There were gasps and a few chuckles.

"Creepy," Lieutenant Gerald murmured. "Why didn't you or anyone else notice this on any of the other tapes?"

"Because it was nowhere to be seen in the other sessions. By then Jesse had learned to open his eyes wide and position his head so that he was always blowing downward, away from his upper eyelash."

"Someone had to have coached him," Howe said.

"Someone did." Joe told them about his conversation with Janey Clary.

Fisher nodded. "So she not only helped him refine his technique, she also taught him some new tricks to round out his repertoire."

"You got it. But all of his telekinetic tricks were accomplished by forcing air through his eye socket. Periorbital respiration."

"Sorry to burst your bubble," one of the FBI agents said, "but Jesse Randall wears eyeglasses."

"Except when he's about to cause objects to move. Then he takes them off. Check the tapes. It happens every single time. And you'll also notice that he likes to hear loud music in almost every session. That's to cover up the sound of him blowing."

Lieutenant Gerald walked to the front of the room. "The question now, gentlemen, is whether we go public with this."

Fisher ejected the videocassette. "If Jesse is still alive, this could help him. If he's being held by an extremist group who fear his powers, they may be more willing to let him go."

"But if his abductors want to use his powers, this announcement could be a death sentence."

"He may already be dead."

Joe shook his head. "If that's what they wanted, they could have hired a sniper to pick him off. They wanted him alive, and he'll stay that way as long as they think he has these powers."

"We'll see."

"I want that tape." Gerald reached for the videocassette.

Fisher tossed the tape into his briefcase and closed the lid. "We need to analyze it."

"That's police evidence."

"The mayor promised the bureau total cooperation."

Gerald held out his hand. "Now, Fisher."

Everyone in the room suddenly tensed, and Joe noticed that

the cops were on one side of the room, the feds on the other. It looked like a beer brawl waiting to erupt.

"You guys have enough to worry about," Fisher said. "You still can't even tell us how Nelson was murdered."

Joe stepped forward to face him. "I can." If he didn't have everyone's attention before, he had it now.

"How?" Fisher asked.

"We'll go to Nelson's house right now and I'll show you."

"Okay. Let's go."

"After you give me the tape."

"Jesus, Bailey . . ."

"Give it to me. It's my evidence, and it stays in police custody."

Fisher glared at him. Finally he reached into his briefcase, pulled out the videocassette, and handed it to Joe. "Expensive show you're putting on."

"Satisfaction guaranteed. Let's go to Nelson's."

18

Charles paced in the narrow aisles of the Stone Mountain General Pharmacy, a mom-and-pop store in a small neighborhood strip center. It was taking forever to get that damned prescription filled.

He'd managed to have a doctor friend write it up for him. Ness had assured them that Jesse's condition was not life-threatening, and that he'd soon get an inhaler from one of his own discreet sources. Screw that. It was taking too damned long. The guy was a billionaire, for Christ's sake. Couldn't he just buy a pharmacy?

Charles and Myrna had discussed it and decided to get an inhaler of their own and keep it nearby. If Ness came through with one, fine, but at least they'd be prepared if Jesse had a sudden attack.

He admired Ness, but he'd seen his weaknesses as a leader in the past few weeks. Charles had never met Garrett Lyles, but he'd begun to wonder if the man was such a psycho after all; maybe he was merely rebelling against Ness's timidity.

In any case, it felt good to get away from Ness's estate for a while. Today was the first day he'd been away in almost a week. He'd been spending most of his time in the pit, his name for the elaborate holding facility Ness had built below his main house. It had been worth it for a chance to be near the Child of Light. And things would improve when the permanent facility was completed on Ness's island in the Caribbean.

He glanced toward the back of the store. The ancient pharmacist was in his long, narrow booth, apparently working on the prescription. Didn't those damned inhalers come ready made?

The electronic door chime sounded. Two police officers entered the store.

Charles's heart jumped. He slipped his hand into his pocket, feeling the handle of his revolver. Don't freak out, he told himself. The cops probably just came in for a soda from the vending machine.

Charles tried to appear interested in the laxatives in front of him. The cops were walking his way. Fuck.

They stopped next to him. "Can we have a word with you, sir?"

As Joe and the task force of cops and FBI agents walked into Nelson's foyer, they heard an eerie clanging echoing from down the hallway.

"What the hell is that?" Howe asked.

Joe pointed toward the kitchen, and the group walked in to find the hanging pots and pans swinging wildly and clattering into one another.

Howe walked around the island, gazing up at the rack. "They're moving just like Nelson's girlfriend said they were. How is that happening?"

Before Joe could answer, there was a crash from the hallway. And another.

They rushed into the corridor just in time to see a plate fly through a doorway and shatter on the floor. The remnants of two other plates lay nearby.

One of the feds stepped toward the doorway. He ducked as another plate flew out and shattered against the wall behind him.

"A little too close for comfort," Joe said.

The agent leapt into the room and switched on the light. The others gathered to see what he'd found.

Nothing. Just the dining room set, china cabinet, and wet bar. The agent went to the windows, drew the heavy blinds, and checked the windows. "Locked from the inside."

Fisher grinned. "There aren't too many windows that lock from the outside, kid." He turned to Joe. "Okay, how'd you do it?"

The pots and pans were clanging in the kitchen again.

"I didn't do it," Joe said.

Howe tried to ignore the sounds from the kitchen. "You expect us to believe it's Jesse Randall?"

"No, but somebody wanted Dr. Nelson and his girlfriend to believe that in order to lay the foundation for his supposedly psychic murder."

"Who would want to do that?"

"I'm not positive yet. But I can tell you how."

Another plate flew out of the dining room and shattered. Everyone turned to look. This time they saw that a ceiling panel had been moved aside and a hand was waving at them from above, just inches from the china cabinet and a stack of plates.

Joe moved a dining room chair under the opening and helped his assistant down. Suzanne, dressed in a black body suit and covered with dust, hopped to the floor.

She smiled. "Sorry about that third plate. I threw it a little closer than I realized."

"This is Suzanne Morrison," Joe said. "Believe me, she's an expert in the art of illusion."

She made a face at him.

He smiled. "I'll let her explain how she did this."

Suzanne described the suspended ceiling and her technique just as she had discussed with Joe the night before.

After she finished, Howe nodded. "I'm impressed, Bailey. Not only that you guys were able to figure this out, but also with the fact that you were able to find a beautiful woman who's just as interested in this weird stuff as you are."

"Yeah, but was she able to tell you how Nelson was murdered?" Fisher said.

Joe put the chair back at the table. "No, but in a way, Jesse Randall did."

Fisher gave him a strange look.

"And after we get the results back from a search warrant I had issued this afternoon, we may even know who did it."

Gerald's portable phone beeped, and he answered it. "Gerald here." He listened, then said, "Okay, we're on our way." He cut the connection.

"What is it?" Joe asked.

"There's a hostage situation at a pharmacy in Stone Mountain. The perp just tried to get the same corticosteroid inhaler that Jesse Randall uses."

Charles crouched behind the pharmacy counter and tried to decide how many cops he'd spotted in the parking lot. Twelve? Fifteen?

Too damned many.

He'd screwed up big-time. He'd killed a cop and let the other one leave to call in the entire squad. He should have killed them both.

No. He shouldn't have drawn his gun in the first place. They'd only wanted to ask a few questions about the prescription. He could have bluffed his way through it.

There was no way out of this.

Now, taunting him behind the counter, was the bulletin urging area pharmacists to call the local police whenever a first-time Pulmicort Turbuhaler prescription was presented. If he'd only known.

Ness probably knew. That's why he was being so damned careful.

At the far end of the counter, bound by threaded packing tape, the elderly pharmacist was trembling. "There's a back way out of here," he said.

"I'm sure they have that covered too."

Charles stared at his gun. The same gun he'd used to kill the helicopter pilot that morning. It was all Ness's fault. If he hadn't decided to kidnap Jesse, none of this would be happening.

He peered over the counter again, and a chill ran through him. The cop he'd shot was gone. He was sure he'd killed him. Where the hell was he?

Charles turned to look at the small black-and-white security monitor just in time to see the wounded cop rise from behind a coin-operated blood pressure machine and take aim with his revolver.

Joe, the Atlanta P.D. task force, and the feds arrived on the scene as the wounded officer was being transported to a waiting ambulance.

A burly local cop introduced himself. "Chief Edward Pine, fellas. We got everything under control here."

"Where's the suspect?" Joe asked.

"Inside with the paramedics. My man put two bullets in 'im. You know, we've been running down these prescriptions for a couple days now, they've all been legit. You don't think this guy—?"

"Who is he?" Gerald asked.

"We think his name is Charles Lane. That's who his car is registered to anyway, and—hey!"

Joe, Howe, and the others bolted into the pharmacy.

They ran past the racks and stopped abruptly at the back counter.

"Jesus," Howe said.

The suspect's torso was sopping in blood. A paramedic team was trying to stop the bleeding.

"We have to talk to him," Joe said.

"He's busy," one of the paramedics replied.

Joe knelt beside Charles. "Where's Jesse Randall?"

Charles looked at him and his oxygen mask fogged.

Joe glanced back at Gerald. "He's trying to say something."

The paramedic pushed him back. "Let us do our jobs, Detective."

Joe leaned forward. "Where is he? Where's Jesse?"

"Child of Light," Charles murmured through the clear plastic mask.

"Yes, the Child of Light. Where is he?" Joe edged closer. "Tell me."

Charles blinked several times, then froze.

The paramedic grabbed Joe's arm. "Enough."

Joe didn't fight him. At that instant he realized Charles Lane was dead. He stood as the alarms and flatline tone sounded, watching the paramedics try to resuscitate him. It wasn't going to happen.

Gerald pulled Joe back. "We'll fingerprint him and find out if he's who we think he is. Maybe there's something he can still tell us."

Ness stared in total disbelief at the wall-mounted flat-screen monitor. The local TV stations had been covering the hostage standoff for the past half hour, and a newscaster had just reported that the wounded suspect had been attempting to get the inhaler prescription that Jesse Randall used.

Before Ness had a chance to absorb that, the camera cut to a car in the parking lot. Charles's Cutlass. He was positive.

That son of a bitch. What the hell was he thinking?

Ness strode to the intercom panel and punched the P.A. button. "We're evacuating, everyone. Prepare to leave in twenty minutes."

Myrna burst into the room. "What's happening?"

"Charles got caught trying to get the inhaler prescription. It's only a matter of time before the authorities link him to me. You didn't know anything about this, did you?"

She was stunned. "Of course not. Where is he?"

"Wounded and possibly dead. We have to get out of here."

Ness's estate generally ran with incredible efficiency, but for the next fifteen minutes chaos reigned. He'd recently winnowed down his large household staff to just a half-dozen devoted Millennial Prophet followers, and they weren't prepared for the evacuation order he'd given them. They were now rushing around, loading Ness's mobile office and two smaller trucks.

Damn. He'd hoped to keep Jesse here until the Caribbean facility was finished, but fortunately he had a backup ready.

Ness climbed down the stairs to the holding facility, which, only the month before, had been a massive wine cellar. He hoped Dunning was correct about Jesse not being able to consciously use his powers against them. There wasn't time to "Jesse-proof" the new holding area he had in mind, a forty-room mansion in South Carolina that he had secretly purchased from a trusted business associate.

He walked down the narrow hallway and stopped. Something was different tonight. It was usually darker down here. There were no windows and only a few lights in the corridor, and as he glanced around, he realized where the light was coming from: Jesse's room.

The door was ajar. Had someone already come to prepare Jesse for the journey?

Ness slowly moved into the containment room. Jesse still made him nervous; what if the boy was dreaming right now? Ness peered through the open door. He couldn't see Jesse. He stepped through the doorway, turned, and found himself face-to-face with Garrett Lyles.

"Hello, Vicar," Lyles said.

Ness frantically glanced around the room. Jesse appeared to be fine, thank goodness, but was huddled in the corner.

"Lyles . . . what do you think you're doing?"

"I'm through *thinking* about doing things, Vicar. I should have known that you were the one who took him, but it just didn't seem like your style," he said bitterly. "I thought that kind of bold, aggressive action could get a guy removed from the sect."

Ness tried to compose himself. Christ, the son of a bitch would kill him. Think of a way out. . . .

Lyles smiled. "I assume you still have a panic button on your cell phone. If your hand even looks like it's heading that way, I'll shear it off at the wrist."

"Don't be foolish. There's a place for you here, you know. You can play a part in the boy's development."

"Is that why you sent Teague and Manning to find me with their cattle prods?"

Ness glared at him. "Teague's body was found washed up on a riverbank. I assume you killed Manning too?"

"You shouldn't have sent them."

"We've missed you, Lyles." He moistened his lips. "We realized how right you are. It *is* a holy war, and we need good soldiers."

"I haven't come back to rejoin you."

"Then why are you here? It couldn't have been very easy getting inside."

"Easier than you might think. I've been to your house before, remember? I have a bad habit of imagining ways to circumvent security systems in every place I visit. It's gotten me through some excruciating dinner parties. Plus your people are running in and out of the house, loading up the trucks, so they've shut down your systems. You're down to a skeleton staff, everyone's in a state of panic. You've made my job a lot easier."

"And what is your job?"

Lyles raised his hand to show Ness a large knife. "It begins with this."

In one smooth, effortless motion, Lyles slid the knife across Ness's throat. Blood instantly poured from the wound, drenching Ness's shirt and jacket.

Lyles glanced at Jesse. "Turn away. It will be over in a few seconds."

But Jesse couldn't take his eyes off the gurgling, gasping man whose blood-soaked hands were trying to stop the fountain at his throat.

Ness fell to his knees, then tumbled facedown onto the padded floor.

. . .

Joe stared at the blotchy thermal fax paper that Fisher had torn from the console in his car. "Paltak Innovations?"

"Charles Lane was an employee stockholder in that company."

"You found this out in the last ten minutes?"

"More like fifteen. I called in the license plate as soon as we realized it was his car. There'll probably be some more info coming any minute now. Our guys at the office are whizzes at this stuff."

"I believe it. But did they give you any information about what this Paltak Innovations does?"

"No, but it's a subsidiary of"—Fisher consulted another fax page—"Oasis Holdings."

"Oasis?"

"Yeah. Heard of it?"

"That's a Roland Ness company."

"One of many."

Joe's mind raced. "Ness's estate is just a few miles from here."

"You don't think—?"

"I'd bet on it."

19

Stewart Dunning paced around the large fountain in the center of Ness's circular driveway. He checked his watch. What the hell was taking so long?

He wasn't concerned for Ness; a guy with that kind of money could buy any brand of justice he wanted. But what happened in the next few days would go a long way in shaping the power and reputation of the Millennial Prophets.

Shit. Now everything was going downhill. If the cops knew that it was Charles Lane in the pharmacy, it would be all too easy to trace him to Ness. Jesse had to be removed from the premises at once.

Come on, dammit.

He heard a car at the back of the house, roaring up the narrow service driveway. As it blew past him, he could see that it was one of the white pickup trucks the gardeners and groundskeepers used.

His heart jumped in his chest. Lyles was in the driver's seat.

"Mr. Dunning . . ." Myrna was at the front door.

"Myrna, tell Ness that I just saw Garrett Lyles on the premises."

She was dazed. "Ness is dead. And Jesse's gone."

After taking a moment to comprehend what she'd told him, he
jumped inside Ness's large mobile office, slid behind the wheel,
and leaned out the open window. "Get the team together. Tell
them to lock on to the mobile office's security tracking system."
He started the vehicle and took off.

Jesse checked his seat belt as Lyles sped around the sharp
curves of Rockbridge Road. The first time he'd seen the giant, he
had felt safe and protected. This time was different. Lyles was
drenched with sweat, and he looked . . . crazy. It was one thing
to watch him push a bully around, but he had killed that man.
He jerked his thoughts away from the memory. "Are you taking
me home?"

"Not right away."

"Then where are we going?"

"Someplace you can be safe from people like Ness. Okay?"

"I want to see my mom."

"I know you do, and maybe we can arrange that. But Roland
Ness had a lot of powerful people on his side. We have to go
someplace where they can't find you."

"Why don't we go to the police?"

"We can't trust 'em. We have to be very careful about who we
trust, Jesse."

"I know who to trust."

"How do you know?"

By then Jesse knew what kind of language these people responded to. "I can sense it. My power will show us the way."

"It will?"

"Yes." Jesse stared at a small Hawaiian doll hanging from the rearview mirror. He opened his eyes wide and pushed a blast of air through his left eye socket. The doll twirled and bobbed up and down, almost as if it were dancing.

"Amazing," Lyles whispered.

"You must not worry. The power within me will be our guide."

Lyles nodded.

Jesse tried to look calm, in control. Lyles was buying his act, just as everyone else had. He hadn't wanted to do any more demonstrations, especially after he had to blast that poor mouse's head with air every time it went off track in the maze. This was it, he told himself. His last performance.

"I am here to serve you," Lyles said.

Something hit them.

"Shit!" Lyles fought with the steering wheel as the truck fish-tailed. He finally regained control and Jesse spun around. The entire back windshield was filled with the chrome grille of an RV.

"It's Dunning," Lyles said. "Shall I take care of him?"

Jesse bit his lip. Would Lyles really kill a man because he told him to?

"You must do what you feel is right," he replied.

A broad smile illuminated Lyles's face. "You trust me." He drew his gun. "I used this to take care of that TV reporter, Jesse. I honor you with my every thought and action."

Reporter? At first Jesse didn't understand, then a cold sickness rushed over him. As much as he'd hated that reporter, he hadn't wanted her dead.

Mama. He wanted to be home with Mama.

Lyles lowered the window, thrust the gun outside, and fired four shots at the RV. It didn't even slow down.

Lyles squinted in the rearview mirror. "Bulletproof. It's a god-damned tank."

It rammed them again.

Lyles unbuckled his seat belt. "Jesse, I need you to apply pressure on the accelerator. Try to keep us over seventy. Can you do that?"

Jesse wasn't sure if Lyles wanted him to use his powers on the accelerator, but the man didn't look surprised when he slid over and pressed his foot on the pedal.

"Like that?" Jesse said.

"Yes. Try to keep the speed constant."

With one hand still on the wheel, Lyles leaned out the window and fired at the RV's tires. Jesse glanced in the rearview mirror. Several direct hits. But the RV kept coming.

"Self-inflating tires," Lyles said. "You'd almost think a billionaire built that beast," he added sarcastically.

It hit them again. Lyles gripped the steering wheel. "We have one advantage. We know he can't do anything to seriously hurt you."

"He doesn't care."

"Well, if we keep trying to fight that thing, we'll lose. We need to pull off the road and make a run for it. Once he gets out, I can handle him."

The RV rammed their right rear bumper, sending the truck into another fishtail. Lyles struggled to correct it, but the passenger compartment's left side swung squarely into the path of the RV.

The last thing Jesse remembered seeing was the RV's chrome grille and Lyles's intense expression reflected in it.

It struck them. Jesse heard the sounds of breaking glass, groaning, twisting metal, and shrieking tires on asphalt.

Then nothing. Darkness. Silence.

Jesse couldn't breathe. Was this what it felt like to die?

Two strong arms were suddenly under his armpits. He was being pulled out.

He could breathe again. He could see, and he could hear the chirping of crickets. He looked down and realized that he had been encased in an airbag. He glanced up, expecting to see Lyles saving him once again.

It wasn't. It was Dunning.

"Relax, Jesse. You'll be all right now."

He looked back at the pickup truck, and only then did he realize what a twisted wreck it had become. The RV had flipped over on its side, but incredibly, there didn't appear to be any body damage.

Lyles was lying a few feet away, soaked in blood. His arms and legs were twisted at odd angles, but he was conscious. "Jesse . . . help me."

Lyles thought he had the power to help him. Just like those people who had stood in front of his house.

"Jesse, please . . . I know you can do it."

Tears ran down Jesse's face. "I can't."

"Try. Please. Jesse, you're the Child of Light."

"I'm sorry," he sobbed. "I really, really can't—"

"Can you stand?" Dunning leaned over Jesse.

Jesse nodded. "Yes."

"Rest for a minute. There's something I need to do."

Dunning walked toward Lyles. Jesse was sure he was going to kill him, but he didn't. He just whispered to him.

When Dunning was finished, Lyles turned to look at Jesse. The giant was gazing at him with such hurt that Jesse had to look away.

Jesse wiped his tears with his sleeve. "I'm so sorry," he whispered.

He turned back to see that Lyles's stare was still fixed on him. It was an expression he knew he could never forget, frozen on the face of a dead man.

A helicopter roared overhead, hovering over the accident scene.

Dunning grabbed Jesse's arm and pulled him toward the forest that lined the road. "Let's go."

"We may have a visual on the boy, do you copy?"

Joe was on his cell phone, taking a call from the station. He handed Howe the walkie-talkie. They were still in the car, only a mile from Roland Ness's estate. The police chopper had spotted Ness's overturned RV on the roadside.

"I copy, aerial," Howe said. "Where is he?"

"He and an adult male just proceeded west from the Rockbridge Road accident site into a forest to the mountain's south side."

"We're almost there. See us yet?"

"Affirmative. Two more bends in the road, and you're on the scene."

Howe put down the walkie-talkie as Joe finished his call. "Who were you talking to?"

"A guy in the A/V lab."

They skidded to a stop near the overturned RV and wrecked pickup truck. "Jesus," Howe said. "This kid's lucky to have survived that." They climbed out of the car and approached the demolished vehicle. "Somebody's not so lucky."

They stood over the corpse. "It's the man from the church," Joe said.

Howe opened his car trunk and produced a pair of flashlights. "The other guys should be here any minute now."

Joe took a flashlight and aimed the beam into the woods. "They'll know where to look for us."

Dunning stumbled through the woods, shoving Jesse to keep him in sight. It was an uphill climb, but fortunately, he was in excellent shape. The chopper roared overhead again, but he knew the trees blanketed him. He was sure that others would soon be following on foot, however.

He needed to revise the plan again. As a trial lawyer, that was his specialty—rolling with the punches and adjusting the game plan on a minute-by-minute basis. But in everyday life he hated surprises.

What could he do now? He couldn't let himself get caught with Jesse. The boy would tell everything about the previous few days, and that would be disastrous for him and the Millennial Prophets.

The ideal solution would be to make it off the mountain with Jesse, then arrange a rendezvous with the other followers. Perhaps they could arrange a boat trip to the Virgin Islands, then maybe to England, where Jesse could be accommodated by that sect.

But if that scenario was not possible, there was one more that could work. He would play the part of Jesse's savior, the attorney who begged Roland Ness to release the boy and turn himself in to the authorities. And who, after a psychopath killed Ness and took off with Jesse, risked his own life to save the boy and take him to safety.

But one thing had to happen for that scenario to play out: Jesse Randall had to die.

A real tragedy, he'd tell everyone. While fleeing from who he thought were Ness's minions, Jesse met with an unfortunate accident on the mountain.

Voices behind him. Flashlight beams spearing through the trees. Shit.

He emerged in a clearing and found himself staring at the Atlanta skyline in the distance. He turned and saw the Appalachian Mountains silhouetted against a sea of blazing stars. He hadn't thought he was up this high.

There was a building just a couple of hundred yards down the

embankment, and he could just make out a sign: STONE MOUN-
TAIN SKYLIFT.

He grabbed Jesse's arm. "Come on. We have to get to that
building."

They half walked, half slid down the embankment until they
reached the small plaza, where a snack stand and picnic tables
were set up. Dunning stared at the Skylift cable, which descended
into the darkness below.

He turned. More voices. More flashlights.

He pulled Jesse toward the Skylift shack, where he could see
the forty-person Swiss cable car docked inside. He examined the
tall chain-link fence that protected the Skylift area. Rolls of
barbed wire topped the fence. He bent over, gripped the fence's
lower links, and pulled. The metal fasteners separated from the
posts, giving him and Jesse a small passageway to slip through.
They rolled underneath the fence and sprinted toward the cable
car. Dunning opened the door and lifted Jesse inside. "Wait here
and leave the door open."

Dunning crossed back to the control station. He needed keys
to activate the panel. There was a drawer under the panel, but it
was locked. He found a small spanner and used it to force the
drawer open.

Keys. Right on top.

He tried one after another until he found the key that activated
the control panel. He studied the switches. If a goddamned park
employee could operate this thing, *he* certainly could.

He turned on the power, and the main engine roared to
life. He tried to judge the distance between himself and the cable car. Maybe forty feet. He'd have to move quickly to pull this
off.

He pulled a lever, and gigantic gears began to turn above him.
The cable was pulled through the shack, jolting the red car.

Dunning bolted for the car's open door before it hit the chain-link fence.

He had to make it. Jesse couldn't be allowed to reach the bottom by himself, free to tell his story. Dunning dove inside and rolled onto the tram's sticky floor just before it broke through the fence and left the shelter of the shack.

Joe ducked to avoid the pieces of wood, metal, and chain-link fencing as they fell around him. He'd heard the roar of the Skylift motors when they were activated, but he didn't know what was happening until he saw the cable car burst through the closed fence.

He knew he could radio for backup, but the cable car would probably reach the bottom before the police units could get there. Even the helicopter would be hampered by the trees and foliage down below.

But there was one thing he could do.

He ran down the embankment, trying to convince himself he could actually do this. He knew Howe was several yards behind him, probably thinking he was totally insane.

The car dipped below the embankment, starting its long journey down the mountain.

Now or never . . .

He leapt onto the roof, reaching out to grab anything that might prevent him from tumbling off the other side. He gripped the white steel fin that connected the car to the long cable.

A gunshot exploded on the far side of the car. And another.

Joe ducked behind the steel fin. The cold wind howled around him. For a moment he thought someone was on the roof with him, but he finally realized that the shooter was leaning out of one of the car's open windows and firing upward.

Joe spun around, waiting for the gun to appear. When it did, he struck the shooter's forearm with a hard kick. He heard an anguished cry as the gun went flying. Now's the time, he told himself.

Still gripping the fin, Joe thrust his legs over the edge and kicked in two windows. He swung into the car. Before he could draw his gun, he found himself face-to-face with Stewart Dunning.

Dunning held Jesse in front of him. "Stand back, Bailey."

"You wouldn't hurt the Child of Light, would you?"

"Don't try me." Dunning pushed open the door and the cold wind whistled through the compartment. "Pull out your gun with your thumb and index finger, then throw it outside."

"I can't do that."

"Either your gun goes out or the boy does."

"You'll lose your shield."

"I can take care of myself."

"Like you took care of Nelson?"

Dunning stared at him. "What are you talking about?"

"I know you killed him. And even if you manage to get away from every cop and FBI agent on this mountain, they'll know that you killed Nelson too. Your life is over."

"Everyone knows Jesse killed him."

"I *didn't*," Jesse said.

Joe spoke to Jesse without taking his eyes off Dunning. "I know you didn't hurt Dr. Nelson, Jesse, and this man knows it too."

Dunning smiled. "Because I killed him? Believe me, if I had telekinetic powers, we would not be having this conversation."

"I know about the Windsor wall in Nelson's house. You knew about it too."

"You're flying right over my head."

"You knew that Jesse wasn't the genuine article, and what's more, you knew that *Nelson* knew it. You tapped into the wireless video feed of Jesse's Landwyn tests, and you saw all the sessions, even the ones Nelson and Kellner chose not to document. It makes sense that you'd want to keep tabs on your Child of Light."

"Are you making this up as you go?"

"Nope. That day in the Randalls' backyard, you mentioned the sealed box card reading test. I hadn't seen that in any of Jesse's session tapes, so I looked it up. It wasn't in any of the files, but it was listed as a T.A.—test abandoned. Kellner told me it would have been too easy for Jesse to cheat on that test, so they removed it rather than face the wrath of people like me. The only way you could have known about it, Dunning, is if you had intercepted that original video feed. Nelson and Kellner erased their tapes and didn't tell anyone about it. But you knew. And if you knew about that, you knew about the electric halo test, which is when Nelson had to have found out that Jesse was actually blowing on the objects through his eye socket."

Jesse gave Joe a surprised look.

Dunning paused as thunder rumbled in the distance. "You don't know what you're talking about."

"I think I do. The wires from the halo dangle over the subject's face and eyes. It would have been impossible for Jesse to blow through his eye socket without disturbing those wires. That's when Nelson found out, wasn't it? And since you'd tapped into the video feed, you found out too. Was Nelson going public with it? Was that why you killed him?"

Dunning half smiled. "You give me a lot of credit."

"You deserve it. Not only did you kill him, you did it in such a way that made Jesse seem more powerful than ever. Maybe you got Cy Gavin to help you lay the groundwork with the levitation stunts at Nelson's house. For a fix, I'm sure he would have helped you with almost anything. And with another fix, you were able to finish him off."

Dunning held Jesse closer, using him as a shield. "Those weren't the only unexplained occurrences."

"You're right. When I started to take a look at Nelson's murder, you tried to kill me too, but in other supposedly psychic ways that would have only boosted Jesse's reputation. I think you used blast caps in the elevator floor, and maybe a nitrate acid derivative on the floor and base of the first set of the library bookshelves. With one side eaten away, it became fairly easy to tip over and bring the rest down."

Dunning shook his head, but his cool veneer was melting fast. Lines of tension were etched across his face.

Joe took a step closer. "When all that didn't work, you came after my daughter and killed one of the best, most caring people I've ever known. That was your biggest mistake."

Dunning's face was covered in sweat, even though it was freezing in the drafty cable car. Lightning flashed and it started to rain. "You don't have a single bit of proof to back up any of this."

"Yes, I do. I got a search warrant for your house, garage, and storage unit in Tucker."

"You had no right—"

"You can explain that to the D.A. the same time that you explain why you happened to have a videocassette of the electric halo test. It was in your safe, which they had to drill, by the way. The tape was labeled with the date, and since that's one piece of information I did have about the test, it was pretty easy to identify. According to the A/V guys at the station, it's very clear how Jesse was pulling off his miracles. The wires in front of his left eye were flapping. Since you had the tape, you had to have known."

"This—this is insane. Why would I do any of this?"

"You tell me. I guess for the same reason you made up the strange occurrences at your house. You wanted to preserve Jesse's reputation as the Child of Light. But if you knew he was a fraud, why would you even want him? If you care so much for your religion, why would you want to base it on a lie?"

Dunning gripped Jesse's shoulders. "The powers don't matter. The *symbol* matters. It's what we've needed all this time."

"But Nelson was going to take it away from you. Just like I'm going to do."

"No, you're not." Dunning pushed Jesse toward Joe's left side, where his gun was holstered. Before Joe could regain his balance, Dunning tackled him to the floor.

The open door swung back and forth as the rain fell harder. Lightning flashed outside, followed almost immediately by a sharp clap of thunder. Jesse ran to the far corner of the cable car as it swayed in the storm.

Dunning was on top of Joe, squeezing his throat and sliding him headfirst toward the doorway. Joe stared upward as another bolt of lightning flashed in the sky overhead. Rain pounded his face. Thunder filled his ears.

He strained to reach for his holster. Dunning's hand was already there, and he was unfastening the safety catch. Can't let it happen.

The cable car rocked violently and water began to slosh from one end to the other. Joe reached out with both hands and gripped the metal seat support bar. He raised his knees, and then, summoning every ounce of energy, he flipped backward and forced Dunning out the open door.

Joe's legs dangled outside as the rain pounded him. Still gripping the support bar, he struggled to pull himself up. Just a few more feet. His head jerked back as a hand closed on his collar.

He glanced over his shoulder. Dunning. He was hanging from the open door's interior metal rail. He kicked outward and struck Joe in the upper back.

Joe couldn't breathe. Dunning kicked him again. Joe's shoulders went numb.

He heard something and looked up. Jesse was on all fours, slowly crawling toward him.

"Stay back!" Joe yelled.

Jesse extended a small, trembling hand.

The Skylift lurched. Jesse almost lost his balance.

"Get back to the corner, Jesse. Now!"

"I'll help you!"

Dunning pulled him back even farther.

"Listen to me!"

Jesse backed away.

In the next flash of lightning, Joe saw something rolling toward him. A chrome fire extinguisher. It struck his forearm, sending spasms of pain through his fingers. With one hand still firmly gripping the seat support, he grabbed the extinguisher's nozzle.

Do-or-die time . . .

He ripped out the pin, aimed the nozzle toward Dunning's face, and squeezed the trigger. White foam shot into Dunning's mouth, nose, and eyes. He screamed and tried to turn from the blast.

Joe felt his fingers separating from the support bar. He couldn't keep this up. . . . The Skylift lurched again, and the screaming abruptly stopped.

Joe glanced back. Dunning was gone.

Joe looked down just in time to see him disappearing into the rain and shadows, hurtling toward the dark forest hundreds of feet below.

Joe swung his feet up, trying to pull himself back into the Skylift. His wet bandages were making it hard to keep his grip. He tried again. Another miss.

Shit.

He finally swung both legs up and caught the doorframe with his heels. He pulled himself inside, crawled to the middle of the car, and rolled onto his back. He lay there for a moment, listening to the rain pounding on the metal roof.

Jesse moved toward him. "Mr. Bailey?"

"Are you all right, Jesse?"

"Yeah."

Joe sat up. "Your mother will be glad to see you."

He shook his head. "I caused her lots of trouble."

"She doesn't care. You make her very happy, you know that?"

"I'm so sorry, Mr. Bailey."

Joe drew him into his arms as he looked out at the approaching Skylift ground station. The rain was starting to taper off.

"It's all right, Jesse. Everything's going to be all right."

20

"I wasn't sure if I was going to be here," Howe said as he followed Joe upstairs at Nelson's house. "I bet I could have sold my spot for a small fortune."

It had been almost twenty-four hours since Joe's demonstration had been interrupted, and tonight he led a much larger group of cops, feds, and journalists to the crime scene. He'd been fielding calls all day from reporters and curious coworkers who wished to attend, forcing Lieutenant Gerald to limit the number to thirty.

If only he'd been this big a draw in his performing days, Joe thought ruefully.

They walked into Nelson's study, where Joe had cut a large piece of Styrofoam into the rough dimensions of the sculpture. Nelson's chalk outline, which had once been so high on the wall, was now at floor level.

He turned toward the group. "I said last night that in a way Jesse showed me how this was done. I had a tough time figuring out how he did his tricks, because I assumed the only way he could possibly blow on those objects was through his nose or mouth. I was presuming that his anatomy was put together in a way that it wasn't. When I found out about Jesse, I realized that I'd also been making assumptions about this house. So, I pulled the architectural plans from the county building permit office."

"What could that tell you?" Fisher asked.

"I discovered the downstairs living room has what's called a Windsor wall. Has anyone heard of that?"

No one replied.

"I hadn't either. In the early thirties, Chester and Klauss Developments built several houses here and in northern Florida that had a special feature: a wall that could be raised up and out of the room, so that a separated living room and den could easily become one big room. It worked with a motorized pulley system that operated a lot like our electric garage doors. It was actually based on a design used in some castles in the Middle Ages. These houses were built only during an eight-month period, because they were noisy and prone to mechanical failure. They probably don't work in most of the houses where they still exist, and I'd guess that a lot of the homeowners don't even realize they're there. I brought Nelson's girlfriend here today, and she didn't think he knew about it. The entire residence has been sealed off as a crime scene, so there was no way she or anyone who was familiar with the house could have told us that two downstairs rooms had suddenly become one large one. Dunning may have been planning to return and restore the wall to its original position."

"But the wall is downstairs, right?" Howe said.

"Yes, but it needs somewhere to go. It can't just pop up in the middle of a second-story room, so the wall runs up two floors. The first-story wall rises up into the second story, and the top of the second-story wall runs into the attic."

"Just the top?" Gerald asked.

"As you may have noticed, the second story has a much higher ceiling than the first." Joe pointed to the chalk outline. "And you've probably noticed how low this is now." Joe picked up the Styrofoam sculpture. "The second question is, how could you pick up a statue that heavy and run someone through with it? Here's how Dunning did it."

Joe walked to the piano and placed the Styrofoam sculpture on top. "If you'll look carefully, you'll see there are marks on the piano that line up perfectly with the statue's base." He pushed the piano toward the wall. "And the piano is on wheels and rolls easily. Either Nelson was so drugged he didn't see it coming—Dunning may have slipped him a mickey—or he was somehow forced to stand there. Maybe he was held at gunpoint. His girlfriend was coming over soon, and maybe Dunning threatened to kill her if she didn't go along. Anyway, the sculpture and piano rolled toward him and impaled him to the wall."

Joe rolled the piano forward and the tip of the Styrofoam sculpture lined up perfectly with the gouge in the wall. He gave it an extra push to wedge it inside.

"Then Dunning went downstairs and raised the Windsor wall. The motor doesn't work anymore, but it's counterbalanced by pulleys. It's not difficult to grab the chain and do it by hand." He spoke into a walkie-talkie. "Okay, Suzanne."

There was a sharp click within the wall, and suddenly it began to rise, taking the sculpture with it. The cops and feds watched in amazement as the outline reached the height it had been the night of Nelson's death.

"There's your psychic murder," Joe said.

Howe was still staring at the Styrofoam sculpture. "Abracafuckingdabra."

Half an hour later, Joe escaped the reporters' questions and left the house. It had been a hell of a day, tying up the loose ends and—

"Hi, Daddy!" Nikki ran up the front steps and hugged him.

Surprised, Joe held her close. "What are you doing here? I thought you were staying with Grandpa until the weekend."

Detective Carla Fisk was standing on the sidewalk, smiling broadly. "I decided to come home from Savannah early, and she took a notion to come with me. Imagine that. I guess she must like you or something."

"I missed you," Nikki said.

"I missed you too, honey. So much."

Carla faked a grimace. "Okay, I've had enough of this family togetherness. I'm joining the gang at Manuel's Tavern. See you, guys."

"Thanks, Carla," Joe said. "I owe you."

Nikki pulled away. "I've been watching the news on TV. Jesse really doesn't have any powers, does he?"

"No, sweetheart."

"I was kind of hoping he did."

"Why?"

Nikki didn't answer.

Joe caressed her cheek. "For the same reason the rest of the world wants to believe in this stuff, huh?"

"I didn't think he killed that man, but I still thought maybe his powers were real. Magic is sort of . . . nice. You think that's stupid?"

"Maybe not. Have you seen Suzanne?"

"Yeah, she left a few minutes ago. She's really cool."

"I think so too."

A few minutes later, Joe knocked on Suzanne's front door. She answered it and stared at him with a puzzled expression. "I thought you'd be with those reporters for the rest of the night."

He shrugged. "They can get what they need from the press release. Why did you take off?"

"I saw that Nikki was back. I thought you'd want to spend time with her." Suzanne glanced around. "Where is she?"

Joe pointed to his 4Runner on the street. Nikki waved from the front passenger seat, and Suzanne waved back. Joe moved closer. "Thanks for helping out these last couple of days. You were a big help."

"There's still one mystery we haven't solved."

"How you do your séances?"

"That's not a mystery to me."

"Of course not."

She smiled. "Where do we stand, Joe? With each other, I mean."

"That's the mystery?"

"Yep. And I have an idea that it's one you haven't the faintest idea how to solve."

"Did your dead friend tell you that?"

"She didn't have to. And she prefers to be called Daphne."

"My apologies."

"I liked helping you on this case, but I liked spending time with you even more."

"Yeah, me too."

"Then why the mystery?"

He was silent for a moment. "Kellner and the spook squad will be continuing your trials at the university next week. I'll be there to watch you."

She nodded. "Good."

"Good?"

"Yes. Every time you see me in action and can't explain it, you'll believe in me a little more."

"I *will* find out how you do it."

She leaned toward him. "Take your best shot."

He gazed into her confident, sparkling eyes, knowing that he'd probably expose her techniques within the next week or two.

And yet . . .

There was doubt, he realized. Even though he was 99.99 percent sure of himself, there were infinite possibilities in that other .01 percent.

Magic is sort of . . . nice.

Now he knew how Nikki felt. It wasn't bad.

He took Suzanne's hand in his own. "Join Nikki and me for dinner?"

She stepped outside and pulled the door closed behind her. "Are you sure?"

He smiled. "Yes."

After all, he decided, everyone could use a little magic in their lives.

ACKNOWLEDGMENTS

In the larger sense, this book would not have been possible
without the many defenders of reason and rationality who have
entertained and enlightened me over the years, including James
Randi, Martin Gardner, Joe Nickell, Michael Shermer, and the
great Harry Houdini.

More directly, my wonderful editor, Beth de Guzman, has provided me with sage guidance, infinite patience, and boundless enthusiasm ever since I first told her this story on that autumn
morning in Philadelphia. She's truly a marvel.

I owe a huge debt of gratitude to my terrific agent, Andrea
Cirillo, whom I depend on for her business savvy *and* amazing story
sense. I am also grateful to her associates at the Jane Rotrosen
Agency, including Stephanie Tade, Annelise Robey, Don Cleary,
Ruth Kagle, Meg Ruley, and Margaret Roohan.

And finally, much thanks and appreciation to Alan Ayers and
Yook Louie for the fantastic job they did with the book jacket. I'll
try not to take it personally that the corpse on the cover looks sus-
piciously like me!